THE
WINTER
VISITOR

THE WINTER VISITOR

B P WALTER

bookouture

Published by Bookouture in 2025

An imprint of Storyfire Ltd.
Carmelite House
50 Victoria Embankment
London EC4Y 0DZ

www.bookouture.com

The authorised representative in the EEA is Hachette Ireland
8 Castlecourt Centre
Dublin 15 D15 XTP3
Ireland
(email: info@hbgi.ie)

Copyright © B P Walter, 2025

B P Walter has asserted his right to be identified
as the author of this work.

All rights reserved. No part of this publication may be reproduced, stored in any retrieval system, or transmitted, in any form or by any means, electronic, mechanical, photocopying, recording or otherwise, without the prior written permission of the publishers.

ISBN: 978-1-80550-353-8
eBook ISBN: 978-1-80550-352-1

This book is a work of fiction. Names, characters, businesses, organisations, places and events other than those clearly in the public domain, are either the product of the author's imagination or are used fictitiously. Any resemblance to actual persons, living or dead, events or locales is entirely coincidental.

For Leno, for always making the Christmas season so magical.

PROLOGUE

The man and the boy are looking at the screen in shock.

'That can't be...' the man says very quietly, his words drowned out by the noise of the boat.

'Dad, what is it?' says the boy, pulling at his father's sleeve. 'Dad!'

But his father is busy stopping the engine. Navigating back, trying to find the spot where he saw it. The evening is drawing in. They should be home by now. His wife will be worried. She doesn't like it when he's out late on the loch. It's not safe, she says. And she doesn't approve of his new hobby, searching deep lakes, canals and lochs with state-of-the-art camera technology. He'd seen it in a TV series and found the idea fascinating. It had taken him just a week to get his boat kitted out with the expensive set-up. To his disappointment, his son hasn't shown much interest in the 'camera combing' of the depths, as he calls it. But now he seems interested. Something about the way his dad is acting has caught his attention.

'Just hold on a second, son, let me try to...'

He can't find it. After all this time, he's finally seen something interesting and he's managed to lose it. He steers the boat back along the same stretch of the loch again and again until eventually his son gets bored and starts saying he's hungry. 'Let's go home,' he says to his father. 'Maybe it wasn't anything.'

'It was something,' his father says. 'I think it was—'

But he stops himself. He isn't sure he wants to say what it was. Perhaps he shouldn't involve his son in this discovery. He's only eleven. And what he thinks he may have seen isn't nice. Not nice at all. Not something he'd want a child to see.

But despite this, he can't go to shore without proving to himself he isn't mad. He stops the boat, goes to the iPad, locates the recordings from that afternoon and starts to scroll.

'I said I'm hungry,' his son says.

'Just a moment,' his dad replies. 'I just wanted to check if...'

He stops speaking. Finishing the sentence isn't possible. Not now he has proved he really isn't going mad. The camera did pick it up. And it's more horrible than he remembered from the quick glimpse earlier.

'What are you looking at?'

He looks up from the iPad. Blinks, trying to think what to say.

'Did you find it?' his son asks. 'The thing you saw?'

'I did,' he replies. 'We need to get going. I have to phone the police.'

He sees the word 'police' cause the boy's face to light up with excitement.

'Why?'

'Because,' he says, slowly, 'I've found something.'

The excitement appears to grow in his eyes. 'Something good?'

'No, not good, son,' he says, taking out his phone. 'Something very, very bad.'

As he lifts the phone to his ear, he tries to free his mind

from the images he has just seen on the iPad screen. The image of a wrapped package, open at one end. A woman's head visible. Like a scene from a horror film.

'Hello, police please. I'm on Lemire Loch, Inverness. I think I've found a body.'

ONE

THE VISITOR

CHRISTMAS EVE 2025

The storm is worse than he could ever have imagined. But despite the wind and the snow, he just keeps going, his need to reach Lemire Castle driving him on. Occasionally he shelters underneath a tree or a bus stop along the road, but the cold makes him want to keep moving. And at last, he arrives. A place that he's never visited but has been in his mind for months, now. A destination. A beacon to aim for. He'd looked it up online, but it doesn't compare to seeing it in real life. It's like something from a children's storybook or fantasy adventure film, complete with snow-dusted conical spires and imposing grey walls.

He doesn't have any luck with the doorbell. It either isn't working or nobody can hear it. He walks around the side of the castle, heading towards an area of light falling on the fresh, undisturbed snow around the side of the magnificent building.

That's when he sees them.

All gathered there, in front of a roaring fire, a massive Christmas tree covered with baubles and presents underneath it. He can see a plate of mince pies on a coffee table, one half-eaten.

A family Christmas. Something he's never known. Not properly.

It's time, he tells himself. *It's time*.

He hammers on the window.

He sees them all jump and look around. One of them, the older lady, has been making her way across the room, but comes to a stop and stares over at him, clearly alarmed. The person nearest the window, a teenage boy, jumps up, as though he imagines the visitor might produce a gun and shoot his way through the glass. One of the men also gets to his feet and comes to the French windows. He knows who he is at once. George Weyman, the politician. Blonde, attractive, the hot-shot member of parliament, always smooth, always charming. Well, he doesn't look so smooth right now, he thinks as he watches him fiddle with the latch and open the door. The curtains inside immediately start to billow as the cold air rushes into the room.

'Can I help you?' George says, his voice almost drowned out by the roaring wind.

'I'm... I've come here because—'

'What?' George shouts, leaning outside, his eyes creasing against the wind.

'I'm here to – sorry, can I come in?'

George looks at him as though he's mad. He lowers the hood of his jacket, hoping that will make him seem unthreatening. There have been many times in his life when he was pleased to be born with boyish good looks. People react differently if you're handsome or beautiful. The Weyman brothers have probably benefited from this, even if they aren't aware of it. But he has always been aware. And he sees the look in George's eyes soften, even if he still seems confused and suspicious.

'Who *are* you?' George says loudly.

He wipes some ice from his face and says, 'My name's

Tommy. I've come to talk to you. I started walking from the nearest village where I'm staying before the storm got worse. I would have turned back when it got so late but I wasn't sure I'd make it. The snow is insane. It's taken hours. I'm so sorry, I know this is weird, but can I come in and explain?'

George continues to hesitate. He looks back at his family behind him. Tommy can just make out a female voice saying, 'Who is it?' but George doesn't answer. He turns back and says, 'OK, come in.'

Tommy smiles gratefully and steps over the ledge into the room. George closes the door and suddenly there's peace. A sense of silence and stillness he hasn't heard or felt for so long, due to the hours spent outside, that at first he wonders if there's something wrong with his hearing. But then he notices the crackle of the fire. The rustle of feet on carpet as the people on the sofas in front of him shift position. The boy is still standing, now on the other side of the room, and another of the men has got to his feet too. Ken Weyman, the action movie star, taking up a protective stance next to the lad. How strange it is, Tommy thinks, seeing him in this cosy, Christmassy, fireside setting.

'Go on, then,' George says, his tone brisk. 'How can we help you?'

Tommy takes a deep breath and says, 'Maybe I could sit down. I've come a long way and this is very difficult for me. And it may be difficult for you too. It's just...' He raises a hand to his temple.

'No, you tell us first who you are and what you want,' George says. When Tommy doesn't reply immediately, he adds, 'Right now.'

His gruff tone earns him a tut of disapproval from the old lady. 'George, let the poor boy sit down and warm up. He looks half frozen to death.'

George still looks unsure. 'I'd like him to explain himself.'

She ignores this, walking past him and putting a hand on

Tommy's shoulder. She steers him to the armchair the teenage boy vacated and says, 'Now, when you're ready, tell us what you've come to say.'

Tommy gathers his thoughts. Unsure which member of the family to focus on, he fixes his eyes on the fire, then says, 'This is going to sound mad. It will come as a bit of a shock... but, well... I'm a member of this family. Your family.'

They all stare at him. Eventually, the lady to his left, the younger of the two women, leans forward on the sofa and says, 'I don't understand. How can you be? I don't know you. Do my sons know you?'

He bites his lip, looks at the three men in the room, one by one. Then he looks back at the woman and says, 'I'm your grandson.' He pauses and swallows awkwardly. 'One of your sons is my father.'

He hears her take in a sharp breath. 'But... which one?' He watches her turn to look at her children. The eldest, the film star standing with the boy near the bookshelves. The middle son, the MP, taking up a commanding stance next to his grandmother. And the youngest son, the famous GP, sitting next to his mother, his eyes red and wide.

'That's the thing,' Tommy says. 'I don't know. And that's what I'm here to find out.'

TWO

GEORGE

TWO WEEKS EARLIER, 9TH DECEMBER 2025

George sits in the sleek, silver-toned office, watching the woman before him reading the terms and conditions on the sheet she's just been handed. He's feeling a little bit light-headed. He shouldn't have skipped breakfast this morning. But when he came downstairs, Delia asked what plans he had for the day, and he just couldn't face sitting down at the table and lying. He could have told her a bunch of things he was actually doing, things that would have been entirely truthful. Meetings with civil servants about policy drafting, a Zoom call with a fellow MP along with representatives from various educational establishments, drinks with a family friend. But he would have been leaving out the part of his day he knew he was going to find the most difficult, and he just couldn't do it. So he left the house without food and it is now well into the afternoon and all he's had is coffee. And Marianne is taking her time reading those terms and conditions.

'I know this might seem a bit...' George starts to say.

'Cold?' she asks, without looking up. 'Callous? Impersonal?'

Oh shit, she's taking it like this, he thinks. 'Er, yes, I suppose, if that's how you feel,' he says.

She does look up then. He's relieved her eyes aren't full of tears, but the anger that's plain to see makes his chest constrict a little.

'Yes, it *is* how I feel, George.'

He should never have started up this latest little fling. His closest friend, Raymond, thinks he's got an addiction – a 'womanising addiction', he calls it. George doesn't think so. His older brother, film star Ken Weyman, with his debauched celebrity parties, is the womaniser. He'd never put himself into that category. And it isn't his fault that he likes women's company. He likes his wife, too. Just because he sometimes sleeps with other women doesn't mean otherwise. It isn't an either-or situation. Never has been, in his eyes. It was the same when he was at university in America and had to make sure his roommate didn't let slip to the girls he brought home that he actually had three others on the go. Although he'd always found in the US they had a more free and easy approach to dating. But things became more difficult when he came back to England. Then he rose through politics, Delia at his side. While having the occasional affair was possible, it became harder and harder as time went on.

'Mr Weyman?'

He pulls himself out of his thoughts and looks at his lawyer, Jacob Wakefield. 'Sorry?' he says, blinking.

'He does this,' Marianne says, in a steely voice. 'He zones out. It usually happens when I try to talk about myself or what I'd been doing with my day or share my opinions on, well, anything.'

George feels bad when she says this and finds he can't properly face her. He hears the sound of papers being dragged along the surface of the table. Then the scribble of a pen.

'There we go, it's done,' she says, clicking the pen lid and placing it on the desk. He steals a glance at her. For a moment he's worried she'll be crying now, but she isn't. But she does look hurt.

'You didn't have to do this,' she says quietly. 'You could have just told me. I think you need to have a good, long sort-out in your head about what you want from life. Because I think you're spending a lot of time and energy making it more complicated than it needs to be.' She stands up, pushing her chair back under the table. 'There we are. I've said my piece. Here's your fucking non-disclosure agreement.' She slides the paper back across the desk. Then she moves towards the exit.

Jacob gets up and smoothly opens the door for her, offering a thin smile which she doesn't return. As she's about to pass through the door, she stops and looks back at George. 'Do you know, one day, George, I think a woman's going to be your undoing. You'll be too busy trying to keep everything nice and palatable, you'll probably miss it happening until it's too late.'

Then she's gone.

Behind George, Michael Allerton stirs. 'When it comes to parting shots, I thought she worded that one rather well,' he says, mildly.

George turns to look at him, surprised. It isn't often his godfather criticises him, but he feels a ghost of a dig in his words. 'Do you think she's right?' he asks, a little nervous about the answer.

Michael smiles at him. 'No, not at all. I think you're taking a very sensible step, drawing up legal boundaries. And remember, for all her bold words, she *has* taken the money. A not ungenerous amount.'

George nods, slowly, still not feeling entirely reassured. 'Well, as ever, I'm very grateful for your services. I suppose a simple NDA is small fry for your firm these days.' He stands, and Michael gets to his feet too.

'From experience, George, I never underestimate any situation which involves a member of parliament's reputation. We live in difficult, challenging times. It is my job to help you navigate them.'

George bids both men goodbye, walks out of the anonymous-looking building on Stable Yard and heads down towards St James's Palace. It's a cold December day, but bright and pleasant, and he's just about to head back to Westminster when his mobile rings. It is his wife.

'My love,' Delia says when the call connects, 'there's a message on the answerphone.'

George frowns, crossing the street to avoid a throng of talkative tourists taking pictures of York House. 'What do you mean, the *answerphone*?' But as he says it, he realises he has a pretty good idea who it must be from. They only get two types of messages on the landline answerphone in his house: ones from automated scam operations, or ones left by his mother. Despite having an iPhone and various messenger apps and all her sons' mobile numbers, she still considers the landline her first port of call if she wants to get hold of them. And since they are all busy people who regularly forget landline phones exist, they often either miss her calls or fail to pick up on her messages.

'I'd just popped back after a trip to Harvey Nichols, I was looking for some more gifts for my parents and brother,' Delia is saying, 'Gosh, Cyril is so hard to buy for. Anyway, I wanted to drop the shopping off before I had afternoon tea with Anita Nightly. Did you know she's split from her new man? He actually sold her horses.'

'What was the answerphone message about?' George asks, trying to keep the irritation from his voice. Delia has a habit of straying off-subject if given too much silence to fill.

'Sorry?' she says, the line a little crackly.

'The *message*,' George says. 'The bloody message.'

'It's a bit odd,' she says, the sound breaking up, words

becoming hard to make out. 'If you've got time... think you should come back and listen to it... I think...'

In spite of the distortion, he can tell she sounds troubled. 'I don't... probably imagining the worst, but... think it's bad. Awful, in fact.'

'Awful?' he repeats back, feeling worried now.

'Yes. In fact, I think it might ruin everything.'

THREE
CLAIRE

9TH DECEMBER 2025

Every morning when she wakes, Claire makes a point of walking to her bedroom window and taking in the view of the Scottish countryside stretching out in front of her. Previously, she and her husband occupied the master bedroom at Lemire Castle, which is very grand and spacious, but the view from its window is just trees and the car park. Whereas the guest bedroom she switched to after he died twenty-five years ago offers a wonderful view of the loch and the mountains behind it. Very much worth the compromise of reduced floor and wardrobe space.

The view of the loch was painful at first. Memories – sore and uncomfortable – were never far away when she looked at it. Moments she'd rather forget, burned onto her soul for eternity. But, for some reason she wasn't sure she'd ever really understand, the thought of avoiding the loch and the beauty it lent the surroundings felt like the worst of two evils. No matter what had happened, no matter how raw the trauma still remained, it was part of her home. So over the years, she made a point of not just looking at the view, but enjoying it. Being thankful for it. Embracing it. And eventually, over time, she found room in her heart to love the loch in her own way and allow its presence to soothe rather than trouble her.

But not even the loch can raise her mood today. After a few seconds of staring out of the large window, she decides she can't keep quiet. Can't let things lie. The shock from the night before still burns fresh and painful within her. *How could she do this? How could she be so cruel?* Her own mother.

She dresses quickly and walks out of the bedroom and down the corridor. She takes the four steps to the upper flat, situated in one of the towers, two at a time and raps on the door with vigour. 'Mother, are you awake?'

Silence comes from within.

'Mother?' she calls again. It's only 7.15. Her mother usually wakes around now but keeps to her little flat until later in the day, with their housekeeper Alexandra bringing her breakfast on a tray. Maybe she's died in the night, Claire thinks, then feels a pang of shame when she catches herself hoping this might actually be the case. It would be the answer to all their troubles.

She reaches for the handle and goes inside. There's no sign of her mother anywhere – not in the bedroom or bathroom or connecting kitchenette. Leaving the flat and going back down the stairs onto the landing, Claire comes face to face with Alexandra.

'Oh, good morning, Mrs Weyman, you're up bright and early. Couldn't sleep?'

Claire can't help but frown at this. She knows this isn't the era of *Upstairs, Downstairs*, but still, she doesn't think it appropriate for a housekeeper to comment on what time she gets up or how well she rested. Ignoring the question, she says, 'I can't find my mother. Is she—'

'She's downstairs in the kitchen. She wanted to make her own porridge this morning.'

Claire rolls her eyes. While this particular activity is unusual for her elderly mother, the unusual itself is usual. She can always be relied upon to subvert expectations or suddenly do something that seems wildly out of character. Anything out of character is very much within character for Eileen Weyman.

She mutters a distracted thank you to Alexandra and heads down the main staircase in the direction of the kitchens. The long corridors and thin stairwells of 'below stairs' would, once upon a time, have bustled with servants, but that is long gone. Almost gone before Claire was born. Indeed, it would have gone even earlier if her father hadn't been a stickler for tradition. Behind the times, her mother always said, and as soon as her father died, her mother dismissed the remaining servants ('relics of the past') and kept the staff to one live-in housekeeper and a twice-weekly cleaner.

'Mother, we need to talk,' Claire says, sweeping into the kitchen. Her mother has her back to her and is in the process of stirring a large saucepan of porridge.

'Good morning to you too, darling. Did you rest well?'

'No I didn't,' she snaps back.

'Shame. Cinnamon or nutmeg?'

'What?'

'For the porridge. I think cinnamon,' Eileen says, reaching towards the spice rack above the hobs and taking down a small glass jar. 'It is Christmas after all. Or nearly.'

'I'm not here to discuss seasonal spices,' Claire says, folding her arms and assembling her face into a look of stern determination.

'No?' Eileen says, turning to look at her daughter, an eyebrow arched.

'You bloody well know what we need to discuss,' Claire says, feeling a rush of anger.

Eileen turns back to her porridge and ladles some into a bowl, then fetches another and repeats the process. She then places both onto the stained, scratched surface of the large wooden kitchen table. 'Sit down,' she says, gesturing towards one of the chairs nearest Claire.

'We don't eat down here, Mother. Bring your porridge to your room if you must.'

Eileen ignores her daughter and sits down at the table. After a few seconds of silence, she nods at the second bowl and says, 'Don't let it get cold, dear.'

'Mother, I don't know what games you're playing—'

Eileen laughs. '*Games,*' she repeats with scorn, then proceeds to blow on a spoonful of porridge as though the activity requires a lot of precision and attention.

'Mother, you can't do this. I know what you said last night. I know you made it sound... I'm not sure if you said it to rile me or get my attention, but it's worked. Here I am, wanting to discuss it.'

Silence returns while Eileen swallows her spoonful. Then, in a calm, pleasant voice that Claire finds maddening, she simply says again, 'Your porridge is getting cold.'

Claire pulls out the chair with enough force to make it screech across the floor. She sits down, takes up the spoon next to her bowl and eats some of the grey-white mixture. It is very good and in spite of herself, she takes another mouthful.

'I thought you might be hungry,' Eileen says. 'It's what comes from leaving half of your dinner.'

Claire takes a deep breath, trying to force herself to remain calm. 'I found I couldn't stay in the same room as you any longer.'

Eileen lets out another short laugh, although this time Claire thinks she hears a 'tut' within it. 'You always were a high and mighty one, Claire. You got it from your father. He liked to be the voice of law within this house. He used control to hide his weaknesses. Something he had in common with most other angry, damaged men. Gosh, it was freeing when he died.'

Claire drops her spoon. It clatters onto the table, sending flecks of oats over its surface. 'Don't say that about Father. His death...'

'Was the worst thing that ever happened to you, yes, yes, I know the tune, you've been humming it all your life. And do you know what, my love, I think you've used it as an excuse? An excuse as to why your music career faltered. An excuse as to why you stopped playing. An excuse as to why you got rid of all the pianos in the castle so you couldn't be confronted by your own failure to get over your grief. An excuse as to why you've spent the best years of your life holed up in a castle with your mad old mother for company. Such a waste.'

Claire stares at her. 'You know why...'

Eileen waves her free hand, rolling her eyes again. 'Don't give me your excuses, they don't wash with me. It isn't the arthritis that stopped you from performing, you were determined to pack it in long before that. And it all started with your father's death. It was cruel that he was taken from you when you were getting into your stride, managing to prove yourself in his critical eyes. It was always his approval you wanted. Never mine. You didn't care what I thought.' She gives a sad little shrug.

Claire doesn't know whether to shout or cry or both. This isn't an unusual dilemma when dealing with her mother, but today it's particularly strong. She stares at her, tempted to take the bowl of porridge and fling it across the room. But she doesn't. She gets up and says, 'I can't talk to you when you're being like this. But I'll just say one thing. I've given up hoping you'll start loving me like a normal mother one day. It's not for me I'm fighting against this mad decision of yours. It's for my children. *Your* grandchildren. It's so incredibly hurtful. It will destroy them. Especially George. He looks up to you, you know.' When this doesn't get a response, she continues. 'I'm going to phone him. Even if he's at the commons, I'll leave a message. I'll tell him what you're doing.'

Claire sees the spoon in her mother's hand come to a pause on its journey to her mouth. Her eyes move over to look at her. 'He's one of the reasons I'm doing this. I'm doing it to help them all, can't you see that? After this Christmas, all three boys are going to see the world in a different way. I think it will be the making of them.'

FOUR
GEORGE

9TH DECEMBER 2025

George ends up walking to his home on Lowndes Place. There are no taxis anywhere in sight and traffic is typically solid in the nearby streets anyway. Each step feels painful, as though he's walking barefoot on knives. He's furious that he wasn't able to properly hear what his wife was saying over the phone call. But he heard enough to disturb him. Enough to chill him from within.

I think it might ruin everything.

It can't be, he thinks to himself as he crosses the road at Hyde Park Corner. It can't really be happening. Not now. Not after so long.

He tries to stop his mind from taking him back. Tries his best not to remember that terrible night, years ago, when he was nineteen. He gets out his phone and calls his wife again but just gets voicemail. He then tries the landline but finds it to be engaged. Feeling more desperate as the seconds pass, he phones his brothers. Ken first, but he doesn't get through. This isn't anything unusual. He's often either on a film set or in the bed of some woman who isn't his wife. Next, he tries Ralph, the youngest of the three. When his mobile doesn't elicit any success, he taps on the number for his brother's Harley Street practice. His secretary answers and tells him that he's out of the building, but a couple of minutes later his phone buzzes, Ralph's name on the screen.

'Hey! What's up?' Ralph says, the usual bouncy, happy tone filling his earbuds. It's the friendly, approachable voice that's helped him carve out his successful career both as a private GP and as a regular participant on TV chat shows, like *Good Morning Britain* and *This Morning*. It gives George hope. It makes him think the thing he's feared – the biggest fear he holds deep within him – isn't about to be realised.

'I'm worried, Ralph. I think something's happening. I just got a very strange call from Delia. She... there's been a message on the answerphone, she says it could ruin us. I wondered, have you heard anything?'

'No,' he says. 'What's wrong, you sound odd?'

He feels his throat tighten. He can't have a panic attack. Not here, on a central London street. Someone would photograph it and post it on social media, then it would likely get picked up by the papers. He loosens his collar and takes off his tie.

'George? You there? What's all this about?' Ralph is sounding worried now.

'I think you know what this could be about,' George says.

Silence follows. Then Ralph says, quietly, 'I'm coming over. I want to hear what it is. Could it be a journalist? Or police?'

'I don't know,' he says, turning the corner and quickening his pace, nearing the house. 'I think the police would have just come to us directly.'

'When Delia told you about it, did it sound like she knew? Like she was shocked or upset?'

'She sounded worried,' George says. 'But I couldn't properly hear.'

'Have you googled it?'

He comes to a sudden stop, causing a man walking behind him to mutter a swearword and dodge around him with a huff. 'No, I haven't,' he says, taking out his phone. He types in three words.

Loch Lemire Inverness

Nothing. Just the sort of results one would expect to see. A short preview from Wikipedia about the loch and his family's estate, along with various other sites like 'A History of Scottish Lochs' and 'Lakes and Lochs of Great Britain'. Nothing on recent news stories.

'I can't see anything,' he says. 'I may have overreacted. This might not have anything to do with...'

'What we did,' Ralph says, finishing the sentence for him. Saying the words that haunt them both. Always on their minds, like an echo you can't silence.

'I'm almost home,' George says. 'I'll call you later. Keep calm. I'm sorry to worry you.'

His brother starts to say something, but he's already cut the call. He pockets his phone and hurries the short distance down the street to his home.

When he bursts through the door, he sees Delia straight away. She's sitting at the kitchen island, tapping at her iPad. George closes the front door and almost runs down the hallway to the side table where the answerphone is.

'Darling, thank goodness you're here,' she says, getting down from her seat and walking over to him. 'It's the first message on the recordings.'

He presses a button and his mother's voice sounds out of the phone docking base. She sounds odd, distracted, as though she hasn't successfully ordered her thoughts before picking up the phone.

'George, something's happened... oh, I suspect you're in parliament... maybe I should... it's your grandmother. She's...' There's a ghost of a sob in her voice then, then she says, 'I think she's gone mad. She says she's going to disinherit you. Us. All of us. Your brothers. She says she's going to give away most of the money soon, though she hasn't said to who or what. And she's implied the castle will be *sold*. The home that's been in our family for generations. You might need to talk to her, she won't talk to me anymore. I might have got a bit cross earlier. I'm worried I've made things worse. Oh God... I said what if you were to speak to her when you come for Christmas... maybe talk things through. She wants to see you and your brothers and she says she won't be moved on the whole thing, but I think it's worth a try. She did mention how she doesn't want wives or girlfriends, you know how odd she is... bloody rude if you ask me. I realise Delia usually spends Christmas with her family anyway, but I think this year especially just make sure it's just you. I'll let your brothers know. Or maybe you could. Christ, it's all such a mess. It's revenge, I just know it. Punishment for me being close to your father and her always feeling like I let her down and... sorry, I shouldn't be telling you these things. Oh, Jesus, I've just realised this is on your answerphone. Could you delete this before Delia hears it... unless you're listening now, Delia? I'm sorry. Maybe it's good you both know. It's going to affect all of us. Ruin us.' The recording ends.

George is stunned. Stunned and relieved. He turns to look at Delia. She doesn't reference the mention of her name within his mother's message, nor show any offence to her not being keen on her daughter-in-law hearing it. Instead, she just says, 'See what I mean? It's awful, isn't it?'

George nods, trying to think. He's struggling to digest all the information that's just been thrown at him, coupled with the relief that's now truly setting in. She didn't mention the loch.

Didn't say anything had been found. Nothing to do with what happened back then.

She still doesn't know.

'I can't decide what's best,' Delia says. 'Do you think we should go there today? Fly up to the Highlands?'

George pauses, feeling awkward. 'Well... she did say she wants me there alone. And besides, you're going to your parents', aren't you?'

Delia stares at him, eyes wide. 'Yes, but not for two weeks. Do you really think this can wait that long? We need answers now. We need to know we're not going to lose the house. And what if I got pregnant next year? We can't survive on just your MP salary, they pay you such a pitiful amount, it's truly a scandal, and—'

The doorbell rings. Then a hammering follows.

'Oh my, who's that?' she says, looking alarmed.

George turns around and walks over to the door. He can tell from the outline behind the frosted panes of glass that it's Ralph.

'God, that was fast,' George says, looking at his brother, whose normally pale skin is red, his shoulders heaving as he pants from exhaustion.

'I wasn't far. Had a meeting with a team at another practice on Lennox Gardens,' he says. He starts unbuttoning his cuffs and rolling up the sleeves. 'I ran most of the way.'

'Come in, Ralph,' Delia says. 'Go and get him some water, George.'

George disregards this. Instead, he steps closer towards his brother, just as Ralph says, 'Is it happening?'

George falters. He glances over at Delia, then widens his eyes at Ralph, his meaning clear. *Shut the fuck up.* 'It's not good, it's to do with our inheritance,' he says, putting a hand on Ralph's shoulder and guiding him down the hallway, pulling the door closed. 'Come into the living room, Delia will get you a drink.'

'Inheritance?' Ralph says, still breathless, allowing himself to be led through into the meticulously tidy living room and steered in the direction of a cream sofa.

'Yes,' George says. 'It's odd. You can listen to the message if you want, but basically, it's about Granny's will. It seems to be her aim to make sure none of us get anything at all.'

Ralph blinks at him, the perspiration on his forehead glinting in the afternoon sun coming from the front window. 'But... why?'

'I don't know. I don't think Mum knows. She said something about how she feels it's revenge for being close to Dad. She said that Granny was always jealous about how close they were, that this is punishment for that. She was rambling a bit, to be honest.'

'You haven't phoned her back yet?'

George shakes his head. Delia enters the room with a large glass of water and hands it to Ralph. She stays standing near them, which makes George feel uneasy about continuing. He's never talked at length about his complicated family to her. He thinks it unlikely she'd understand. The relationship she has with her parents and siblings has always come across as effortlessly uncomplicated. Plus, he's always suspected the distance that exists between him and his immediate relatives provides her with a source of drama – like a front-row seat at a live, ever-developing soap opera. He's not sure he likes this.

'Why don't you listen to the message?' George says to Ralph.

'I'll set it up for you,' Delia says, as though the system is way more complex than just a simple 'Play' button. She strides out of the room and Ralph follows. George stays inside the living room, but can hear every word of the recording. He sets himself down in the single-seater chair opposite the sofa. By the time

Ralph returns, George has leaned back and closed his eyes. He's exhausted. It isn't even the evening, and yet it feels like the clock's pushing midnight. When Ralph sits down on the sofa, George just says, 'See what I mean?'

Ralph nods. 'Yeah. It's—'

'A mess.' George completes the sentence for him.

'Yeah, a fucking mess,' Ralph says, pulling his hands across his smart grey wool trousers. George thinks how old he suddenly looks. He's always been the baby brother, and usually looks like it too. He's stayed looking boyish, even though he's nearly thirty-six. Put him in jeans and a hoodie, he looks like a sixth former. But today, dressed for his GP practice, but untidy, scruffy, harassed-looking – it's like he's aged over a decade in front of George's eyes.

Ralph then does something that surprises him. He laughs. A short, sharp, yap of a laugh, then puts his hand to his mouth, as though he's sneezed. 'Sorry, I just... this past hour has been a bit of a headfuck. I don't think you realise...'

'I do,' George says, then lowers his voice. 'And I need you to shut the hell up about—'

Delia comes into the room and George sits up straighter. Ralph seems to clock his meaning and coughs, then says, 'I bet it's just one of Granny's games. She's done weird power plays before.'

This is true. When the brothers were teenagers, she'd expressed a view that young people didn't read enough anymore. None of them agreed. They were too busy surfing the web to mount much of a defence. The next day, she removed all the cables from the backs of the castle's two computers. The brothers were incensed, as was their mother, who had recently become quite involved with various gardening chat rooms. The cables magically reappeared two days later after outrage ensued, but the point had been made. Both the point that they were indeed slaves to the internet, and that there was one real boss in the house. Granny is queen.

'I'm going to pop out,' Delia says, cutting through George's thoughts. 'If that's all right with you both? I was supposed to be meeting Julietta and Clara for our little pre-Christmas meet-up but I could cancel if you'd like me here. All hands on deck, so to speak?' She laughs lightly, then coughs, adding to the awkwardness.

'It's fine, darling,' George says. 'You go, enjoy yourself. Don't worry about this. It's under control.'

He looks up at his wife, offering her a smile. He can tell she doesn't find it convincing but she doesn't say anything further. She just lays a hand on his shoulder and nods. She looks over at Ralph, who is sitting with his head in his hands, then leaves the room.

After the front door has clicked shut, George gets up and goes to sit next to his brother.

'I go through periods where I can't stop thinking about the past, George,' Ralph says, in a strange, faraway voice. 'Does that happen to you too? Where sometimes you can shut it out. Almost like it all happened to someone else. But at other times it's like it happened yesterday. All this stuff today... I'm worried it's dragging me into one of those periods. Like a spiral I can't get out of.'

George shakes his head. 'Well, it doesn't have to.' Ralph starts to say something, a mixture of annoyance and fear in the expression on his face, but George talks over him. 'No, really. I mean it. As far as we're aware, this thing today involving Granny has nothing to do with... all that stuff. It's my fault for scaring you. I'm sorry for that. Now we'll have no more of that. We're going to have a few beers and chat about the best way to convince Granny not to follow through on whatever threats she's winding Mum up with.'

When George gets to his feet, taking out his phone to clear

his evening plans, Ralph glances up. 'I can't stand it, George,' he says.

'Well, you'd better,' he snaps back at him. 'I've gone through twenty years hiding this from my wife. We're hoping to have a baby. I've kept quiet all this time to protect my future. And I'm living that future now. This is what I was preserving. My chance at happiness. I'm not having you spoiling that for me.'

He's just out of the living room, about to walk down the hallway, when he hears Ralph say, out of sight, 'And are you? Are you happy?'

George pauses. Thinks for a moment. Then walks away without answering.

FIVE

KEN

9TH DECEMBER 2025

'Ken, I'm sorry to say it, but if there's much more of all this, I'll quit,' Seb says.

Ken rolls his eyes. 'Oh, stop your moaning. You're the best PA in Beverley Hills, or so you told me when I took you on.'

Seb drops the bag he has been holding onto the table between them. 'I never said that, you decided that's what I was. I was just eager to get in on the film business. I thought I could learn from you.'

Ken looks in the black sports carry bag his assistant has just deposited in front of him and reaches inside. He pulls out a pair of Hugo Boss boxer shorts, a toothbrush and a small silver case.

'Don't open that in my presence, please. Just hide it away somewhere,' Seb begs.

'Lighten up, this is nothing,' Ken says, struggling with the clasp at the side.

'I mean it. I'd like plausible deniability,' Seb says, backing away as if the object were liable to explode.

'Plausible deniability? God, the youth of today. Do you

know what you need, Seb? You need to get fucked up more often.'

'You're only ten years older than me, so don't talk as if you're this wise old man,' Seb says.

'Bingo,' Ken says, getting the sachet case open.

'If you're going to take that, I'm leaving,' Seb says.

'Christ, Seb, you've been in this game long enough to know this is how the whole thing works. This stuff is the blood of the industry.'

Seb sighs – a little dramatically in Ken's view – and throws his arms in the air. 'It really isn't. It's like you still think this is the eighties or something.'

Ken laughs. 'You weren't even born in the eighties. And anyway, I was at a party last Friday where no fewer than three household names were competing to see how many lines they could do before they blacked out.'

'I mean it, Ken. You're a wreck.'

Ken's too busy looking for something to inhale the white powder with to care about what he's hearing.

'You are. And it's horrible to see it happening. You have a son, you know.'

This triggers his anger. 'I fucking know I have a son, you twat. I love that boy. I'd do anything for him.' He rubs at his face and for an awful moment thinks he might cry. He breathes deep and blinks until the feeling passes. 'What makes you think you can talk to me like this? You're my employee, not my life coach. And I'm not a wreck. I got my sea legs for intoxication when I was doing repertory theatre in the UK. Though then it was more about the drinking, I suppose. But that's beside the point, what I'm trying to say is I'm... I'm not...' He feels a wave of dizziness come across him suddenly. He stands there, swaying a little, one hand rubbing at his stubble, the other clasping a small metal straw.

Seb shakes his head, sadly. 'You're standing there in your

underwear at four o'clock in the afternoon jabbering away like a madman, about to wreck your nose and brain. Why aren't you out Christmas shopping with your son?'

Ken's eyes widen. 'Because I'm at work!'

Seb sits down on one of the chairs in the small table-booth set-up. It's a sizeable trailer. Bigger than anything the other actors get. But Ken hasn't noticed that. He's stopped noticing these things.

'Ken, they shouted "cut" hours ago. So tell me, why aren't you with your son?'

Ken brings his hands to his face again and tries to breathe deeply. 'I've got some family shit I'm working through. I got a call from my brother earlier. It looks like my family is disinheriting me. My grandmother, that is. So Kite and I are going to have to head over to Scotland to try and convince the old bag not to withhold the cash.'

'Oh, I see,' Seb says. It's clear he wasn't expecting this answer.

'Let's just say amiable conversation isn't my son's forte at present. In fact, I'm worried he's becoming a poisonous little prick.' He winces. 'Sorry, I shouldn't call him that. God, that's an awful thing to say. He's nice. Or used to be. Fuck...' That feeling of crying is nearby once again. In order to avoid the tears spilling over, he quickly cuts a line and sniffs the cocaine into his nostril. He notices Seb look away, revulsion on his face.

'I know why you're still here,' Seb says. 'It's because it's easier to do that shit here than somewhere Kite might see you. Then you'd have to explain to him what he already knows. His dad's an entitled smackhead.'

Ken grabs Seb by the lapels of the cheap suit he always wears. He feels rage pumping within him, a furious energy that fuses with the cocaine he's just taken. That extraordinary sensation, both strange and familiar, rushing through him, white hot, powerful.

Then... nothing.

'Ken... Ken... do I need to call an ambulance?'

Ken groans. He blinks for a bit, unsure where he is. All he knows is his head hurts like fuck and he has a pain in his nose. He opens his eyes. The lights on the ceiling of his trailer feel harsh, like they're burning his retinas.

'You're worrying me, you were out for like...'

'What?'

'For, like, ten seconds,' Seb says. 'I thought you were going to hit me, then you just, well, collapsed.'

Ken sits up. He's on the floor of the trailer between the kitchenette area and the table booth. Did he pass out, or did he just have a really good high? Is he able to tell the difference these days? He's not so sure. The boundaries of pain and pleasure are growing harder and harder to tell at this point.

'By not reporting this, I feel I'm a contributing factor in your fucked-up-ness. That my clearing up your mess when you go around sleeping with women and men across Hollywood is enabling you to carry on doing it. It seems like I'm condoning it, even though I criticise you for it. And when I criticise you for it... well, I guess that makes me a fucking hypocrite.' He gets to his feet and picks up his phone and laptop from the table. 'Do me a favour, Ken. Please consider getting therapy.'

Not this again, Ken thinks, as he too gets to his feet, his whole body aching. 'What would be the point?' he says.

Seb straightens his shirt and tidies up his collar. 'It might help you work some things out. Like why, even though you're the lead star in one of Hollywood's biggest movie franchises, you're putting it all in jeopardy with your risky choices, your messy sex life, your burgeoning drug dependency, all the unpredictable behaviour on-set, your rows with your co-stars. I could go on. Not to mention the fact you'd rather be off your face in a trailer on a film lot than at home with your son.'

Seb reaches the door. Before he opens it, he pauses, then

turns back to look at Ken, a sad look on his face, 'Or maybe it would help you confront what made you so self-destructive. Because for some reason, deep down, you don't think you're worthy. I don't know if that's because of something someone did to you. If they hurt you in some way. But you need to let it go.'

Then he opens the door and steps out of the trailer, leaving Ken alone. Digesting what he's just said. Thinking. Those final words have hit home. Seb's right in many ways. Ken doesn't think he's worthy. Not really. But it isn't because of something somebody else did. It's because of something he has done. And there is no way he can ever let it go.

SIX
GEORGE

9TH DECEMBER 2025

Ralph ends up staying for dinner. When Delia returns, she says she'll cook something, but George suggests an Indian takeaway in front of the TV. His wife accepts this without protest but barely eats anything, and after finishing her tiny portion of rice and herbed chicken she retires upstairs with a book, leaving the two brothers lying back on the sofa in front of *Die Hard* while they moan about their family.

'Ken might be able to charm her,' George says, hopefully. 'He might be able to convince her not to go through with it. He's got more skin in the game than us at the moment, what with Kite.'

Ralph makes a noise that suggests he's unconvinced. He picks at some fragments of leftover poppadom, then says, 'I've heard rumours that Ken's career is in trouble.'

George frowns. 'Rumours?'

Ralph nods. 'Yeah, within the showbiz world. People say things at parties about him taking drugs, shagging around. I've had a few journalists asking me questions.'

George laughs. 'I'm failing to spot the news flash here. He's always done that.'

'Yeah, I know, but he needs to be careful. I think people's tolerance for the wild hellraiser lifestyle is way lower than it was even ten years ago.' He straightens up. 'Do you mind if I clear the takeaway things away? The mess is... it's bothering me.'

George rolls his eyes, ignoring the request. 'I rather miss the days when Ken was a serious *actor*.' He emphasises the last syllable of the word with an exaggerated posh voice. 'He used to want nothing more than to play King Lear at the Globe or do Chaucer at an open-air arts festival somewhere rural. The whole Hollywood thing has messed him up.'

Ralph sighs. 'He was always a bit of a dick. You know that. But I think he's edging towards being something else. Maybe you should talk to him a bit more.'

George shakes his head. 'He finds me boring. I can see it on his face whenever he sees me. And I think his son's horrid. He can probably see that I think *that*, so we just opt for mutual avoidance to save the awkwardness.'

Ralph shrugs. 'If you say so. It's just... you were worried I was going to let something slip earlier when I was panicking. Well, I can't help think that a drugged-up idiot on a path to self-destruction is unlikely to be very tactful. Who knows what he might be saying?'

George gets up and starts clearing away the empty takeaway trays. Ralph's right, he thinks. It's a danger they all live with. That's part of life. But accepting that doesn't make it any easier.

Once they are onto their third movie, empty beer bottles cluttering the coffee table, Delia starts to make her presence known, tidying up things George has missed. She then starts her nightly wipe-down of the kitchen, making more noise than usual, clattering around in a way that indicates she is annoyed about something. Once she's finished, she says she's off to bed. George feels she's trying to impart some meaning with the announcement, but whatever it is, it's lost on him.

'Can I call you a taxi, Ralph?' she says. Even in his semi-drunken state, George thinks this sounds a little rude.

'No, we're not finished,' George says. 'Besides, he can stay the night. I'll make up the guest room.'

Delia tuts. 'The guest room is already "made up", as you put it.' She then walks out into the hallway without saying goodnight. George hears her climbing the stairs, each footfall making more of a thud than usual.

Ralph has always been a lightweight when it comes to drinking, in George's view, and he thinks it's a bit ridiculous that he needs to help his brother to the guest room forty minutes later.

'I'm good... I'm good,' Ralph slurs, stumbling towards the bed and sitting down with a slight bounce on the edge. He bends down and starts removing his shoes and socks.

'Just get some sleep. We'll sort everything out,' George says, looking back at his brother. 'Don't worry, we'll sort it.'

Ralph's head moves up to look at him with remarkable speed, considering the state he's in. 'But... *how?*'

George winces, regretting not being clear. 'I meant Granny's will.'

Ralph's expression falls. 'Oh, that. Yeah, sure.'

George bids him goodnight and walks down the landing to the master bedroom. Delia is sitting on the bed in her underwear, scrolling on her phone.

'Finally,' she says, casting it aside. 'Come on, I don't want to be up into the early hours.'

George begins to unbutton his shirt. 'You could have gone to sleep,' he says. 'You didn't have to stay up.'

'*George,*' she says, and he notes the frustration in her voice. 'I'm ovulating. We need to do it, *now.*'

This isn't what he had expected. 'Oh... what... now?'

She stares back at him as though he's an idiot. 'You forgot, didn't you?'

'No,' he lies. 'I just... it's been a stressful day.' He steps out of his trousers and lays them over the chair in the corner of the room.

'Yes, I know,' Delia says. 'But surely it would be really helpful if I was pregnant, wouldn't it? Surely it would seem even more heartless, her cutting us off from the inheritance?'

George takes off his pants and walks towards the bed. 'That isn't the only reason you want a child, is it?'

Delia looks shocked. 'Of course it isn't! How can you ask that? I'm just saying, it would make the campaign a little more *persuasive.*' She raises her eyebrows, as though expecting him to agree.

George sighs. 'I guess. Come on then, let's get this done.'

A few minutes into their love-making session, George stops. He's aware he's been going at it with all the enthusiasm of a man checking a car's engine oil and the creak on the landing firmly pulls his mind out of the task at hand.

'Don't stop,' Delia says.

'I can hear something outside,' he says.

'It's probably only Ralph, going to the bathroom,' Delia says.

George's head turns to the door, even though it's closed and there's nothing to see.

'George, come on.' She pats his shoulder.

George continues to thrust, but mutters, 'He might hear.'

'He's a doctor,' she says. 'I'm sure he's aware of how babies are made.'

He grunts in agreement, but then there's the sound of a smash, and someone saying 'Shit!'

George extricates himself, gets off the bed and pulls his boxers back on.

'Oh for goodness' sake,' Delia huffs.

'Ralph?' George calls, opening the bedroom door and walking to the bathroom across the hallway.

Inside, his brother is on the floor. He's still fully dressed, but his white shirt now has drops of something red on it. Blood.

'Careful... the glass.' Ralph gestures with his hand to the floor of the bathroom. 'The mess... I'm sorry... Can you clear it up? I don't... I don't like it, George.'

'It's OK,' George says, considering what to do.

'Don't step on it,' Delia says from behind him, appearing in her dressing gown. 'I'll get the dustpan and brush.'

'I'll just get some shoes,' George mutters. He returns a few seconds later with sliders on his feet. Ralph hasn't moved. He's a little alarmed that his brother is just sitting there, staring at his cut fingers, mumbling something, as though talking to himself.

'What did you say?' George asks, stepping forward. Ralph doesn't get louder or acknowledge his question. But he carries on muttering.

'Hinge. Saddle. Condyloid. Ball and socket. Plane.'

'Ralph, stop it,' George says, realising what he's saying. He gives his shoulder a little shake.

'Hinge. Saddle. Condyloid. Ball and socket. Plane.'

'Stop it,' George says again, more forcefully, tilting his brother's head up by his chin so Ralph's now looking at him. 'You don't need to say all that. You don't need... just, come back to the present.' Ralph stares at him, blinking. He stops his quiet, methodical muttering and swallows.

'I think I'm still drunk,' he slurs.

'Well, yeah, we only came upstairs about half an hour ago,' George says. 'Come on, let me get you back to your room.'

'There are things... *things*.'

'No, there aren't,' George says, bluntly.

'There are. I sometimes think someone's following me... watching me...'

'That's just paranoia,' says George.

'I worry every day that someone will find out...'

Even though they're broken up, the words are said loudly and clearly, and getting louder by the second.

George slaps his brother across the face. 'Watch what you're fucking saying,' he hisses. 'Do you want to ruin your life?'

The slap doesn't seem to have done much more to Ralph than make him blink a bit. He gets to his feet, swaying a little, then says, 'It sometimes feels like it's already ruined.'

'That's not true,' George says. He guides Ralph around the obvious bits of glass on the floor and onto the safety of the carpeted landing. Delia is standing there holding a dustpan and brush.

'I'll do that,' he says. 'I'll just get Ralph to his room.'

'No need, I'll sort it,' she says in a businesslike way, going into the bathroom.

George deposits Ralph onto the bed. He appears to fall into a deep sleep as soon as his head hits the pillow. The sound of sweeping can be heard from the bathroom. He pokes his head around the door and asks, 'All right?'

'Yes, I've got most of it up. I might just get the vacuum. Katie comes tomorrow, but I don't think we should leave it until she does her full clean, just in case Ralph goes back in during the night. We can keep to our en suite of course.'

Once the bathroom has been sufficiently swept and hoovered and they're both back in bed, Delia puts an arm around him. 'Right, let's carry on. Don't take long, though, five minutes max, I need to get to sleep.'

For a moment, George doesn't have a clue what she's referring to, then remembers what they'd been doing before the interruption. 'Oh... no, sorry, I... I'm exhausted. Can we just sleep?'

Delia turns angry eyes upon him. 'I don't know if you need to brush up on your school-level biology, but conception can't happen unless there's ejaculation. How do you think fertilisation is going to take place if you don't finish?'

'I'm sure waiting one more day won't make a difference,' he says.

He sees her expression soften. 'Oh, all right. I suppose this wasn't going to be a great night for it after all that stress earlier.'

Relieved, George reaches for the lamp, but before he can turn it off, Delia says, 'What did Ralph mean, just now?'

George freezes. He hopes she can't hear his heartbeat, which feels to him as though it's increased in volume tenfold.

'I heard him,' she says. 'He says he worries people will find out about him... something like that? What does he mean?'

Trying to urge his brain to think up a believable and simple excuse, George says the first thing that comes to him.

'He's having an affair.'

As soon as he hears Delia's gasp, he knows he's made a mistake. This is too big. Too shocking. A lie that might unravel before his eyes. The sort of genie you can't put back in the lamp.

'Oh my God,' Delia says. She sits up and stares at him, mouth open. 'I can't believe it. Are you sure?'

George nods, slowly. Now he's said it, he's not sure what else he can do other than go along with it.

'Who with?'

'His... receptionist.'

When Delia's eyes go wide, George knows he's made his second mistake. Ralph's receptionist is male.

'He's having an affair with *Lance*?'

George opens his mouth, then closes it, trying to think how to navigate his way out of this escalating mess.

'Oh my God,' Delia says again before George can respond. 'Do you know, I noticed him being quite tactile with Lance at that drinks thing. Poor Mara. She might have no idea. Many people don't. I read a book once about wives who marry gay men and don't realise it, even though everyone says they should have known. Well, no wonder he's terrified of people finding out. And these days, it doesn't look good, does it? A receptionist? And isn't he quite a bit younger than Ralph? I mean, Ralph's always looked like a teenager, you'd never guess he was over thirty, so maybe he can get away with it. Thank God it isn't with anyone at the morning talk shows he's sometimes on. He'd have to do one of those extended interviews with Amol Rajan to explain how sorry he is.'

Delia has said so many things within the last minute, George feels like his head is about to melt. 'Can we not run away with this,' he says, quietly.

'Run away with this? Darling, this is huge news. My gosh, this coupled with your granny's bombshell... you do have quite the family.'

She lies back and George takes this as his cue to turn the light off. Though there's no danger of him going to sleep now. He might have put out one fire, but he has a terrible feeling he's just lit the kindling for another.

And his wife is right. He does have quite the family. A family connected by blood, but other things too. Money, tragedy, secrets. Secrets that could float up from the depths of the past and taint the present at any moment.

SEVEN
GEORGE

CHRISTMAS EVE 2005

George has heard about the risk of a storm on the news, but doesn't give it much attention. When he hears one journalist describing a Met Office report as 'the most dire prediction of weather-related chaos Scotland and Northern England has seen in half a century', he laughs and rolls his eyes. 'They're overreacting,' he says. He watches as the news presenter's expression and tone switches from grave concern to a more cheery air when he begins to describe the crowds of stars who had been in attendance at Sir Elton John's civil partnership to David Furnish.

Ralph, who has been gripped by the developing news stories about the coming storm with increasing intensity, jerks around from his spot on the sofa and looks at George as though he's just denied the earth is round. 'It's not a joke, there's a chance we could be snowed in completely. Mum and Granny may not be able to get home for ages.'

George hadn't quite appreciated the impact severe weather, if the worst were to become true, might have on them and their family Christmas. Ralph, on the other hand, looks very worried. Even at seventeen, he's still very much the baby of the family. 'Don't worry,' George says, reaching forward and giving his shoulder a squeeze. 'It'll be fine. I promise.' He walks towards the door, then calls back, 'I'm off for a quick trip down to the village. Might get a drink.'

He sees the look of worry in his brother's eyes. 'Isn't that a bit of a stupid thing to do? You've only just passed your test—'

'I passed it three weeks ago!' George objects.

'And you haven't got any experience of... I don't know... perilous conditions.'

George scoffs at that, but Ralph carries on. 'What if the snow starts before you get back? What if you crash and die in a ditch somewhere and Ken and I are left here wondering where you are? Mum would blame us, I know that much, and—'

'It will be fine,' George says firmly. 'I'm not going to crash. And before you start on the alcohol side of things next, I'll have one drink. I won't be over the limit.'

Ralph looks like he's about to argue further, so George leaves. He nips upstairs and has a quick shower and change, opting for a nice dark green shirt and smart jeans and a spray of the Ralph Lauren aftershave he nicked out of Ken's room. Then he heads back downstairs and calls out, 'See you soon!' in the direction of the living room. He sees that Ken has joined Ralph now and they're sitting at either end of the sofa, watching the TV. He's pleased to see the viewing choice has changed from doom-laden weather reports to a DVD of *Harry Potter and the Prisoner of Azkaban*. George goes to open his mouth again to repeat his goodbye, then decides against it. Best not give either of them further opportunity to object to his little trip.

Although the sky is starless and overcast and the temperature very cold, George is relieved not to see a single flake of snow as he drives his Porsche down the long, winding private road leading away from Lemire Castle. For all his confidence earlier with Ralph, now he's behind the wheel in the darkness, he realises he'd rather not encounter blizzard conditions when he's alone, less than thirty days after getting his licence.

By the time he gets to the pub in the village, a mist is starting to form, and he wonders if he's been foolish heading out. He wasn't thinking with his sensible brain, as he sometimes thinks of it. He was thinking with his show-off brain, playing into the part of him that likes how his new Porsche makes him feel. Smooth, attractive, grown-up. And, if he's honest with himself, he was also thinking with his dick. He likes the way girls in the village look at him. One of the Weyman brothers. The middle boy. The normal one, or so he likes to think of himself.

Just as he hoped, he's only in the pub a matter of minutes before he's in the midst of flirting with two local girls. He's met both of them before, and he's fairly sure the night will end with him getting friendly with at least one of them. Then his eyes wander over to a dark corner of the pub. Part-illuminated by the glowing coloured fairy lights of the Christmas tree, a girl is sitting reading a book. No, not a girl, a young woman. She's curled up, as though at home rather than out in public, her outfit looking wonderfully soft and cosy: a pale blue jumper with white snowflakes and a thick black winter coat resting on her knees. There's something oddly familiar about her. She shoots her eyes up, then looks back down. He gets the feeling she's very much aware of him – perhaps she's been checking him out. Hoping he'll come over.

The eyes flick up again. Clock that he's aware of her. And then it hits him. He knows why this girl's familiar.

'Oh my God,' he says, standing up.

The two girls he's with look put out. One of them was halfway through a story about how she was at least fifty per cent sure she'd seen Neve Campbell eating a pizza crunch on Sauchiehall Street during her last trip to Glasgow, and she looks thoroughly annoyed when George doesn't stay to hear how it ends.

'Sorry, I'll catch you later,' George says, vaguely aware he's probably being a prick, but he can't wait to be polite. He can hardly believe what he's seeing. Who he's seeing.

'Well, hello, George,' the woman in front of him says with a shy smile. It's the smile that nearly floors him. It conjures up so many memories in a split second. They dash through his brain, like flipping a stack of photographs very fast, but each one hitting home. Memories of him seeing her for the first time, eight months ago, on a spring trip to Florida. He'd been at a beach rave with his Gordonstoun friends – they'd got a house by the sea for two weeks and were thoroughly making the most of it. But none of their fun and exploits could compare to the time he spent that first night with Sherie. They'd only chatted for about half an hour before he led her to a secluded part of the beach behind some storage sheds, the pounding music causing the corrugated iron walls to vibrate as he pushed her up against them and ran his hands through her hair, her lips on his, her perfume making him feel so exhilarated and aroused, he half-suspected it was laced with some secret drug. Two hours later, after a lot of dancing and drinking, she went back with him to the rental house overlooking the sea and they barely came out of his bedroom for the following week. There were times during that week when he wondered if he was in love with her. Barely at the start of adulthood, he'd presumed love was a concept he'd embrace later in his twenties, perhaps thirties, and it took him by surprise when he found himself looking at her sprawled on his bed in the morning light, thinking *This is it, I've found the one*. The feeling didn't last. His mates started to complain he was spending their 'whole spring break shagging one girl', as though even the monogamous nature of this situation was a thing to resent. He could tell Sherie had begun to feel unwanted in the villa. And when she didn't take this as a sign to go, it made him question his feelings entirely. Couldn't she take a hint? Wasn't it clear this situation was awkward? Why was she still there? Perhaps this whole love thing was overrated, he decided. Or at least not something he wanted to explore yet. So he began suggesting she spend some time back in her villa with her friends – a group of girls she'd befriended during her first months of university. She said she understood, but looked a little sad as she walked down the road away from his villa in the direction of the budget hotel where she was staying. And that was that. He didn't see her again during that trip. They hadn't exchanged phone numbers or email addresses.

And now here she is. Right in front of him. In a small country pub in the Highlands of Scotland. He knew she was Scottish, they joked about him sounding English and 'posh' compared to her Glaswegian vowels, but he'd never in a million years thought they'd run into each other. That sort of thing didn't happen outside of corny Hollywood films, surely?

'Sherie?' he says, disbelief clear in his voice.

'Oh, put your eyes back in your sockets,' she says with a laugh as he stands there in front of her. She sets aside the book she was reading: a Mills & Boon romance called *Blackmailed into Marriage*. 'I'm not an apparition. Or a stalker.'

He shakes his head. 'I can't believe it. This is...'

'Serendipity? Fate? A happy coincidence? All of the above?' She laughs, apparently finding George's shock amusing. 'Sit down. If only to block the view of those two young ladies you've left looking seriously ticked off.'

He does as she says, dropping down onto the little stool in front of her table, then glancing back at the bar. The two women are indeed shooting daggers over at the corner. 'Do you think they'll attack?' George asks, turning back with a laugh.

'Hmm, hard to say,' she says, playfully tilting her head. 'I reckon the strawberry blonde might have a violent streak in her. The fact her chances of getting into your pants has diminished substantially is hitting her hard. I'd best make sure to lock my door here tonight.'

'Here? You're staying here?'

'Yep. They have rooms upstairs.'

George knows this. In fact, he's made use of them on a number of occasions, though he isn't about to tell Sherie this.

'Yeah, I've been visiting a friend on the Shetland Islands and had stopped over in Inverness on the journey back. I've never been here before, so I thought I'd have a look around, then get the train back to Glasgow on Christmas Eve. But for now, I'm here. With a room upstairs.'

'Well, that's...' George starts, but he can't think how to finish the sentence.

'Convenient?' She keeps her eyes locked on his.

'Isn't it just,' he says.

EIGHT
EILEEN

10TH DECEMBER 2025

Eileen has gone for a walk. After the row with her daughter yesterday, she can't face being cooped up in her rooms. She goes through phases of liking the seclusion, the feeling of being a recluse, the eccentric dragon locked away, out of sight but never out of mind of the rest of the family. Then she goes through periods when she just wants to relish the beauty of the estate and drink in the landscape and wildlife that the Highlands of Scotland have to offer. Today, she's come down to the edge of the loch, of the part which comes up close to the back of the castle, with a little jetty at the shore and a bench to the side of it. She sits on the bench and stares out at the dark, rippling surface of the water. It isn't one of the deepest lochs, not quite in the league of Loch Morar or Loch Ness, but even so, deep enough to have secrets. Things out of sight. She isn't sure she believes in the mythical beasts or monsters that people like to talk about. But she wonders about pieces of history. Artefacts that may have been confided to its depths over the centuries. Perhaps she will ask for her ashes to be scattered over it when she's gone.

She's never really thought about it in the past, but now she finds the subject of 'after' occupying her mind more often. Only natural, she supposes. And she expects this Christmas it will become *the* topic of conversation now that she's let the cat out of the bag. One of the cats, out of one of the bags. There are still more to let loose. All in good time.

She lets her mind wander into more tranquil territory, enjoying the dull ache the low temperatures are causing in her limbs. She's always loved the cold, welcomed the harsh bracing strength of it. It makes her feel invincible, healthy, alive. Even when she can only seriously claim to be one of those things. She lets out a deep breath and savours the peace. Her phone remains in the castle upstairs. No calls from her grandsons demanding to know if she's gone insane. A rest from it all, before the chaos begins.

'Mother!'

She hears her daughter's voice approaching from behind. She can't help but roll her eyes and think, *Now what?*

'Mother, it's too cold for you to be sitting out here,' Claire says, coming up to her side. 'You'll catch a cold. Or flu.'

Eileen tuts. 'You can't catch a cold from a breeze, my dear. Or flu. Influenza is a *virus*. Can you imagine if people started to say "Come in from the outside air, you'll catch Covid from the breeze" – that would be pretty ridiculous, wouldn't it? Well, apply that to colds and flu and you'll sound less foolish without much effort at all.'

Claire sits down next to her mother with a sigh. 'OK, if you say so.'

'I do,' says Eileen. 'Though I'm aware people don't take what I say very seriously. Not unless I'm threatening to withhold millions of pounds from them.'

'Oh, so it's a threat, not a certainty, then. That's good to know.'

Her daughter's tone is harsh, as though she's seconds

away from flaring into a rage. Eileen doesn't have the energy for any further fighting. She's said all she needs to say at this point.

'If that's the tone you're going to take, perhaps we shouldn't talk for a while. Not until the boys get here.'

'I've told them of your plan,' Claire carries on, ignoring her statement. 'Well, I've told George. And I suspect he's told the others.'

'He's told Ralph, at least,' Eileen says. 'I've had missed calls from both of them. I haven't heard anything from Kenneth. But even if he did try to call, I wouldn't answer. This isn't a conversation for a phone call. You should have realised that before you spoke to George.'

Out of the corner of her eye, she sees her daughter raise her hands to her face. She looks distressed. Eileen doesn't want to cause any of her family undue upset. She's not cruel, or so she tells herself. But sometimes one needs to be harsh to be kind. She's about to put her hand on her daughter's shoulder, try to offer some comfort, but then Claire speaks. 'What sort of grandmother does this?' She turns to look at her mother with anger in her eyes. Perhaps hatred, too.

'The sort of grandmother who feels her family have sponged off her for too long,' she says, slowly. 'And it hasn't made them into nice people.'

They sit in silence for a few seconds, then Claire says, 'Well, I hope you're not expecting a very peaceful Christmas. Not after this.'

Eileen shrugs. 'So be it. And quiet Christmases aren't exactly our style, are they? Especially when your father was alive. He'd usually find some grievance, something I'd say would upset him, then he wouldn't talk to me for the rest of the day. Do his best to try to control me. Then he'd realise I'm not easily controlled, and blame me for that too. He certainly wasn't immune to doing that on Christmas Day.'

'Don't start on Dad,' Claire says, sounding as though she is trying to stop herself from shouting.

'But then,' Eileen continues, 'you always did take his side. Daddy's little girl, through and through. Not that I blame you exactly, I was the same. Always trying to please my father. Just like you. At least you succeeded, to some extent. You managed to get through to him in a way I never did.'

'Mum, please. Let's not.'

'I'm not being critical. He was a difficult man, after everything he suffered in the war. The torture he endured. Horrible to think about.'

'If it's horrible to think about, why are you bringing it up? It upsets me to think about it and he never liked to talk about it, so I'm not sure why you're—'

'Oh shush, Claire. This may surprise you but I'm doing my best to be empathetic. Explain away his demons. Not that he's here to appreciate it now. He was proud of you, back when you were still playing. When you'd go shopping for pianos. Concerts at the Wigmore Hall. He loved all that.'

'As I said, I don't want to talk about him,' Claire mutters.

'I know it's hard, this time of year. They shouldn't have gone out on the loch in that storm. Tragic, for you to lose your father and husband on the same day. Traumatic. People are quite *into* trauma, these days, aren't they? I hear them on the radio and on TV, constantly talking about it. But if what they say is true, that trauma does shape us, change us... well, I suppose that explains why you are how you are. And why I am how I am. But all the same, you didn't have to stop playing entirely. It was a bit dramatic of you.'

Claire gasps. 'Dramatic? Do you think it was some kind of act, like I was making some kind of point? It killed me to give up my playing. But I just... didn't want to do it anymore. It reminded me too much of Dad, too much of the past.'

'Selling your piano was a ridiculous thing to do. It wasn't

going to bring your father or husband back. It wasn't going to lessen any grief.'

'I'm in charge of my life. I can do what I want.'

'A grand total of nothing, of late,' Eileen mutters.

'I've asked you to change the subject,' Claire says. 'I'm not going to sit here while you go through some highly selective retrospective of the past few decades of grief and difficulty and—'

'And yet you're still sitting here, aren't you?' Eileen interrupts. 'Interesting, that.'

This seems to silence Claire, something Eileen regards as a victory, then feels sad for doing so. Eventually, she decides a change of subject might indeed be best. 'I trust they're not bringing those awful women?'

'If you're referring to your grandsons' wives, I can't promise anything, but both Delia and Mara usually go to their own parents' for Christmas. And when it comes to Ken, I think it's highly unlikely he'll bring his ex-wife, so you needn't worry there.'

Eileen nods. Claire stares at her, as if waiting for her to say something more, then gives up. With another frustrated exhale of breath, she stands. 'Please come into the house, Mother,' she says. 'I heard on the news that a storm is on the way.'

'That it is,' Eileen says, getting shakily to her feet. 'That it is.'

NINE

RALPH

16TH DECEMBER 2025

'Can't you just stop and we can talk about this!'

Ralph's voice rings through the hallway of Green Row Mansions, the block of flats where he and his wife have lived fairly happily for the past two years. They originally considered buying a house, but they couldn't make the finances work, not if they wanted to live in the City of Westminster. Indeed, for a period, it looked like they wouldn't be able to afford even a flat, but he had dropped a lot of comments to his mother and grandmother about how it would be stressful to have to commute into London, which itself would be an expense. How having a flat close to his practice and only a short car ride from the TV studios would make things much easier. By the end of that visit, his grandmother presented him with a cheque, telling him to put it towards an apartment that would suit. He was very grateful, of course, but he could have done with a bit more. It was odd, travelling back to London with a cheque for more money than most people would earn in their lives burning a hole in his pocket, feeling hard done by. It felt as if either his grandmother or mother or both were, by not giving him quite enough, teaching him a lesson in some way. He was fairly sure George had received an even bigger handout for his Lowndes Place house. Mara was very happy with the donation to their property fund, wrote a thank you letter to his grandma and received a nice note back in return. This made Ralph feel even more guilty for being disappointed. 'Cheer up,' Mara said. 'Even if it's not a big place, we'll make it our little palace of happiness.'

But now, as Mara chucks the travel case down the hallway, it looks as though their palace of happiness is crumbling around his ears.

'I *knew* there was something odd going on. All those random late-night "walks" you take yourself off on. It's all been a lie, hasn't it?'

Ralph is so stunned by this, he finds he can't talk for a moment. He can only watch as his wife disconnects her phone charger from the plug next to their gorgeous dark-green sofa and crams it into her handbag.

'You're not even going to deny it, are you?'

'What do you think I've been trying to do while you've been unloading your wardrobe into your cases? I am *not* having an affair. Where are you getting this from?'

He is so disoriented, he feels he has to sit down, otherwise he'll faint. He pulls one of the stools by the breakfast bar in the kitchen area closer to him. He'd come home from work to find Mara in the middle of packing, tear streaks on her face. She didn't speak at first, just packed in silent fury, clothes in disarray around her. Ralph tried to clear up the mess, but that caused her to scream at him, telling him to get out of the room. 'That's another fucking thing, I'm sick to death of your bloody tidying! There's being a neat freak and then there's being totally insane! But will you get any help for it? Will you admit it's been getting worse, for years now? No, Doctor Ralph knows best.'

'Is this what this is about? Me being too neat and tidy?'

She pulled at a zip on her case so hard he was surprised it didn't tear off. 'No, it's fucking not, and you know it.'

He stared back at her, astonished, and refused to leave until, eventually, she said something that shocked him. The accusation that he had been having an affair: and not just that, an affair with a man. His secretary.

'I have no idea where you've got this from,' he says again now, shaking his head.

'I just *know*, Ralph. That's enough.'

He laughs. It's so preposterous, so out-of-nowhere, so *untrue*, he can't help it. And then there's the relief. A similar confusion-tinged relief to what he felt the week before when he found out the crisis his brother had phoned him about had been about his grandmother's will. Relief that it wasn't about something else. The other thing. The ticking time bomb he thought had exploded when he saw Mara cramming her Louis Vuitton with cashmere jumpers. But once again, it appears to be another crisis unfolding in his life. And he isn't sure how to deal with this one, either.

'Do you know, so many things make sense to me now, thinking about it. You've always preferred to do it in the dark. Back when we dated at uni and weren't exclusive, you liked to watch me with other guys. I thought you enjoyed... you know... the dynamic of seeing me with another bloke. But it was the other bloke you were more into, wasn't it? God knows how many more guys you saw in the years we weren't together after uni. And now I find out you've been screwing your male receptionist behind my back... do you have any idea how sad and pathetic that makes me look?'

Ralph gapes at her, then says, pleadingly, '*Please*. Tell me where you heard this.'

She grabs her NutriBullet blender, a device she uses at least twice a day, winds the cord around the base and shoves it into a spare Waitrose shopping bag. 'Fine. It was Delia.'

Ralph doesn't know what he was expecting, but it definitely wasn't this. 'Delia? As in... George's Delia?'

'No, Delia Smith,' Mara says, in a faux-calm voice, then starts shouting, 'Of course George's Delia! How many other fucking Delias do we know?'

'But why would she...?'

Mara's lips go thin, surveying him with disdain. 'Your brother told her last week. Apparently, she's felt bad keeping it secret, so she sent me a WhatsApp.'

'Can I see it?' Ralph asks, holding out his hand.

'No,' she says.

'Well, I can assure you my brother would never say anything so preposterous to his wife. He'd never...'

Then his mind goes back to the night he spent over at Lowndes Place the week before. How he let things slip. Things that would be hard to explain to Delia.

'Oh... oh fuck,' he says, feeling himself lean forwards, the impact of realising what might have happened draining him of energy.

'Looks like something's clicked,' Mara says. 'I presume he either saw something, caught you doing something, or you confessed something. To be honest, I don't really care. I'm just so disappointed, Ralph. So bloody disappointed.'

She walks out of the flat, slamming the door behind her.

'No... wait,' he calls after her. He opens the door in time to see her disappearing out of the main entrance to the building. 'Mara, stop,' he shouts.

'Why should I?' she shouts back.

'Because I...'

Because I love you. That's what someone should say in this sort of situation. It's what someone would say in a TV soap or movie, the man calling after the woman, perhaps as she's about to board a plane. Or in this case, a London taxi. But he doesn't shout it. The words, right now, feel almost redundant. Pointless.

Because he's disappointed too. Disappointed he's married to someone who'd rush so quickly to believe hurtful lies about him, rather than give him the time and space to explain.

He watches the taxi leave. And as he does, he's accompanied by the uneasy knowledge that, even if he had been given the chance to explain, he wouldn't have done. Not fully. Not honestly. He wouldn't have told his wife why George had made up that ridiculous story. Why he must have offered it to Delia in place of the truth. And how terrible that actual truth really is. He wouldn't have told her any of this. In that moment, it's this fact that breaks his heart the most.

Even if he can understand the reasons behind this misunderstanding, that doesn't stop Ralph from setting off in the direction of his brother's home. The cold December air cuts at his face as he strides forward through the evening mixture of commuters, Christmas shoppers and food delivery cyclists. It's a half-hour walk to Lowndes Place, but Ralph's feet take him there without him having to really think about it. If anything, the biting cold and darkened streets do something to soothe him. Lessen the impact of his world turning upside down. He can just walk and walk and not think about it.

And he doesn't think about it. Not until he arrives at his brother's house, hammering on the door, not bothering with the bell.

'George!' he yells, all his outrage flooding back, as though the sight of the house has pressed a button in his brain. He's about to shout a second time when Delia opens the door.

'Ralph, George isn't here, he's at the Commons – why are you shouting...' The sentence trails off when she looks at his face. 'Ah,' she says.

'Yes, *Ah*,' says Ralph. He suddenly feels very hot under his winter coat. Delia looks awkward, then assembles her features into what Ralph presumes is supposed to be a consoling expression. 'It's for the best, Ralph, she had to know.'

He feels something snap within him. 'You fucking mad witch!' he shrieks. He hears gasps from the pavement to his left, sees two people stop and then edge around him.

Delia looks shocked. 'There's no need for that,' she says, pulling her cream cardigan around her. 'I'm sorry if you and Mara have had a row about it all, but she deserves to know the truth about her husband.'

'Oh yeah?' Ralph says, the words sounding like a sneer as he steps closer to her. 'Why don't you repeat those words to your precious husband.'

She looks shocked again, but this time there is something else in her expression that confirms he has touched a nerve. Said something that worries her. And perhaps that worry isn't entirely new; perhaps it's built upon concerns she already harbours. How much of his brother's fear of the past has seeped out over the years, he wonders. Patches of guilt and dread here and there, showing up like stains upon their perfect lives. 'What's that supposed to mean?' she says.

'Just that George Weyman MP has his secrets, like the rest of us.'

She wavers on the doorstep, and for a second, he wonders if she's going to invite him in, perhaps to interrogate him. But then she draws herself up, pulling back her shoulders. Her face, still free from lines at thirty-six, suddenly looks like it belongs to someone much older. 'Just because your own flawed marriage has finally crumbled, don't come around here blaming me.' She then slams the door in his face.

Ralph ends up waiting outside in the cold, on the doorstep, for the best part of an hour until his brother gets home. He knocks on the door and rings the bell a couple of times but Delia doesn't let him in. A few passersby look at him, but mostly people hurry past. Until someone comes to a stop in front of him. Dark trousers, shiny leather shoes.

'What on earth are you doing out here?'

Ralph looks up to see his brother towering above him.

'Delia... she... I came to...'

Concern widens George's eyes. 'What the hell have you told her?'

Ralph leaps up, which is difficult since his joints have seized up in the cold, and he stumbles, grabbing hold of George's coat to steady himself. 'I haven't told her anything, I came because she wrecked my fucking marriage. As have you!'

Ralph sees confusion turn into realisation in his brother's face, similar to his wife not an hour before. 'Oh shit.'

'What is *wrong* with you?' Ralph shouts. 'She's gone. You know that? Mara's gone. Pissed off to her parents' or somewhere.'

George shrugs. 'Well, go and find her then. She might find it romantic.'

Ralph grabs his brother's shoulders. 'She thinks I've been having an affair with my secretary. My *male* secretary. Of all the things to make up!'

The door opens behind him and Delia steps out. 'Come inside, both of you,' she hisses. 'You can't be having squabbles on the street like this. It's like some sordid soap opera.'

Ralph looks at his brother, then at Delia. 'The two of you have ruined—'

'Delia's right, inside,' George says, guiding his brother to the front door and over the threshold.

Delia comes in behind them but doesn't close the door. Instead, Ralph watches as she takes down her coat and steps back out into the night.

'What are you doing?' asks George, turning back.

'Giving you both time to talk,' she says. 'I think I'll pop over to Harrods. There are some last-minute Christmas presents I've been meaning to pick up. They're open until late. I'll take the car.'

She closes the door before George can say goodbye. Ralph sees him hesitate, putting his hand out for a second, perhaps to go after her. But he doesn't. Instead, he turns back to Ralph and says, 'I was clutching at straws. You were letting too much slip.' He shrugs his shoulders. 'What else could I do?'

He takes off his coat and hangs it up.

'Er... maybe not make up such an outlandish weird lie about my private life.'

George thuds his hand down on the side table, causing the landline phone to jump out of its dock. He doesn't set it back in its place, too busy staring at Ralph with furious eyes. 'If you hadn't been going to pieces, it wouldn't have been necessary. Like I said at the time, I'm sorry to have panicked you, to have... well, brought it all back up. But Granny's inheritance nonsense has nothing to do with that. We'll get through this Christmas, have it out with her, and not mention anything about the other thing. It doesn't need to be on our minds. It isn't important, not now.'

Ralph can't help but stare back at his brother, as though he's just been asked to decode lines of an obscure foreign language. 'Doesn't have to be on our minds? How can you say that? Christ, it feels like I'm unravelling. It's like this whole being disinherited thing is the prelude to a disaster.' He feels tears slip from his eyes and he rubs furious hands into them, wiping them away.

'Ralph, I'm sorry about Mara,' George says. 'I'm... I'm worried about you.'

Ralph sniffs loudly. Wipes his eyes again. 'There are things...' he says, quietly, 'things I didn't tell you about... things you don't know, about what happened back then.'

George steps forward. 'What do you mean?'

Ralph pauses. Opens his mouth to continue. But then

decides against it. He pushes past his brother, opens the door and steps back out onto the street, colliding with Delia.

'I've come back for my bag,' she says, rubbing her arm where Ralph bumped into her.

'Don't worry, I'm going,' he says, gruffly.

As he goes, he hears Delia say to George, 'God, he's a piece of work. And everyone thinks he's so lovely.'

On his walk back home, Ralph can't help but think she's right. He is a piece of work. And everyone thinks he's lovely because they believe what they see on TV. They believe he's the kind, approachable GP, offering people health advice from the comfort of a brightly lit studio or comfortable Harley Street surgery. They don't know what he's done. And neither do his brothers. They think they do, but they have no idea. They don't know the full story. And hopefully, they never will.

TEN

KEN

22ND DECEMBER 2025

'Why are you always on my case? Just leave me alone!'

Ken isn't often embarrassed by his son, but right now, in the first-class lounge of LAX airport, he gets an insight into what more hands-on dads must feel when they take their stroppy teenagers out in public. His lack of experience with this situation isn't down to Kite's usual good behaviour, but simply because he rarely goes anywhere with his son – or at least hasn't for a while. Throughout his sixteen years of life, Kite has been parented by a succession of nannies and childminders, housekeepers and personal assistants. Ken might share a house with his son, but that is about all they share. Somehow, without him really noticing it happening, he's managed to bring up a little stranger he feels thoroughly unconnected to. A boy who likely considers himself abandoned by his mother and seems resentful of his father. Ken doesn't know how to fix this. But he has been hoping the boy might seem a bit more enthusiastic – even grateful – for a trip to the Highlands of Scotland to stay with his family.

Before departing for the airport, he hadn't told Kite the real reason for their travels. He hadn't confessed there might be more to the trip than just 'catching up with your granny and great-grandma'. The boy hasn't seen either of them in years. Ken feels annoyed with himself about that now. If only he kept more in touch, had been more present, showed off his adorable little boy to them all, made it clear the family wealth would be channelled into a good cause: his son's future. But now, it all feels a bit too late. The adorable little boy is an angry youth on the verge of manhood. And he is hardly in the running for being father of the year. The truth is, his family wouldn't understand how hard it is being famous. How isolating and lonely it makes one feel. It doesn't put you in a good position to be the perfect parent. If anything, it makes it more of an uphill struggle.

'I'm not on your case,' Ken says to his son in a hushed voice, aware that one of the Real Housewives of Beverly Hills is watching them over the top of her *Vogue* three seats away. 'All I said was go easy on the pastries, it's not polite to pile your plate high and not leave any for others.'

Kite makes a scoffing sound, flakes of croissant falling to the carpet in front of him. 'Like you care about others. And why does it matter if I eat, like, ten of these. It's not as if I'm overweight. Have you seen how much I can lift? Oh no wait, of course you haven't, because you don't give a fuck.'

Ken clenches his hands. 'I do give a fuck. I got into weightlifting around your age too. I used to be the skinny one, you know, in the theatre group I was part of.' He pauses to wipe some of the fallen crumbs off his son's jeans. The boy twists to get away from him. 'I know you think I'm on your case, I'm just saying that this is the sort of behaviour that won't fly when we're in Scotland. Your great-grandmother doesn't look fondly on bad manners.' *Not unless she's the one displaying them*, he thinks to himself.

Kite swallows his mouthful and rolls his eyes. '*Look fondly?*

I don't see why I should care what some old Scottish lady thinks. I barely remember her. She didn't speak to me much when I was last there. Why should she care about me?'

'For once in your life will you just fucking listen!' Ken shouts. If every person in the lounge wasn't watching before, they certainly are now. He even sees one young woman he recognises as a prominent social media influencer take out her phone and begin tilting it towards him.

'Right,' Ken says, seizing his son's arm and leading him past the now empty pastry station, coffee machines and the staff attending to people in booths. He takes him into the corner at the side that leads to the bathrooms, then shoves him through the door into the men's.

'Hey, get off me,' the boy protests, but Ken carries on pushing until they're into a large open space surrounded by gleaming blue marble sinks.

'There's no more money,' Ken says.

He sees confusion fill Kite's face. 'What? What are you talking about?'

'I've... I've made some decisions... unwise financial decisions. And there's a question mark over the next movie. The one I'm shooting now will be finished after the Christmas break, but it looks like the decision to shoot the next in the series back-to-back is about to be re-evaluated. The studio has doubts after the last one underperformed domestically. And to be honest, I'm not sure if I want to carry on with them.'

Kite blinks at him, taking in this information. He reaches up and brushes his blonde fringe away from his forehead, then looks at the floor. 'I don't understand. You're fucking loaded. Always have been.'

Ken feels a sense of shame as he tells his son that it's all gone. All the family money that came to him upon his father's death went on the LA house and the Malibu summer home and the New York flat and the holiday property in the Hamptons. 'It's all because of some investments I made. A friend's restaurant business. And an app startup that went nowhere. I thought we'd be billionaires, but the money just kept on melting away, so I remortgaged and... well, there's barely anything left. Most of the houses will go. We might be able to keep the house here in LA, but even that's not certain. There are some other scripts for movies I've been thinking about. But I'm starting to hate it. I used to be an *actor* actor, you know?'

'What the fuck's an *actor* actor?'

Ken shrugs. 'I don't know. One who enjoys getting his teeth into *Richard III* in some shabby town theatre rather than pointing a machine gun at a burning truck in front of a blue screen on a Burbank soundstage. I'm just saying, the money isn't good at the moment and I'm not sure I know how to make it better. Not anymore.'

Kite looks shocked. 'So... what are you saying? We're not just going to Scotland for Christmas? We're going to beg for cash?'

Ken takes a deep breath. 'It's worse than that. When your great-grandmother dies, my brothers and I, along with my mother, should inherit a lot of money. Huge amounts. But she's threatening to disinherit us.'

'Why?' Kite says, horrified.

Ken hesitates. He remembers what George said on the phone about Granny apparently deciding they weren't worthy of the family fortune. That they weren't very nice people. Something like that. Something that hurt him, in spite of himself. Up until he heard those words, he hadn't appreciated how much he cares about what his family thinks of him. 'She's just... strange,' Ken finishes up. He's aware Kite has transferred his gaze back to him, but he finds he can't meet his eyes.

After a few seconds, the silence between them is broken by an announcement that their flight is now ready to board. 'Come on,' Ken says, and they go back into the main lounge, ready to follow the rest of the first-class passengers onto the plane. As they pass it, Ken sees the pastry and cakes selection has been thoroughly well restocked. That is the problem with their lifestyle here, he thinks to himself. It doesn't matter if Kite eats all the pastries. Someone's always there to refill whatever need or desire takes their fancy.

On the flight, things get worse. About four hours in, one of the cabin crew staff comes to Ken and politely enquires if he's 'the father of the boy currently in the first-class bathroom'. Ken, who was dozing lightly without fully reclining his seat into its bed position, looks over to his left and sees Kite's seat empty. 'I guess,' he says, rubbing his eyes. 'Why?'

The young man looks awkward. 'Well, you see, sir, he's been in there for quite some time. We can gain access, and will if we think there's a medical emergency, but decided it might be more appropriate if we asked you. You might be able to talk to him. Persuade him to open up. He sounds... upset.'

Unnerved by this, Ken nods in thanks to the flight attendant and gets shakily to his feet. Walking down the aisle, he's led to the loos to the right of the refreshment station. He taps lightly on the door. 'Kite? You in there?'

He hears the boy say 'Fuck off,' followed by a loud sniff.

'Have you got the key?' he asks the flight attendant. He sees the man hesitate, then he steps up and unlocks the door.

'Could you give me a moment with him?' Ken whispers.

The attendant nods discreetly and walks away back down towards the main seating area. As soon as he's gone, Ken opens the bathroom door and looks inside.

Kite is on the loo, although the lid is down and his trousers are up. He just seems to be sitting there, his arms around his head.

'Kite?' Ken says, going in and nudging the boy's shoulders.

Kite sits up, jerking back as though Ken's made him jump.

'How'd you get in?' he says, rubbing at his nose. That's when Ken sees the powder around it.

'Jesus, Kite, are you high?'

'Yeah, I'm high,' he says in a dramatic stage whisper. 'High. As. A. Fucking. *Kite*. Do you get it?' He laughs to himself, although it sounds more like a loud squeak. Ken turns around and shuts the door quickly. The small space is cramped and uncomfortable with the two of them inside, but he can't risk anyone overhearing this.

'Are you fucking *insane*?' He does his best to add force to his words while keeping the volume low. 'You've brought drugs onto a plane? You're bringing illegal substances into the UK? You're a kid. This is fucking unacceptable.'

'You're a hypocrite, Dad. A goddam hypocrite. You know that, right?' He stands up, swaying, holding onto the walls to steady himself.

'How did you even get them on here?'

'How do you think?' Kite says. Ken notices his flies and belt are undone. He zips himself up, fumbles with the buckle. Ken spots a condom on the side of the sink, and a small little plastic bag of white powder next to it.

'I don't believe this.' He shakes his head, stunned.

'Hypocrite,' Kite says again, bluntly. 'You're welcome to some, you know – I can see you looking.'

Ken's mouth widens in surprise at the words. Then he looks back to the little bag. 'Go on,' Kite says, his voice taking on a tone of amusement. 'Moral high ground be damned, Dad. Moral high ground be fucking damned.'

It's these last few words that cement his resolve. Ken picks up the little bag and empties it into the sink.

'Hey, you prick!' Kite says, stepping forward.

Ken ignores him. He turns on the tap and watches the powder wash away down the plug hole.

'Come back to your seat,' he says to Kite quietly. He sees

now the boy's eyes are red. Not just messed up from the drugs. Red from crying. He remembers that the flight attendant said he'd sounded upset. Feels awful this child of his has come into the bathroom to poison his body and shed his tears. He pulls Kite into a hug. Holds him close. He hears his intake of breath, feels the surprise in him, but his son doesn't resist the embrace.

Ken leads him back to his seat. He sees the flight attendant look over as he walks down the adjacent aisle. 'He's fine,' Ken mouths at him and smiles. He wonders what the flight attendant will tell his friends and family. Probably share stories over his Christmas dinner about how he worked a flight with action movie star Ken Weyman as a passenger and he had to help break his messed-up cokehead offspring out of the bathroom. 'Like father like son,' he might say, and his friends and family will nod, expressions of performative shock and sadness on their faces while secretly loving the celebrity gossip.

Kite seems content to get into his pyjamas, put the seat back into its bed position and go to sleep. Ken is relieved. He has been worried the boy would be too wired after his lines. He knows full well what that feels like. Then again, perhaps it wasn't coke in that bag, but something else. It could have been anything. He has no idea. There is so much he doesn't know. So much about this strange life he's slipped into that has caught him unawares. He lies back and tries to sleep himself, but finds it impossible to get comfortable. As the plane takes them across the Atlantic, in the direction of his homeland, Ken is haunted by the words George said when he broke the news about their grandmother and her plans for her will. *She doesn't think we deserve it, apparently. We're not worthy. She's punishing us for some reason. I don't know what for.* When he heard those words, they astonished him. Now, sitting in his seat, counting down the hours until he sees his family for the first time in years, they don't astonish him at all.

ELEVEN
GEORGE

22ND DECEMBER 2025

George disembarks his flight at Inverness airport and is greeted by the family driver, Hamish. 'Very good to see you, Mr Weyman,' he says as he takes George's bags and walks around to put them into the Range Rover's boot.

'Good to see you too, Hamish. And for goodness' sake, call me George,' he says, smiling at the man. He's known Hamish all his life and the formality has always jarred.

Hamish smiles, but says, 'It wouldn't be proper, it wouldn't be right. As soon as your father died, God rest his soul, you ceased to be George and became Mr Weyman. That's the way it is in my mind.'

George gets into the car and settles back into the comfortable seats. 'I'm not sure I can cope with someone who used to catch me skinny dipping in the loch calling me "Mister".'

Hamish laughs. 'That was a long time ago, Mr Weyman, and you were a wee lad. Better not go saying it too loudly, though, or the *News of the World* will find a way to splash it across the front page.'

George doesn't bother telling Hamish that the *News of the World* hasn't existed for the best part of two decades. Not for the first time, he wonders if the driver lives in his own secluded and separate reality. He might drive a state-of-the-art car, but he's a man of the land, living in one of the small cottages in the forest on the Weyman estate with his father, the estate manager, Robbie. He wonders if the man knows who the prime minister is or what party is in government or if he could name three recent movies or famous musicians born in the twenty-first century. And as he thinks this, George is surprised to realise he's more than a little jealous. He could have done this. Not driven people, exactly, but stayed in the Highlands, buried in the elemental landscape, the trees that block out the sky, the sprawling estate that feels endless, the huge castle that feels like a country in itself. He could have just helped run the estate, worked with Hamish and Robbie, been like a CEO or something similar, making sure it turned a profit. He could have lived a quiet and secluded life too, never leaving the boundaries of his family's land, sheltered from the rest of the world. But he knows he would have gone steadily mad. And after what happened twenty years ago, it would have been impossible for him to stay. Loch Lemire, vast and menacing, right next to the castle, would always be there, like a threatening beast, ready to pull him back to the worst days in his life. The day of his father and grandfather's deaths. And, years later, another moment that haunts him. One that binds him and his brothers together in the worst of ways, never to be let go.

'Mr Weyman? Are you all right, sir?'

George looks up, realising Hamish has been talking while he was lost in his thoughts. 'I'm sorry,' he says. 'What were you saying?'

'I asked how your brothers were. I didn't get a chance to ask young Mr Weyman, he drove himself all the way up from

London. I said to your mother I'd have happily gone to get him, but he apparently wanted to do it himself.'

George is aware Ralph came up early. Driving across the country by himself on a spur-of-the-moment whim wasn't surprising after their row. They'd planned to fly up here together, but his brother messaged the day after his fraught evening visit to Lowndes Place, saying *Driving up tonight. See you at Christmas*. George was worried he'd drive recklessly and crash, but no news of disaster reached him.

'If it isn't impertinent to say, he doesn't seem to be in the best state. I've seen him sitting outside in all weather, just staring out at the loch. We were supposed to be having a major storm but it just missed us, thankfully. But I've heard rumours there's another brewing. Something about pressure systems and arctic air. I've told him he should take better care of himself, stay inside in the warm, but he seems... preoccupied.'

George nods. 'Yes, he has had things on his mind. I think the TV business probably isn't easy. He sometimes doesn't know when his next booking is until just before it happens, depending on the items they discuss, and the demand isn't as frequent now we're not in the midst of Covid anymore. And his GP practice takes up a lot of time.'

He doesn't mention Ralph's marital issues. Or the part he's played in them. He feels a pang of guilt thinking about it. Over the past week, he's spent a lot of effort justifying the fiasco to himself, thinking that Ralph's marriage has always seemed mismatched and doomed from the start. Mara was his girlfriend when he was fifteen – the sister of a boy at school, they had an innocent-seeming teenage relationship. Then they broke up when he was seventeen. George knew what that was about. The guilt Ralph struggled with after what happened during that terrible Christmas. What all three brothers did. But to George's surprise, Ralph and Mara found each other again, many years later, their paths colliding through business contacts. They struck up their relationship again and married shortly after.

Something about the quick way it happened made George wonder at the time about its chances of survival. He suspects his brother married her in a hurry in an anxiety-driven attempt to grab a respectable married life while he could. Even before he voiced his drunken fears a couple of weeks ago, George knows Ralph has spent his life running away from the sins of the past. All three of the brothers have in their own way. George has always seen Mara as a prop in Ralph's attempts to create a happy, safe, stable existence. And now it has all fallen apart. Directly or indirectly, his past horrors have caught up with him. Never far away, never free from their grip. The secret they confined to the loch.

As if on cue, the row of trees out of the window to George's left gives way to a view of it now. An expanse of water that looks like a sheet of crinkled foil in the darkening late-afternoon light.

'It's a beautiful sight, isn't it?' Hamish says, mistaking George's transfixed gaze for something a lot more positive than it is. He can't imagine a world where he feels anything other than repulsion towards this body of water. It feels like a malignant tumour on the landscape, a fuel for his anxieties, the source of his worst nightmares. Yet it hadn't always been so. Before the two traumatic, life-changing events, Loch Lemire was just part of his home. Not exactly a thing he loved, just something that had always been there. He finds he can still just about access those memories now, just as he did when he made his innocuous comment to Hamish earlier about his youth spent swimming in there with friends or going out on the boat when his father was still alive. Then his father and grandfather drowned out there on a cold November afternoon. Then, of course, a few years later, there was that fateful Christmas. The night that has come to define his life. Even so, it isn't as though these traumatic experiences have obliterated those early memories. But it has archived them, like precious objects, only to be handled occasionally.

He and Hamish lapse into comfortable silence for the rest of the trip. The dramatic view of Lemire Castle comes into view after ten minutes of the drive around the perimeter of the loch. Situated on the raised side of the ground across the water, the Z-plan castle looks like a sculpture against the purple-grey evening sky. Home. George feels both affection and trepidation towards the building. Throughout his life it has been the scene of various difficulties. This Christmas promises to be another challenging chapter.

When the car winds its way up the drive, he sees the front door open and someone walks out. His mother. She looks stressed. She's put on weight since he last saw her, and this change is disturbing to him. She's always been so disciplined about her health. Her hair, a natural red-brown, maintained with hair salon treatments, is streaked with grey. Perhaps the two weeks since his grandmother's declaration have been all it took to trigger a breakdown. He wonders if this is just old age setting in, or if he's just being inexcusably sexist to notice such things, but figures he would have noticed the same changes in his father, had he been living. He forces himself not to get lost in thoughts about his father and gets out of the car.

'Mum,' he says, going over to embrace her.

'Darling,' she says, taking him in her arms. 'I'm so glad you're here, it's been terrible. Truly.'

She lets go of him and looks at him. 'You're looking thin, darling, are you eating?'

After thinking just the opposite about his mother, the comment surprises him. But it makes sense. When he's stressed, his appetite disappears. Delia has commented on it.

'Err, yes, I am.'

'I'll take these inside for you, Mr Weyman,' Hamish says, holding George's bags.

'No, I mean... yes, sorry, thank you, Hamish. Just the hallway will do.'

Hamish walks inside with the bags. Claire's expression changes. Whatever guard she's been keeping up slips. He sees her eyes growing tearful, the ends of her mouth tensing. 'That bloody awful woman,' she whispers, tilting her head at the tower to the right of them. George looks up at it. There's a light on in the window. It feels ominous. He's not scared of his grandmother, but the power she wields has always been felt by each and every one of them. And power breeds tension.

A strong gust of wind hits them, suddenly. Claire pulls her hair out of her eyes. George puts his hands in his coat pockets and says, 'Come on, let's get out of the cold.'

'Ralph's here too, I presume you know that,' she says, taking his arm as they walk towards the door.

Hamish comes out of the house and says he'll head off home. 'If these storm warnings get worse, I can check in on you all?' he says.

'We'll be fine, but thank you,' Claire says. George sees her trying to smile and act naturally. She fails, but Hamish doesn't comment.

'I'll be back tomorrow morning,' he says.

'Sorry? Oh, yes, of course. With Ken and Kite. I sometimes forget... it's been so long since they've been here.'

Hamish smiles. 'Hopefully, they land before the storm hits.'

Claire nods, distractedly, 'I'll let you know if I hear anything.'

Once Hamish has gone, George turns to his mother and says, 'Do you think I should go and see Granny now? To, um... say hello.'

His mother looks doubtful. 'I don't think you'll get anywhere. Although you're more likely to than Ken. Subtlety isn't exactly his thing. I'm worried he'll go stomping in there and make things worse. But if you tread carefully, I suppose you could... I don't know... update her.'

George frowns. 'Update her? On what?'

'On your arrival, I suppose,' Claire says. 'How's Delia doing?'

George sighs. 'She's anxious. She flits from telling me it's vulgar to talk or worry about money, then spends most of her time doing both those things.'

'Ah,' Claire says. 'I can imagine that might be a bit difficult. And are you... are you both... um, still trying?' She looks embarrassed and George is mortified to see her eyes flick down to his crotch.

'Yes, we are still trying for a baby, and no there hasn't been any success,' he says, in a way he hopes puts an end to the subject. He's been cursing the day Delia told his mother of their plans earlier in the year. 'I should probably get unpacked.' He looks across the entrance hall, over to the large staircase leading to the upper floors. The sight of a figure leaning on the bannisters makes him jump. 'Oh... Ralph. Hi,' he says, calling up.

Ralph doesn't answer. He's leaning up against the railings of the gallery landing, his hands hidden by the Christmas garland lining the top of the rails. Dressed in tartan pyjama trousers and a navy hoodie, scowling down at them, as though he's a teenager been sent up to do his homework. George feels a pang of guilt, wondering if he's responsible for this, as though their fallout has caused some Benjamin Button-style age reversal, and the more they fight the younger Ralph will become until one morning they will find a screaming baby in his bedroom where a grown man once was.

'Can someone tell me what's going on with you two?' Claire says, causing the surreal edge to George's thoughts to evaporate. Still, though, he continues to stare up at his brother. Ralph doesn't say anything, just stares back at him for a few more seconds, then turns away and disappears off into the darkness of the first floor.

'Go and make up with him,' his mother says, her voice now gentle. 'Please.'

George turns sharply back to her. Narrows his eyes. He's relieved it doesn't seem as though Ralph has told her the details of their falling out, which would make things very difficult. For all of them.

'He says you've had a row.'

'And he hasn't said why?' George asks, tentatively.

Claire shakes her head. 'No. He wouldn't tell me.' She narrows her eyes, and George feels her watching him with more scrutiny. 'I can never make you boys out, sometimes. I do wonder if...'

'If?' George says, dreading what might follow.

'If there's some tension between the three of you that I don't understand. But maybe that's always the case with siblings. I never had any, so what do I know?' She shrugs and smiles sadly. 'Just try to make up with Ralph. This Christmas is going to be hard enough without adding to it. If this is going to be a civil war with your grandmother, it would be nice to know that my sons are all fighting on the same side.'

TWELVE

RALPH

23RD DECEMBER 2025

On the morning of the 23rd of December, Ralph wakes early, gets out of bed, and is halfway down the corridor on his way to the bathroom when a door opens and George comes into view.

'Morning,' he says, his normally tidy blonde hair a mess. 'Happy Christmas Eve Eve.'

Ralph doesn't smile at this reference to their childhood. They always used to call it 'Christmas Eve Eve' as kids, make up stories about this being Santa's last chance to get himself together and check all the presents. He and George once filled a notebook with drawings of reindeer doing warm-up stretches and practising their take-off speeds, complete with candy-cane runways and elves holding glow sticks. He knows George is trying to evoke a sense of closeness in order to thaw the icy atmosphere between them, but Ralph isn't in a forgiving mood. He turns on his heel and walks away from his brother without saying a word.

'For God's sake, Ralph, stop being like this,' George calls after him. Ralph doesn't look back. He just returns to his room and slams the door. It's only 6.50 a.m. and he considers trying to go back to sleep, but instead pulls on his cosy dressing gown and goes to sit by the window, looking out on the lawn, the little steps and pathways, just about visible in the morning darkness. And the loch, of course. Always there. Never free from the landscape or his mind. He picks up a copy of an American medical journal he'd been reading the night before and pulls it towards him. He's only read two sentences of an article about tibia pain when there's a knock on the door.

'Can I come in, Ralph?' George says from the other side.

'Piss off,' Ralph calls out. It's the first thing he's said to his brother since he arrived the night before. He refused to have dinner with him, instead taking a bowl of Frosties to his bedroom, ignoring his mother's protests that it 'wasn't very sociable on the first night they were all together'. But of course, they're not all together. There's still Ken and Kite to come, their arrival probably imminent. Then there is Granny, who has kept to her tower for the most of his week's stay. She was friendly enough to him when he arrived but made it quite clear she wouldn't be discussing the inheritance issue until everyone was there.

'Ralph, I'm... I'm sorry. I really am.'

The word *sorry* causes a flicker of something within Ralph. A sudden ghost of a need to see his brother face to face. Perhaps even hug him, tell him he forgives him. But he doesn't give in to it. His anger is still his dominant emotion.

George knocks again. 'Ralph, I'm coming in.'

Ralph gets up, his reading material falling to the floor, and marches over to the door, dragging the chair he's been sitting in over to it and shoving it under the handle. When George tries a second later, access is impossible.

'Open the door, Ralph,' he says with a frustrated sigh.

'No!' Ralph shouts back. 'I can't right now. I'm too busy sexting my male receptionist. You know, the one I'm fucking!'

There's silence after he says this. Ralph hears footsteps. He pulls the chair away and opens the door in time to see the castle's housekeeper, Alexandra, holding a pile of folded towels. Their eyes meet and they both stand there, Ralph feeling like he might die of embarrassment. 'Have you seen my brother?' he asks.

She points down the corridor. 'He went to his room.'

'Right,' Ralph nods. 'Sorry about the shouting.'

She gives him a small smile.

He's about to close the door, but decides he has to address what she probably just heard. 'Err... that thing I just said. It was a joke. An in-joke with George... that is, he would get it. Get that it was a joke. That I wasn't serious. I'm not... texting anyone.'

Shut up, he says internally to himself. He can feel his face going red.

'Sure,' Alexandra says, turning to go. 'No judgement here, Ralph,' she calls back at him. He hears her chuckling as she walks down the stairs.

Cursing himself, he closes the door. He picks up the discarded journal and places it carefully on his bedside table, then straightens his wallet and positions his water glass so it's equidistant from the other items. Satisfied and feeling a little calmer, he dresses in a tracksuit and thick hoodie, then goes downstairs, through the entrance hall and out into the freezing morning air. He heads for the forest, keeping to the main trail path that runs through the heart of the woods. It's still dark, but there are warm white Christmas lights that run each side of the path – large festoon bulbs that go up every year in mid-November. They could do with being there all year round, but his mother likes the tradition of having them up through the Christmas season. 'The wildlife can enjoy the darkness the rest of the year,' she always says.

He gets tired pretty quickly, his lack of sleep catching up

with him. He takes a shortcut back and walks the rest of the way. He's coming up to the house when his phone starts vibrating in his pocket. He takes it out, impressed he has enough signal to receive a call here in the depths of the Highlands. They're often impossible.

It's his mother.

'Mum, why are you calling me?' he says.

'Because I can't find you, darling, and I know you're awake as I've already been in your room. I was worried about you.'

He stops, panting, and leans up against a nearby tree. 'I went out for a run. I do it most mornings. Don't remember anyone being worried about me before.'

His mother is silent for a few seconds and for a moment he thinks the call's failed, but then she says, 'I heard a row between you and George, then saw you disappearing off into the dark from my window. But if you're OK, then I'll see you when you get home.'

'Well, I'm almost back now,' Ralph says, starting walking again. 'I'm coming up to the outhouses.'

'Oh splendid,' she says, sounding instantly more enthusiastic. 'You can get me some twine.'

'Twine?' he says, not hiding the irritation in his voice. He's aware he hasn't been very helpful since arriving, but he hates being given jobs to do.

'Yes, I've run out, and the garlands are hanging too loosely on the upper bannisters. You know, along the main staircase? Be a darling and see if there's any in the sheds?'

He sighs. 'Aren't there, like, gardeners and people to do that shit?'

He hears his mother tut. 'Darling, we've given most people time off this week, we always do, you know that. If it's too much trouble...'

'No, no, it's fine,' he says. 'I'm coming up to the sheds now.

I'll see you in a bit.' He cuts the call before any further requests can be made.

As he walks across the courtyard, he feels a strange feeling coming across him.

Has he been here since that night? That night twenty years ago, almost to the day?

Of course he has, he tells himself. Stop being stupid. Of course he's been to this courtyard. He must have been.

But not to the sheds.

No, that can't be right. But as he walks towards the outbuildings, with their wooden doors with chipped paint and cobwebs in the corners, he can't remember a time in the past two decades when he's gone into them. Not since...

Just get the twine, just get the bloody twine and go.

He isn't even entirely sure what he's looking for. He's never used twine in his life, but he imagines it's probably like string, or the surgical thread he uses to stitch small wounds in his surgery.

He feels something on his face. Then it happens again. He looks up and it gets in his eyes. It's snow. Snowflakes everywhere, floating down thick and fast, drifting to the stone ground. He suddenly feels very cold.

He reaches out a hand for the main storage building, housing all kinds of gardening stuff, along with the generator. It's the most likely place to find what he's looking for.

That heartbeat is getting loud in his ears. Very loud.

Breathe.

The door screeches and rattles. Inside the scent of paint and dust and damp hits his nostrils.

Twine. Twine. Where the fuck is the twine?

But he can't see any twine. He can just see things. Shapeless, dark things. Messy, untidy. Out of order. Even if he didn't have other reasons to dislike this place, the disorder itself would be enough to spike his anxiety. He should turn on the light, but one of the shapeless dark things stops him. Because it isn't shapeless or dark. It's clear and distinct, lit by the grey morning light filtering in from the doorway. It's plastic sheeting. The sort of plastic sheeting used to cover plants. Protect them from the winter cold.

Or wrap a body.

'Whoa, whoa, OK, I've got you,' says a voice in his ear.

He feels weird and floaty, as though he is dissolving into the ground, about to become one of the dark, shapeless things. But the hands steady him, catch him before he falls.

'Can you walk? Ralph, can you walk or do you need me to get someone?'

'I can walk,' Ralph says and allows himself to be guided by the person holding onto him. Once he's out in the courtyard again, he sees the hands holding onto him are a woman's. It's Alexandra. 'There we go,' she says, the soft Scottish lilt to her voice soothing. Reassuring. Reminding him of one of the nannies who looked after him as a child.

'Inside here. Come and sit down. Let me get you some breakfast.'

He sits down at the long kitchen table without argument. His head still feels a bit strange, but he's quickly getting back to normal. 'Eggs, I think,' Alexandra says. 'I presume you haven't had anything since those Frosties I saw you pilfering last night, and that's hardly a main meal, is it? Better add some bacon, too.'

Ralph isn't sure if the scent of fried food is helping or hindering his uneasy feeling, but he sits, silent and patient, making himself go very still and calm. He sniffs, realising there's a sweet smell in the air, then notices a large jar candle on the table, its lit wick fluttering in the breeze. The front has a colourful, Christmassy image and the label declares the scene to be 'Advent Gingerbread Cookie'. He figures Alexandra must have purchased it herself, it looks a bit too 'mass-market' to be something his mother would buy, but something about its presence helps him feel more relaxed. When the plate of food is placed in front of him, he picks up the knife and fork and starts to eat, feeling better with every mouthful.

Alexandra sits down opposite him and says, 'I haven't seen you on TV much lately. Have your GP patients been keeping you busy?'

He chews for a bit, thinking. Then swallows and says, 'Maybe I'll drop the TV stuff. I'm starting to think... maybe I don't like the idea of people recognising me.' After he says this, he wonders if it's been a mistake, to be so candid in front of staff. Lovely though Alexandra is, she isn't one of them. She isn't family.

Alexandra nods and smiles. 'Oh yes, I'd never become a TV personality. I've got too much of a wild past for that.' She starts to collect things up from the Aga and puts them in the sink. 'Then again,' she says, her words barely audible over the clatter, 'haven't we all.'

THIRTEEN
GEORGE

CHRISTMAS EVE 2005

George is examining the books in the library when he first sees it. A shape moving past the window in the dull late-afternoon light. He wonders if it's Hamish, coming to check on them, and goes to look out of the window.

'What is it?' says Ralph, looking up from the large medical volume he'd been engrossed in.

'I don't know. I thought I saw someone.'

Ralph shrugs, 'Probably one of the groundsmen. Or Hamish. Hey, do you know the difference between synovial, fibrous and cartilaginous joints? It's so interesting that our bodies—'

'No, I don't know,' George cuts him off. He's looking outside. 'Perhaps it was Hamish, but I didn't think it looked like him. I thought it looked more...' He trails off.

'More?' Ralph repeats, sounding confused.

More like a woman, he had been going to say. But he stopped himself because a thought occurred to him. Not just a thought – a memory. A memory of two nights before.

A memory of heading up the stairs at the pub to the smallest of their two guest rooms. Barely making it through the door before they started kissing, his hands running up the back of her neck and into her hair. Just as they'd done on the beach in Florida months before. Inside, they fell onto the bed in a semi-clothed tangle, their mouths desperate for each other's lips, George's heart pumping a beat so forceful it felt celebratory in its persistence and volume. The other girls he'd taken up to these rooms weren't like this. They'd been quick treats at the end of a night out, the landlord's son Jim, a local mate of George's from childhood, slipping him a room key from behind the bar with a wink. Those encounters were throwaway distractions. This was something else. This was passion. How could he have cut things off with Sherie so pathetically, back in the spring, he thought to himself. They could have easily arranged to meet up, to do this very activity, again and again, when they were home in Scotland. All these months without this exhilarating rush in his life felt like a criminal waste.

Then, when they lay back breathless and exhausted an hour later, with grim inevitability, his thoughts changed. Perhaps it wouldn't be wise, he thought as she leaned against his chest, to let this get out of hand. He didn't want a girlfriend. Didn't want to spend university tied down in a long-distance relationship. 'God, I've missed you, George,' Sherie said right at that moment, inflaming his worries. His thoughts switched so quickly from excitement to negativity, the stark change making his head spin.

'Yeah, it was fun,' he said. He could tell immediately that it wasn't what she'd hoped to hear. So they lay in that cramped single bed for what felt like an age until he noticed her breathing become steady and her eyes were closed. He then climbed out of bed and went over to the window. The mist had become thick, and he had a sudden panic about the impending snowstorm – the storm that had seemed like a trivial fuss about nothing a few hours before. Now, it felt like a looming threat. The awkwardness of spending the main days of Christmas here in this pub, unable to drive home, trapped in a tiny room with Sherie, felt as horrific to him in that moment as a prison sentence.

As fast as he could without waking her, he pulled on his clothes and headed out onto the landing. In the dim light, he knelt to tie up his shoelaces, feeling like he was performing some kind of elaborate escape in a war movie. 'Making the walk of shame, mate?' said a voice behind him. He jumped so hard he was surprised he didn't pass out. With relief, he saw it was Jim walking down the short corridor off the landing. 'I thought that bed was going to fall through the ceiling into the kitchen below,' he went on with a grin.

George smiled, slightly embarrassed, then asked in little more than a whisper, 'How many days is she booked in for?'

Jim raised his eyebrows. 'Why? Want to come back for round two? You'd have to be quick, tomorrow's her last night.' George felt relieved to hear she'd been telling the truth, that she'd be gone on Christmas Eve. Irrational fears of her taking up residence in the village had flown through his mind as he'd dressed, and he was pleased this now seemed unlikely. He drove home carefully through the mist, unsure if he'd had a great night or made a big mistake. By the time he was in his own bed, his thoughts were becoming stained with guilt. He'd done the same thing all over again – just like in Florida. She'd think he was awful. A dick. A certified chauvinist who treated women with abominable disdain. The worst example of his sex, a case study in all that was wrong in the world regarding relations between men and women.

The next day, the guilt had more or less abated, although he washed himself extra thoroughly in the shower when he woke up, hoping he might be able to wash away his poor behaviour like shedding an old skin.

And now Christmas Eve is here and he's confined what happened two days before to the past. Or at least, he would, if he hadn't just seen Sherie walking past the window outside. Hood up against the wind and snow, but her face unmistakable.

'George? What's wrong?' Ralph says, but he just doesn't answer him. After a few more seconds of trying to spot movement, he opens the window.

'Hey, what are you doing?' Ralph protests as a snowflake-flecked gust flutters the pages of his book.

'Sherie?' George calls out.

To his surprise, he gets an instant answer. 'Hello?' comes a woman's voice amidst the howling wind. Then footsteps. Someone crunching through the storm, out of sight but getting nearer. From around the side of the building, a figure emerges. It doesn't take long until he sees her smiling at him, relief in her eyes. 'Oh my God, I'm so glad to see you! I thought I was going to die in the snow!' However, for all her alleged fears of death, she doesn't hurry. Instead, she looks up and says, 'I can't believe you live here! Like, for this to actually be someone's home. It's crazy!'

'Yeah,' George says. 'Yeah, this is home. What are you doing here?' He then worries his words sound unwelcoming, so he continues, quickly, 'Come in from the cold, you must be freezing.' He points to his left, where the French windows to the library can just about be seen, snow drifting up to the doors. She nods gratefully, and he says, 'See you in a sec.'

'What's going on?' asks Ralph.

'Just... wait a sec,' he says, running to the door and along to the library.

'Thanks so much,' Sherie says as he lets her in. Some quantity of snow falls into the room and onto the carpet, but he barely notices or cares. His feelings about her arrival are a confused tangle in his head. He wonders, as she pulls down her hood and brushes her long, brown hair out of her eyes, if she's come here to scold him, to tell him how awful he is, how hurt and offended she was that he shagged her then bolted as soon as she closed her eyes. Or perhaps, even worse, she is here to declare her love to him – how the night of passion they shared two days previously convinced her that they were soulmates. That would be a nightmare: a painfully embarrassing situation to unpick, especially with his brothers all nearby and likely eager to revel in whatever drama she might create. Even so, amidst all these fears, he doesn't want to leave her out in the snow to freeze to death. He may not be her future husband or star-crossed lover, but he's not a monster.

'This really is such a relief,' she says, dusting off her sleeves. They watched a movie together in this room earlier and the embers from the fire Ken lit are still giving off some heat. She goes over to the hearth and puts her hands towards them. 'This whole experience has reminded me to invest in better gloves,' she says, with a laugh.

George nods, smiles, stays where he's standing, feeling a little awkward. The door creaks, and he sees Ralph coming in, looking curious. 'Hello,' he says to the room at large.

'Oh, hi,' the visitor says.

'Ralph, this is...' He peters off, feeling embarrassed.

'Sherie,' she says. 'My name is Sherie.'

'I know that,' George says, a little too quickly. Of course he hasn't forgotten her name – what sort of guy does she take him for?

The sort of guy who all but throws her out of his holiday villa? The sort of guy who beds her then leaves without saying goodbye?

He silences his thoughts with a tut, then realises he's made the noise out loud. He sees a frown creases Sherie's forehead, then she turns back to George, giving him a shy smile.

'Okaaay...' Ralph says, amusement at the corners of his mouth.

'I was heading for the station but took a wrong turning,' Sherie says. 'Before I know it, I'm walking up this long winding path and there are signs to Lemire Estate offices and I'm so confused and then I saw the castle. By that point, the snow had turned into a full-on blizzard. I thought – well, the choice is either to die of exposure or throw myself on the mercy of whoever lives here!' She finishes the last line so brightly, with an upturned flick of her hands, George can't help but feel there's something a bit theatrical about the whole thing. The story, the delivery – it has something of a rehearsed narrative about it.

'Are you... friends?' Ralph asks, eyebrows raised.

'No,' George says, at the same time as Sherie says, 'Yes.' She looks over at him, frowning slightly.

'I mean, we've met,' adds George. 'The other night. And before.'

The howl of the storm is the only thing that can be heard for a few seconds, then Ralph says, 'I assume this night was the one a few days ago when you didn't come home until about 3 a.m.? I saw the headlights of your car coming up the drive.'

He looks amused. George smiles, feeling his embarrassment rise. Sherie is grinning too. 'Yes, that is when we met. Although it was two days ago, not a few, if we're being pedantic about it. And that was hardly the first time, was it, George?' There's a weighted edge to the end of the sentence, as though his response to this question might be some sort of test. He resents the spotlight it puts him under. Then, before he can say anything, Ralph pipes up.

'Are you the All-Night Girl?'

Sherie's eyes widen. 'What?'

'Apparently George had a summer fling when he went to Florida. His friends were all talking about it when they came to stay.'

'Shut up,' George says, but his sharp words seem to only cause Ralph to carry on with mischievous enthusiasm.

'You remember – Harvey and Gabriel both joked how you'd keep them up all night. That's why they called the girl you were with the All-Night Girl.'

George feels himself blush and wishes he could disintegrate into ash on the spot. Ralph perhaps realises he's pushed it too far, as he shifts his eyes to the floor and mumbles, 'Sorry, that's probably a bit rude. It was Harvey and Gabriel saying it... I wouldn't... sorry.'

There's an excruciating silence.

'Wow,' she says, and lets out a low whistle. 'That's... quite the insight.'

'Sorry, sorry,' says George. 'Can we just start again?'

She shrugs, then nods. But there's a sad tinge to her smile now.

'So, were you on your way home when you... um... got lost?' George asks, keen to get the subject onto safer ground.

'Yes, the station, as I said. Although I suppose even if I'd made it, I probably would have found all the trains cancelled anyway. So getting lost hasn't made much difference. I doubt I'd have been able to get home in all this.' She nods at the window. 'The loch has frozen. I saw it on my way up to the castle.'

'It does that sometimes,' says Ralph. 'Not every year. Hasn't for a while now, but when I was a boy it did quite a bit.'

'You're still a boy,' George says, wishing his little brother would leave them alone. He suspects there's more going on here than Sherie is saying, and he thinks his brother's presence might have something to do with her reticence.

'I'm seventeen,' says Ralph, sounding affronted. 'Nearly an adult.'

'Emphasis on nearly,' George says.

A thud is both heard and felt, followed by footsteps. George knows what this means. Ken has finished his session of pumping iron in his makeshift 'gym', which is just a set of weights in what is traditionally called the 'Smoking Room', even though nobody in the castle smokes. George hopes Ken will head straight upstairs for a shower, but he hears his older brother go into the library where he left them and say, 'Hello? Where the fuck is everyone?' Nobody in the living room says anything, though this doesn't stop Ken's head from appearing around the doorway seconds later. 'Hello?' he says, smiling and wiping his brow with a gym towel. 'I didn't know we were expecting company.' He comes properly into the room and looks at Sherie, interest clear on his face.

'Hi,' she says. She steps over and holds out her hand. 'I'm Sherie. I was just explaining to your brothers – I presume they are both your brothers?'

Ken nods.

Her eyes linger on Ken's vest top and very short shorts. George notices her taking in his muscled arms and toned thighs for a little too long and feels a stab of irritation. This isn't the first time a girl's interest has moved from him to his older brother. And he knows Ken enjoys the effect he has. Occasionally, they recognise him from the odd bit of TV or theatre work he's done. Say things like, 'Oh, weren't you in that BBC regency drama' or 'You're that guy on those posters on the underground for that play' or variants of these. Or they just care about his abs.

'Well,' Sherie says, clearing her throat and running a hand through her hair a little self-consciously. 'I was just saying to them that I got lost in the storm and have had to throw myself upon your mercy.'

Again, George is struck by her use of language, then realises what it reminds him of. It's like something from a novel, perhaps one of those romances that she was reading in the pub. Perhaps, he thinks, she's trying to engineer her own windswept tale of passion – *Seduced in the Castle, Lust by the Loch* – that sort of thing.

'They *know* each other,' says Ralph, who has apparently overcome his previous embarrassment and is now flicking his eyebrows up at Ken to make absolutely sure his meaning is understood. Ken gets the message.

'Curiouser and curiouser,' says Ken, an amused glint in his eyes. 'Where do you *know* each other from?'

George decides to answer quickly before Ralph can cut in with any further references to the 'All-Night Girl'. 'We met the other night, down in the pub. We had a drink.'

'A bit more than a drink, it seems. Is Jim still slipping you the key to the rooms upstairs?'

Feeling like his plan to decrease the awkwardness is backfiring spectacularly, George says, 'It wasn't like that.'

Sherie grins, without much humour. 'Interesting to know I wasn't the first in that pub. Although from the way he scarpered while he thought I was sleeping, perhaps I should have guessed. One moment he's standing at the window, the next he's grabbing his clothes and bolting for the door.'

George mumbles something about being 'Worried about the bad weather' but it sounds pathetic even to his ears.

'Well, well, well,' Ken says, looking at George with surprise and possibly admiration. 'You are a dark horse. I thought I was the serial womaniser in this family. But I suppose the young ones are growing up fast.'

'Would you like a drink?' says George to Sherie, desperate to change the subject.

She takes a while to answer. 'I'd love a drink,' she says. 'If it's warm and full of sugar, preferably?'

'Hot chocolate?' says Ralph, with the enthusiasm of a nine-year-old being told he can have a treat. George and Ken roll their eyes at him, whereas Sherie smiles and nods.

'I like your thinking, laddy.' She winks at him.

Ralph's face goes as red as a phone box. 'I'll make it,' he says, apparently encouraged by her reaction, and dashes out of the room.

'So is it just you three in this big old castle?' she asks, stepping away from the fire and taking off her coat. 'Have you dismissed all the servants for Christmas or something?'

George is about to answer, but Ken gets in first. 'We don't really have servants as such. We have a housekeeper, but her sister's unwell so she's taken some leave. There was going to be a replacement, some agency person my mum hired, but she's been kept away by the storm.'

'And your parents?' Sherie asks.

'Our mum's stuck in New York with our grandma,' George explains. 'And Dad's...'

'Dead,' Ken says. George notices that he glances out at the loch. Though he's never seen him cry – always the tough guy – George knows Ken is still processing their father's death, five years on. They all are in their own ways.

Sherie looks embarrassed. 'Oh God, I'm sorry.' She turns to George. 'I must have forgotten if you said that before.'

'I didn't, it's OK,' George says.

Ken smirks. 'Yeah, I doubt the story of our father's death is in George's seduction repertoire.'

'Haven't you got a shower to get to or lines to learn or something?' George says to his brother through clenched teeth.

Ken laughs. 'Very well. I'll be back down in a bit. Enjoy Ralph's hot chocolate.' He winks, though George isn't sure if it's aimed at him or Sherie, then leaves.

There's silence for a bit between the two of them. All George can hear is the sound of Ken loping upstairs and the raging storm outside. 'So...' he says eventually. 'Do you... want to sit down?'

Sherie smiles and sits on the largest sofa. She looks invitingly at the seat next to her. George takes a single-seat armchair.

'Don't take this the wrong way,' he says, slowly, 'but something tells me that you turning up here... it isn't quite the random-by-chance situation you made it out to be, is it?'

Her expression is unreadable, her eyes on him. For a moment, he wonders if she's going to take offence, but to his relief, she smiles again and holds her hands up. 'I confess, I might have exaggerated the getting lost part. I just... I don't know... wanted to see you again. Is that so bad?'

George frowns. 'No, not exactly. But, well, it is Christmas Eve.'

'Exactly,' she says, leaning forward. 'When better than to act impulsively, to stride out and find your one true love, no matter the danger, even if death might come as a result of it, better to have tried than to fail. I'd rather perish at the altar of love than never to have known what that felt like. So I battled the elements to find you, to come to you. My one true love.'

George feels like a ton of bricks have just crashed down onto his skull. He opens his mouth but no sound comes out. The earnestness in her face frightens him, her eyes holding his with an intensity that seems to grow by the second.

'Jesus fucking Christ are you that gullible?' She shrieks with laughter, slapping her damp jeans with a hand while pointing at him with the other. 'My God, I really had you going there, didn't I? Your expression. Wow. That was classic.'

George feels embarrassed and disoriented, but chuckles too, mostly with relief more than amusement. Sherie is still laughing when Ralph comes into the room.

'I could only carry one, what with the doors and the stairs,' he says, setting down a large steaming mug on the coffee table in front of Sherie.

'Oh my goodness, I could kiss you,' she says, leaping up. She doesn't kiss Ralph, but she does give him a big hug, prompting further blushes. 'Sit down, sit down,' she says, patting the space on the sofa next to her. She picks up the mug and blows on its surface, then takes a sip. 'It's gorgeous! This is exactly what I needed after that ordeal out there.'

George looks over at the swirls of snow, the whiteness of the surrounding area turning a grey-purple in the late-afternoon light. Night is approaching.

'So are you staying for Christmas?' Ralph asks her, looking hopeful.

'We don't know when Mum and Granny will be back,' George says quickly.

Sherie raises an eyebrow at him. Ralph's looking incredulous, too. 'If they haven't left New York, do you really think they'll be walking through the doors ready for Christmas dinner tomorrow?' He focuses back on Sherie and grins. 'You'll stay for a bit, won't you? It would be dangerous to go back out there with the weather like this.'

Sherie takes another sip of her drink and shrugs. 'Well, if you boys don't mind. And I suppose it's true, I'd prefer not to go back out into the storm.'

'It would be madness to go back out there.' Ralph nods, so vigorously it almost makes George cringe.

'Very well, then,' Sherie says, then looks back at George, a mischievous glint in her eyes. 'For the time being, I guess you're stuck with me.'

FOURTEEN
GEORGE

23RD DECEMBER 2025

George doesn't want to overplay his hand. He went to see his grandmother the night before, just after he arrived, but after a quick, 'Oh hello, my dear,' she said she was tired and needed to go to bed early. But at the same time, if there was a possibility of settling the whole situation before Christmas got underway properly – before Ken and Kite descended upon them and waded into the discussion – he'd much prefer that than stringing it out.

'I'm going up to see her,' George says, rising from his seat at the table, his breakfast only half eaten. He and his mother have been having breakfast together, and the topic of conversation had inevitably drifted towards 'the situation'. It struck him how ridiculous it was that they were sitting there talking about it when he could just go and have it out with her.

'Just be careful,' Claire says, looking worried. 'I told you, darling, I have tried, but she's refusing to be drawn on the subject. I worry you might make things worse if you go in there all guns blazing.'

'I won't blaze any guns,' he says. 'And how could it be worse than it already is?'

His mother bites her lip. 'I don't know... I get the feeling she isn't finished yet. That she has something else up her sleeve to shock us with. I've never understood her.' She says this last sentence almost to herself, her eyes on the table in front of her.

'Do you want to come with me?' he asks, keeping his voice gentle.

She shakes her head. 'No. She's seen enough of me. Doesn't have much choice, it being the two of us rattling around this old place most of the time.'

'Well, I'll report back,' he says.

The tower where his grandmother now lives used to be like something from a fairy tale, the wallpaper vanishing halfway up the stairs, giving way to the exposed wall, the railing at the side switching from the smooth, polished wood of the main part of the house to a rusted metal railing. Back when it was used just for storage, climbing those stairs felt like you were about to be banished to somewhere ancient and cold, never to return. But about five years ago, Eileen decided to move to the tower. The rooms were converted, at great expense, so they resembled a very comfortable apartment. Cream, neutral colours. Expensive fabrics, bed covers and carpets. A selection of paintings was moved from the family's extensive art collection. One of her rooms was furnished as a miniature library, with new books purchased to stock its shelves: brand new paperback editions of twentieth-century fiction, mostly, with a heavy leaning on Virginia Woolf, E.M. Forster and Muriel Spark. Now, Eileen spends her days reading them all. When she isn't doing that, she consumes black and white films from the 1930s and enjoys spending time on second-hand sellers' websites and various international incarnations of Amazon, importing rare or out-of-print Blu-rays from all over the world. George finds this eccentric, borderline reclusive behaviour both endearing and irritating. He sometimes feels like his grandmother pursues interests with a ferocious intensity not because she wants to, but because they send a message to the rest of the family that her focus isn't on them. It is on her. And she'd cope perfectly well without them, even though she is in her late eighties. Still very independent, still capable.

When he reaches the top of the staircase, he knocks on the door and says, 'Granny, it's George.'

He wonders if she'll pretend to be asleep or not hear him, but a second or two later, he hears a 'Come in'.

He enters. The modern-but-homely feel always strikes him as such a major contrast to the older, classical style of the rest of the castle. His brief visit to his grandmother's rooms yesterday was in the evening, with the curtains drawn and the warm lamps on. Now, in daylight, the whole place looks much brighter and larger.

'I'm in the living room, dear,' she calls out.

He walks down to the largest room, which has a long, thin window. His grandmother is looking out of it, watching the snow starting to fall. 'We had a little bit in late November, but that didn't last,' she says, as though they were already in conversation. 'But this promises to be something a lot more interesting.' She turns away from the view of the dark morning sky and falling flakes. She looks perfectly made-up as always, her hair tidy, her cardigan and trousers looking both comfortable and smart at the same time. A photographer could turn up at any moment and she'd look like the perfect lady of the house, ready for a magazine shoot.

'We haven't had any snow in London,' George remarks, simply to have something to say.

'Oh I could never go to London, not anymore. Is the Palace of Westminster dreadfully cold? It looks it.'

George smiles. 'It can get a bit chilly in the winter.'

'I've lost touch with so many people down in England,' she

sighs. 'But I do keep up with some via email. Your godfather, for example. I check in with Michael now and again. And Jacob Wakefield.' Her eyes drift over to him when she says those last three words, and he wonders if this name-checking of George's legal team is her way of saying she knows about his recent scandal-avoiding NDA meetings.

'I hope,' George says, his voice tight, 'that Michael and Jacob would always remain professional and not breach any confidentiality.'

She looks at him, unblinking, for what feels like a very long time. Then she says, in a voice of serene innocence, 'I don't know what you mean, George. I'm talking about catching up with friends via email. Little messages about concerts and grandchildren and the latest Ian McEwan novel.' There's a small smile playing on her lips. 'Paranoia isn't an attractive quality, you know?' She turns her head away and goes over to a pile of books on a table by the window. 'I'm considering rereading all of Iris Murdoch. If I have the time...'

'Granny, can I talk with you?' George says, trying to balance his impatience with his wish to be polite. He doesn't want to spend the morning making small talk about the weather and his grandmother's favourite novelists, or worse, falling into any linguistic traps and mind games she's laid out ready for him.

'George, we *are* talking.'

'Yes, I know, but... I wanted to talk about...' He trails off, but it's clear what he means. He watches as his grandmother drops a pristine paperback copy of *The Waves* back down on the table with a thud.

'Oh dear,' she says.

'I know you said that—'

'That I didn't want to discuss it yet? That I wanted to wait until everyone was all together? My dear, did you think I was lying?'

George chews on his tongue for a few seconds, trying to

think about what to say next. He tries to think of his grandma the same way he would a troublesome constituent. Make them feel like they're having their say, in control, guiding the conversation. 'No, I didn't. And of course, I appreciate that you want to wait—'

'Do you?' Eileen says in a way that makes it clear that she doubts it.

'But I wondered if we could have a little... preview discussion... iron a few details out. Just so I can hear and process your point of view. I want to understand, Granny, I really do. Then maybe I could give you some reassurances...'

His grandmother walks slowly towards him. 'George, you've always been the mediator, confident in the knowledge that you will carve a way through the intellectual and moral woods single-handedly, because you know best. The best man for the job. Well, it pains me somewhat to say it, my dear, but I don't think you are.'

George frowns. 'Don't think I'm... I'm what?'

She comes to a stop. Lays a hand on his shoulder. 'The best man.'

They stand there, him looking at his grandmother, unsure of what to say. This alarms him. He usually knows what to say. Or at least, the words often come to him quickly and easily. But not now. He feels like he's stumbled into a strange parallel world and doesn't know how he's got there. Though he can't shrug off the feeling that he should have noticed the transition happening.

'*Tomorrow*, George,' she says. 'I will talk to you all tomorrow. Christmas Eve feels like a good day to set out some changes. Then we can enjoy Christmas Day – if "enjoy" is the right word. We'll see.'

George's ability to speak returns with force, like a cork bursting from a shaken bottle of champagne. 'We already bloody know the headline! We just want to know *why*! And what we can do to stop it!' He doesn't shout, exactly, but the emotion and frustration is clear, his voice rising in volume. She doesn't look hurt by his outburst. Or even very surprised.

'You think that's all? Oh no, the disinheritance is just the start. But you'll have to wait until tomorrow evening. I want Kenneth and Kite here, too, when I tell you everything. Then the games will really begin in earnest.'

FIFTEEN
KEN

23RD DECEMBER 2025

When Ken walks into the main entrance hall of the castle, he can't help fantasising about the money this place would fetch. He's been thinking of little else over the past couple of weeks, since George told him about his grandmother's plans. Of course, they'd never made a decision to sell. He doesn't even know if his mother or brothers would want to. His mother might want to keep the place on, although he's confident he could talk her around. He's fairly certain George would be keen to see the back of it all. Ralph would probably also take the money ahead of any childhood affection for the place. If it were up to him, the whole estate would be sold off to an American billionaire or a golf course company or private school. The thought of being free of its icy grip is so incredibly liberating.

'I'm so fucking exhausted,' Kite says, letting his bags thud down onto the floor. 'Aren't there people to help us with this?'

'No. This isn't *Downton Abbey*,' Ken says, bluntly. He didn't object when Hamish headed straight off to his home instead of offering to take all their luggage into the house. The poor man was probably keen to get to his bed after the miserable day they'd had. It really had been quite a day of it. Before Ken and Kite even reached Scotland, they'd endured a delayed landing at Heathrow, followed by a missed connecting flight to Inverness. Further delays followed due to a baggage problem. Then more delays in landing at Inverness airport due to concerns about the weather conditions. Eventually, it was managed, only for them to be trapped on the plane due to a fault with the doors. Once Hamish collected them, the journey from the airport to Lemire Castle took four times longer than it should have due to the worsening conditions. The Range Rover got stuck on one of the winding paths along the edge of the forest and Hamish even said they might end up having to walk the rest of the way – which would have been miles. Ken tried to remain calm and polite but Kite made the whole thing so much more difficult, not hiding his irritation and bad temper. Ken ran out of things to say to him, his pounding headache making talking and thinking a painful process. He knew it was down to the withdrawal of the various substances he was used to, but after the shock of finding his son indulging in similar vices, he had a new resolve to get his act together. But an instant detox while stuck in a snow drift in the Highlands with a moody teenager wouldn't have been his chosen method.

He finds his mother in the living room in front of the enormous Christmas tree and a roaring fire. She's sitting in one of the armchairs and appears to be in the process of wrapping presents, traditional carols playing from a radio next to her. 'Oh my darling, I didn't hear you come in,' she says, getting up. 'I can't believe it's been so long since I've seen you.' It has been a long time. Years since he came home to the castle, probably four or five, the Christmas before the pandemic hit. He saw his mother briefly since for the occasional dinner in London if she was in town and his schedule allowed. But even the last of those was over a year ago.

'Lovely to see you, Mum,' he says, embracing her.

'And this must be Kite,' she says, releasing him and going over to his son.

Please be polite, he thinks, as she walks up to the boy, smiling. 'Gosh, you've grown so much. Of course, I see pictures, but a computer screen is no replacement for seeing someone in the flesh, is it? Do you have a hug for your grandma? Do sixteen-year-olds hug? I forget.'

'I hug,' Kite says, stepping forward and allowing his grandmother to put her arms around him.

'Gosh, so strong. Like a tree,' she says, tapping his chest and shoulders. 'Nothing like the little boy who was here last time. Slim but made of stone, just like your father.' She turns back to look at Ken. 'Or at least before he piled on the muscles to play those big action hero characters in those films.'

'Kite's trying to bulk up, too,' Ken says, remembering what he said about his weightlifting.

'Like you know or care,' Kite mutters.

Ken ignores this. 'Where're George and Ralph?'

Claire nods at the door that leads to the library. 'George is in there, calling Delia. Ralph is upstairs, he... they aren't talking.' She lowers her voice as she says this last bit.

Ken raises his eyebrows. 'Oh yeah? Is this to do with the whole Granny business?'

Claire shrugs and goes back to her chair with a sigh. 'Goodness knows. I haven't been able to get to the bottom of it. To be honest, I haven't really tried. I feel my interference might be more of a hindrance than a help. Maybe you'd have more luck.'

'I doubt it,' Ken says.

'Why don't you both come and sit down by the fire and get warm. I'll call for Alexandra to make you some food. It's nearly time for dinner anyway.'

Ken sits down on one of the two-seater sofas, then looks back at Kite, nodding at the space next to him. The boy makes a point of going to a single-seater next to the Christmas tree as far away from his father as possible. 'Is Alexandra the new girl? What happened to Mrs Sopel?'

His mother tuts. 'Alexandra isn't *new*. She's been here for two years, now. If you visited more often you'd know that.'

Ken groans and leans back, closing his eyes. 'Please don't start, Mum, it's been an awful day without the guilt trip.'

This earns him another tut. 'Guilt trip? I don't guilt trip anybody. That's your grandmother's job. Anyway, Alexandra joined us when Mrs Sopel got too old for the job of housekeeper. She carried on as long as she could, but the arthritis made it impossible. Don't worry, she's comfortable. We've paid for her care in a luxury retirement complex in Aberdeenshire.'

'I wasn't worried,' Ken says. 'I never liked her much.'

'That's because she used to smack your bottom when you were naughty,' his mother says.

Kite makes a scoffing sound.

'Mum, please,' Ken moans.

'Well, it's true,' Claire says, putting her glasses back on and picking up the gift she's been wrapping, folding the paper around its boxed sides. 'She'd probably be had up for child abuse now, smacking someone else's children.'

She doesn't notice how tightly Ken begins to grip the arm of the sofa.

'Yes, she was very much of another era,' she continues. 'Your father and I didn't mind, though. It was quite useful having someone else in the role of disciplinarian.'

'Is that so,' Ken says, trying to make his words sound more like a full stop than a question.

At that moment, the door from the hallway opens and a young woman comes inside. Ken is immediately aware of how attractive she is. Small, slim, with gorgeous long dark hair that falls over her red turtleneck jumper.

'Hello,' she says to Ken with a smile. 'You must be the prodigal eldest.'

'Talk of the devil,' Claire says, looking up over the top of her glasses. 'We were just talking about you, Alexandra. And your predecessor. How she used to have to punish my son when he was naughty.'

Alexandra laughs. 'Well, if that falls under my duties too, just let me know.' She smiles at Ken and he's sure he spots flirtation in her eyes. He likes the soft Scottish-accented vowels and the way her voice sounds both bubbly and soothing at the same time. She reminds him of the local girls in Inverness he and his friends used to try to get off with on nights out when he was a teenager. They hold eye contact for a beat longer than he'd expect and Ken feels familiar desires stir within him. Then he reminds himself both his mother and son are in the room. It's no time to be flirting with the housekeeper.

'Er... this is my son, Kite,' he says, gesturing to the chair by the tree.

Alexandra smiles and nods at the boy. Kite nods back, saying nothing.

'They've had rather an awful journey,' Claire says. 'Would you mind bringing them up some buttered crumpets?'

'Of course,' Alexandra says, then leaves the room.

Silence follows, punctuated only by snaps of the fire and the sound of his mother tearing off strips of Sellotape. Then, from his chair over by the tree, Kite says, quietly, 'What's a crumpet?'

Some hours later, Ken is sitting on the end of the bed in his childhood room, staring around him. He took a hot shower and was in the middle of getting dressed when a combination of mental and physical exhaustion weighed too heavy and forced him to sit down. He always underestimates the strangeness of coming back here. That's why he doesn't do it often, why he chooses to keep to the sunny emptiness of Beverly Hills or, if he has to come to the UK, the busy rush of London. Neither are like this. A castle of memories. A castle of ghosts.

'I don't know how you're not freezing,' says a voice at the door. He hadn't realised he'd left the door open, and he blinks confusedly at the figure in the doorway. It takes him a few seconds to realise it's Alexandra. 'This room isn't exactly the warmest.'

'None of the bedrooms here are warm,' Ken says, getting up and pulling on a T-shirt. She looks at him and he sees her eyes rest for a moment on the pyjama trousers he's wearing.

'Those look a little tight on you.'

He isn't sure if the statement is said in a flirtatious way, or if she's just making an observation.

Ken lets out a laugh and pinches the material over one of his legs. 'Yes, I found them in a drawer. They're from when I was young, before I got, you know, all pumped up.' He makes a wrestler-like pose, holding his arms up.

Alexandra smiles, but it feels more like an adult humouring a child rather than actual amusement. She crosses the room and turns the radiator up to full, then picks up Ken's discarded jumper from the floor. 'I'll wash this. And these.' She begins to collect his discarded clothes. He finds, suddenly, he can't bear to see her do it, watch her gather his socks and jeans that he's left like the arrogant, entitled prick he is.

'Don't,' he says, putting a hand out. 'You don't have to do that. I shouldn't have left them like that.'

She laughs and this time she does sound amused. 'Well, it is my job. They pay me money to do this very thing.'

'Hmm,' Ken says. He can feel shame starting to crawl across his skin. He's allowed household help to clean up for him a thousand times before and isn't exactly sure why he minds so much now. He rubs his eyes and is about to apologise to

Alexandra for his odd mood, but he sees that she's moved away from him. She's turned towards the walls, looking at the Blu-Tacked posters.

'At first I thought these were movies, but they're plays, aren't they?' she says, looking around the walls. '*Richard III, The Importance of Being Earnest, The History Boys*. Bit different from the movies you act in.'

Ken takes his head from his hands and looks around too. 'Yeah. Nothing goes the way you think it's going to go. Not in my business.' He watches her for a bit, then says, 'Are you really just here to pick up my clothes, Alexandra? Or for another reason?'

She frowns at him, apparently confused. Then she laughs in a way she hasn't before – properly now, as if something is seriously funny. 'Oh, sorry, I just... you think I'm here to flirt with you? Trust me, I value my job too much for that.'

Now it's Ken's turn to look confused. 'Why would your job be at risk?'

Alexandra rolls her eyes. 'Trust me, flirting with the boss's grandson isn't a good look for a housekeeper. Sorry to disappoint. But I suppose you're used to women falling all over you with your film-star good looks?' She shrugs. 'Maybe that's just how it is with celebrities.'

Ken doesn't comment. He isn't entirely sure he's grasping what Alexandra is trying to say or if there's a criticism within her words. He often feels this way when talking to the opposite sex and once remarked to a sort-of-girlfriend that he felt women sometimes overcomplicated things deliberately. She simply replied, 'What a *male* thing to say,' then didn't come out of the bathroom for two hours.

Eventually, Alexandra says, 'Wow, you're not even going to object to the term, are you?'

Ken frowns. 'What term?'

'*Celebrity.*'

He shrugs. 'Do you want me to deny that I am?'

'It would sound more modest than not,' she says.

'Do you like men to be modest?'

She considers, then says, 'I don't have a very good track record with men. I dated a car mechanic from Glasgow who slept with my mother, married her, then took all her money when she died. I should write a book about that someday. Really messed me up. Then there was the investigative journalist who was coercive and controlling and kept trying to get back with me even though I'd broken it off. Since then, there's only been the owner of a small bar down in the village, who is pleasant enough and absolutely gorgeous, but it wasn't a match made in heaven and now it's bloody awkward if I want to go there for a pint.' She grins. 'Sorry, I didn't intend to give you a sad history of my love life.'

Ken gets up and walks across the room. 'I don't mind. It sounds more stable and normal than my own.' He wonders if he should say he's sorry to hear about the horrible, perhaps even abusive, men she's encountered, but isn't sure how to phrase it.

'Yes. I've heard rumours about you, Ken Weyman. Bad rumours.'

Ken reaches the window and watches the snow, still falling thick and fast, the wind starting to gather speed. He can see the gusts sweeping the snowfall across the surface of the loch, the edges starting to freeze in the bitter night air.

'Oh really?' he says, keeping his eyes on the loch. 'Well. They're probably all true.'

SIXTEEN
GEORGE

CHRISTMAS EVE 2025

George spends Christmas Eve in a state of nervous energy. He wishes he were a runner like Ralph or a gym maniac like Ken. He could have done with an outlet to spend some of his pent-up tension. Instead, he wraps the presents he's brought, answers work emails, eats a lot of Quality Street, and sits through *The Princess Diaries 2: Royal Engagement* on television, not even attempting to follow the plot. His mind is on other things.

The hours drag by, feeling extended tenfold as the clocks around the castle tick slowly towards 8 p.m. Dinner time. Frustratingly late, but he thinks that's all part of the planned suspense. The time his grandmother will at last lower her drawbridge of silence and give them some clarity on their precarious financial situation. He doesn't expect the clarity to be reassuring, but he hopes it will at least give him a platform for discussion.

At last, they are all seated at the large table in the main dining room, watching as Eileen takes her seat, her eyes glinting. She looks excited, George thinks. He's certain she's been looking forward to this moment. All of them ready to hang on her every word, her commanding the mood with her powers of manipulation. Alexandra serves them a dish that involves chicken and leeks, although it could have been a lump of Astroturf for all George tasted of it. None of them speak, aside from Eileen, who compliments Alexandra on her cooking and asks Kite a few questions about his school in Los Angeles. This goes on for an achingly long time until eventually the suspense seems to get too much for Ken. Talking over his son as he's explaining which sports teams he's on, he says, 'Look, Granny, can you just tell us what the deal is with the money?'

George can feel the tension in the room, like a buzzing in his ears. Eileen looks at Ken, her eyes narrowing. 'Your son was telling us about his achievements, Kenneth. Wouldn't you want me to focus on that before we deal with something as trivial as money?'

Ken splutters in outrage. 'Trivial? I don't know if this occurs to you, but that private school he attends, those oh-so-prestigious teams he's talking about, none of that is free. It's not trivial. It isn't trivial for any of us.' He looks around, as if expecting support from his mother or brothers.

George steps in, hoping to rescue the situation before it spirals out of control. 'I think what Ken is trying to say—' he begins, before Ralph cuts in.

'I'm sure Ken can speak for himself, George,' he says, glaring at his brother. 'Don't stick your oar in. You might make things worse. You usually do.'

If anyone else at the table wonders what Ralph means by this, they don't ask.

'I want to finish my meal before we discuss it all,' Eileen says. 'Then we can all go into the living room and—'

'I don't think I can wait any longer,' Ken says. 'Granny, I'm just going to lay it out straight. I'm broke. I'm sorry, but I am. It's my fault, partly. Bad investments, bad choices. The movies aren't bringing in what I'd hoped. Things are really difficult. To be honest, I think I'm at the end of my tether in more ways than one.' George notices Ken rubbing at his nose as he says this and wonders if illicit substances – or lack of – might have something to do with this outburst.

'Ken, calm down,' George says.

'Calm?' Ken says, laughing in a scornful, ugly way. 'Don't you tell me to calm down. You were straight on the phone to me, wailing about how Granny might disinherit us all, and she doesn't appreciate how little MPs are paid.'

'If we're on the subject, GPs aren't paid much more,' Ralph chips in. 'Even private ones.'

'Boys, this isn't helping,' says Claire, putting down her cutlery, then glancing at her mother.

'It's OK, Mum, I've got this,' George says, trying to give his mother a reassuring look.

'You haven't *got this*,' Ralph says, rolling his eyes.

'Oh fuck off,' George says, his patience deteriorating.

'I'm dying,' Eileen says.

That shuts them all up. George freezes, his mouth open, ready to shoot another retort at Ralph. But all his words leave him when he realises what his grandmother has said. Everyone looks at her. Then Claire says, 'Dying? Like... soon?'

Eileen nods. 'Yes. Not long now. A matter of weeks.'

George thinks his mother is about to cry. But instead, she just asks, 'How? I mean... what is it?'

Eileen puts her cutlery down at the edge of her plate and looks at her daughter. There's sadness in her expression, but a stoniness too. Defiance. 'I don't want to say. My medical matters are private. I'm sorry, my dear, it's tough news, but there's no sugar-coating it.'

'How...' Claire says. 'How could you not tell me?'

Eileen gives a little shrug, 'I'm not exactly young. I'm over eighty. It can't be a massive shock.'

'Well, it still would have been nice to know!' Claire says, almost shouting now.

George sees his grandmother's face tighten. She looks around at them all. Then gets up from her seat.

Claire looks indignant. 'Where are you going?'

'Please, Claire, don't shout at me,' Eileen replies. 'I'm going into the living room. I'm feeling a little chilly and this is all becoming rather unpleasant.'

'*Unpleasant*?' Ken says. 'Of course this is unpleasant.'

'How did you think we'd react?' says George, trying to soften his tone, but still stunned.

'Granny... just... *why*?' says Ralph, tears visible in his eyes.

'Come to the living room,' Eileen says. 'I want to sit by the fire. Then I'll tell you everything.'

She leads the way into the large living room next door. Even amidst the intensity of what's happening, it strikes George how warm, festive and cosy the whole place is. An idyllic Christmas setting, with the fire glowing and the lights on the enormous tree in the corner twinkling. There are times when Lemire Castle really does feel like a castle, with its towers and turrets, hundreds of rooms and dark corners. But when George sees the living room looking like this, he thinks of the building as a house, not a castle. A house, a home, one that's been in the family for generations. But not for much longer. Not if his grandmother is about to confirm what they've all feared over these torturous couple of weeks.

Eileen takes a seat in the straight-backed chair by the fire and waits until everyone's in the room. Then she begins. 'As you are all aware, I mentioned to your mother a couple of weeks ago that I intend to change my will. These changes will be substantial. I understand this has led to a lot of rumour and speculation amongst you all.'

'Which is what she intended,' Ken mutters in the direction of George. George doesn't respond and his grandmother doesn't acknowledge the comment, even though it was loud enough for her to hear.

'So,' Eileen says, 'I think the time is right for me to tell you what these changes will be. For starters, there will be no money.'

George both feels the impact of these words and sees it play out across his family. If their faces were pictures of outrage before this point, they now display pure, undiluted shock. George understands. His own mouth is open, his heart thudding and his vision takes on a surreal, almost-liquid quality, as if at any moment the room might all melt away and he'll wake to find it's still November and this whole month has been nothing but a dream.

'No money at all will go to any of you,' his grandmother continues. 'At the moment, if my solicitor's calculations are correct, and not taking into account the value of the castle, the estate and other properties, the total cash amount comes to around £35 million. The original plan was that this money should be divided between you all. But now, I feel differently.'

'Well, tough,' George says. 'Unless you've forgotten, Granny, this is Scotland, not England. You can't just disinherit your family, it isn't as simple as that.'

'You're right, it isn't simple.' Eileen says. 'But I wouldn't get too confident. There are legal mechanisms that my very expensive team have managed to find. Loopholes to exploit. I've had them examine the intricacies of Forced Heirship, and I think we've tied up the cash nice and tight. But you're right, there's a chance not all of it will hold water. But whatever you end up getting, I wouldn't bank on it being "dream come true" sort of money. And I think it has been a dream. For all of you. A tempting pot of gold at the end of the rainbow. And none of you deserves it. Not a penny. The one exception is Kite.' She turns to look at her great-grandson. 'I haven't had a chance to get to know you, since Kenneth has kept you away from us all in

America for most of your life. So it seems unfair to penalise you. For this reason, I am going to put £50,000 in trust for you when you turn twenty-one.'

'Fifty... *what?*' Ken says, his mouth open. 'What the hell is that?'

'About 0.14 per cent, that's what it is,' says Ralph. If George had felt less sick, he'd have rolled his eyes at this. Even in tense situations, Ralph still manages to show off his mathematics skills.

'That's... that's all?' Ken says. 'My son deserves more than that. We all deserve more than that.'

'No, you don't,' Eileen says smoothly. 'And can't you see, my dear, you're rather proving my point with your reaction.'

'So where's the rest of the money – our money – going?' George hears his mother ask.

Eileen looks at her daughter. 'I'm glad you've brought that up, as it's a project I'm quite excited about. A Facebook friend of mine is starting a foundation and is looking for funding. I will provide that funding.'

Claire looks completely baffled. 'Funding for what?'

'The foundation is to support the conservation and care for prehensile-tailed porcupines in South America.'

The silence that greets this feels louder than a bomb blast.

'You're winding us up,' George says.

'You can't be serious,' says his mother.

'What the actual fuck?' breathes Ken.

'This is a joke,' mutters Ralph.

'I'm absolutely serious,' says Eileen. 'They care for sloths too, if that makes any difference. The estate, meanwhile, will be left in the care of my lawyers, who will auction it off to the highest bidder. Early enquiries have already been made. I'm told a hotel company headquartered in Boise, Idaho, is keen to have a Scottish Highlands off-shoot. There has also been interest from a German theme park company and a Canadian golf course chain. One of them wants to build an extensive water slide. The proposals are quite exciting, I'm rather sorry I won't be alive to see them. Not that I've ever really been one for water slides. But I digress. Regardless of who wins the bid, the money from the sale will be donated to a list of charities and academic research organisations I've put together. You'll find the list somewhat biased towards the animal kingdom, especially those from the Xenarthra family. Sloths, armadillos, anteaters. Animals don't exhibit greed in the same way humans do, you see. You'd have found all this out from my solicitors and executors upon my death, of course. I just wanted to pay you all the courtesy of telling you first.'

George really does feel like his skull is going to break open. He feels he should say something, point something out, raise some more legal issues, but he can't get his brain to work. He opens his mouth, deciding he must at least exhibit some sort of protest, but his mother gets in first.

'You really are insane,' she says, staring at Eileen with wide eyes, as though she truly believes this to be the case. 'I refuse to go along with this. You've always liked to play mind games, but this really takes the cake. And it's despicable for you to drag my sons into this... to disadvantage them... you're... you're *warped*.'

'No, I'm not mad or warped. Just tired of my family. And your sons are many things, but disadvantaged isn't one of them. Kenneth is a very successful film actor. George is a member of parliament. Ralph is a doctor. They're very capable young men. I just don't think they're very nice.'

Claire gapes at her mother, apparently rendered speechless.

'Not... not nice?' stammers George. 'As Mum said, I'm an MP. I... I *help* people. And I'm trying to start a family, Granny. Delia and I... we're trying for a baby. Surely that's... that's nice, isn't it?'

'That's lovely, dear,' his grandmother says. 'But if society was to presume the strength of a man's character lies in his ability to fertilise an egg, we'd be forgiving all manner of monsters, left, right and centre.'

'That's a dreadful thing to say,' Claire says, with a look over at George.

'Yes, it is,' he agrees.

'And I want to buy a house,' Ken cuts in. 'A house for me and my son.'

George notices Eileen's eyebrows rise in surprise at this. 'Is that so? I may be mistaken, but I understood you lived in some glass-fronted modern construction in Beverly Hills.'

'Yeah, Ken,' George says, anger now giving him strength. 'And if society was to presume the strength of a man's character lies in having Ashton Kutcher for a fucking neighbour, we'd be forgiving all manner of monsters left, right and centre! Isn't that right, Granny?' He's starting to sound almost manic now.

He sees his grandmother fix a stern look upon him. 'Calm down, dear,' she says, then returns her eyes to Ken. He's jutting out his jaw, looking indignant. 'I'm thinking of moving to a more sensible place,' he says, with a cough. 'One where Kite and I can be more... homely.'

'Oh, the film star wants to be all homely, does he?' George says. 'Convenient you suddenly want to be all fatherly to your son when your inheritance hangs in the balance.'

'Why are you attacking me?' Ken snaps back. 'You're not helping your own cause, George. And at least I've got a son.'

'Granny, *please*,' Ralph says, speaking up at last. 'Please, isn't there some other way?'

Eileen shakes her head. 'No, I don't think so. In fact, watching you all protesting and bickering has made me more certain than ever.'

Silence greets this.

'Well, if that's everything,' she says, 'I'm going to bed. Unless anyone plans to murder me during the night, I shall see you all for breakfast tomorrow morning. Merry Christmas to you all.'

The dark humour isn't out of character for his grandmother, but even so, George is a little offended that she might think someone in the family might kill her in the night. They might be many things, he thinks, but they're not murderers.

Then, with a horrible sense of guilt and inevitability, he remembers that isn't true.

Don't think about it, he tells himself, feeling the back of his neck going red. *Keep it locked away. Turn the key. Just don't think about it.*

He's about to get up and excuse himself, try to free himself from the rising panic and sense of dismay this evening has caused. His grandmother is manoeuvring herself around the coffee table, heading to the door, when there's a loud sound that makes everyone jump. A loud, repetitive knocking.

And it's coming from the living room's French windows.

George swings around to look outside. And there it is. A hooded figure is standing there, outside in the blizzard, knocking on the windows. Asking to be let in.

SEVENTEEN
GEORGE

CHRISTMAS EVE 2025

For a moment, George thinks he may have imagined the sound. But the sight of everyone else starting and looking around tells him this isn't in his head. There really is someone outside. A figure at the window.

His grandmother has come to a stop near the door and is staring over at the storm outside. Kite has jumped up, as though he fears an imminent attack. Neither, though, make any attempt to tackle the problem. And everyone else stays seated. George takes a deep breath and decides to take charge. He rises to his feet, marches over to the French windows, undoes the fiddly metal catch and opens the door. The cold air rushes into the room.

'Can I help you?' George says.

The figure starts to speak. He thinks he hears something along the lines of, 'I've come here because...' But if an explanation follows the 'because', he doesn't hear it.

'What?' George shouts, leaning outside.

'I'm here to... sorry, can I come in?'

George looks at him. He can barely make out the face, and the stranger seems to realise this, as he lowers his hood. A young man stands before him. Blonde, clean-shaven, and extremely good looking.

'Who *are* you?' George says loudly.

The man wipes some ice from his face and says, 'My name's Tommy. I've come to talk to you. I started walking from the nearest village where I'm staying before the storm got worse. I would have turned back when it got so late but I wasn't sure I'd make it. The snow is insane. It's taken hours. I'm so sorry, I know this is weird, but can I come in and explain?'

George continues to hesitate. He looks back at his family. Wonders if anyone else will come to his aid in this dilemma. But nobody does. Feeling a prickle of irritation, George turns back to the open door. As he does, he hears his mother say 'Who is it?', but he doesn't answer. He just says, 'OK, come in.'

The young man smiles gratefully and steps over the ledge into the room. George closes the door, the quiet now the roaring wind has been shut out both a relief and an added tension. He sees his mother and Ralph shifting in their seats, as though they're not sure whether to stand or stay still. Ken's head turns to Kite, who is still standing. He gets to his feet and goes over to him.

'Go on, then,' George says, his tone brisk. 'How can we help you?'

The young man takes a deep breath and says, 'Maybe I could sit down. I've come a long way and this is very difficult for me. And it may be difficult for you too. It's just...' He raises a hand to his head.

'No, you tell us first who you are and what you want,' George says. When he doesn't get a reply immediately, he adds, 'Right now.'

He hears his grandmother tut. 'George, let the poor boy sit down and warm up. He looks half frozen to death.'

George is still unsure. He feels there's something going on here. Something strange, like they've all fallen into a play, with a rapt audience holding their breath. 'I'd like him to explain himself,' George says.

She ignores this, walking past him and putting a hand on the visitor's shoulder. She steers him to the armchair Kite has vacated and says, 'Now, when you're ready, tell us what you've come to say.'

George watches as the stranger furrows his brow and brushes some snow from his hair and eyebrows. He has that prickle on the back of his neck again, only this time it isn't a symptom of frustration. It's something a lot more unsettling. Like déjà vu. A memory of someone else coming in from a storm, showing relief to be in from the cold.

'This is going to sound mad,' the stranger says. 'It will come as a bit of a shock... but, well... I'm a member of this family. Your family.'

Silence follows. George can't think what to say. Hasn't got a clue where this is going and worries he won't like the destination. Eventually, his mother speaks. 'I don't understand. How can you be? I don't know you. Do my sons know you?'

The young man bites his lip, then looks at George, then Ralph, then over at Ken. One by one, as though taking each of them in. Then he returns his gaze to Claire and says, 'I'm your grandson.' He pauses and swallows awkwardly. 'One of your sons is my father.'

George no longer feels like he's in a play. He feels like he's in a nightmare. Not for the first time in his life, it's as though the walls of this castle have become the bars of a prison. And through those bars, he's being made to watch something strange and disquieting take place. He hears his mother take in a sharp breath. 'But... which one?'

There's a pause, then the stranger swallows again and says, 'That's the thing. I don't know. I'm not sure which one is my father. And that's what I'm here to find out.'

EIGHTEEN

KEN

CHRISTMAS EVE 2005

After his shower, Ken dresses in smarter clothes than he might usually wear for an evening lounging around with his brothers. Sherie is, of course, the motivation behind this, and he thinks of her long, brown hair flecked with snow as he takes out a tartan flannel shirt and dark navy slim-cut jeans from his wardrobe and begins to pull them on. Although Sherie is a former conquest of George's, he doesn't see why that should stop him. It's not as if he's trying to steal his girlfriend or anything. And a quick, no-strings-attached Christmas fling with a beautiful woman sheltering from a storm sounds like the perfect alternative to their normal family Christmas. A vast improvement, if you ask him.

He knows George has always been jealous of his confidence. For all his talk about wanting to go into politics after university, he's aware he lacks an integral ingredient: showmanship. He gives it a go, but Ken thinks he's going to need to do quite a bit of polishing when it comes to ease and charm. People don't vote for candidates they find unsure or awkward. They vote for people who have confidence in their veins. He thinks George might have that within him eventually, but not yet. He's still a boy, not a man. Although at least he's not as much of a thin-skinned mummy's boy as Ralph. He's next-level, Ken thinks, as he sprinkles a subtle touch of his favourite cologne on his neck.

The plan for drawing Sherie's eyes away from his brother and onto himself seems promising at first, his smiles and meaningful looks mirrored, with sweet little smiles offered back as they all share some pizzas Ralph found in the freezer. Then, as the evening progresses, he becomes less convinced. She's clearly here to get George – or get him *again*. He watches as she hangs on his every word, her eyes on his mouth as he raises some of the deep-pan American Hot to his lips. She's here for him, it's obvious. He never bought her whole damsel in distress in a snowdrift act. Though he probably shouldn't use the word 'damsel' now, he reminds himself. Ken's wrapped up in his thoughts, trying to think of a more politically correct alternative when he realises everyone's looking at him.

'Is it next week you start, Ken?' George says in a way that suggests he's having to repeat himself.

He shifts on the sofa. His feet touch the slightly baggy heels of Sherie's socks. He sees her notice, her eyes flicking down, but she doesn't say anything. 'No, prep isn't until the second week of January, so I've got a while yet,' Ken says, presuming they must be talking about his latest acting job: the role of a ship's crew member in the third *Pirates of the Caribbean* film. 'They're shooting it back-to-back with the second, which comes out later next year. I was originally cast for that one, so it's been a bit of a wait.'

'Ah, great,' Sherie says, then helps herself to more pizza.

Ken's ego is stung. *Ah great* isn't the reaction he's used to when he talks about his work. Sure, he's still only twenty-one, he's only just graduated, and he knows he's not Tom Cruise, but at the same time, many people find it hard to get into the acting world. Some try for years and never get their break – they either give up and become teachers or shop assistants or accountants, or they settle for am dram at their local town hall because they can't imagine a world where they don't act. Ken would have ended in the latter camp. He loves 'the work' as he and his student friends call it. Loves the learning of the lines, that rush of anticipation when you turn up at a casting call and wait to hear if they want you back. Then the excitement of getting the call back and visibly wowing them. He loves all that. And he loves the attention too. People being impressed. Hanging on his every word when he mentions the famous people he's worked with. Some people don't care, and that's fine. But he hadn't banked on Sherie being one of these. It disappoints him at first. Then decides this must just be part of a game. Playing it cool. Hard to get. He knows this dance. He can do it well.

Later on, when all the pizza has been consumed, save for the odd abandoned crust, and *Elf* is on the TV, Ken starts to become irritated. Perhaps he's eaten too much food or just needs a good sleep. In spite of the storm, the lounge is hot from the roaring fire George built and the radiators are adding to it. It's annoying that the outside is out of bounds, but only a fool would go out there voluntarily.

But then all the lights go out.

'What the fuck?' shouts Ralph. He sounds afraid.

'Shit, the power's gone,' George says.

Ken doesn't say anything at first, hoping the lights will return, that it's just a temporary issue. But no such luck.

'Do you have candles?' Sherie says, leaning forward, her frame visible in silhouette against the flickering light of the fire.

'We do,' George says. 'But I feel like there are things we could try with fuse boxes or generators or something. Dad...'

Ken knows what he's thinking. Dad always used to know what to do during moments like this. This isn't the first time power has failed in the castle and their father would usually fix it in an effortless sort of way, as if it were just a question of flicking a switch. Although he had been a quiet and bookish man, content to spend most of his days listening to Chopin while reading John le Carré novels, he had a practical side, a quiet resourcefulness that Ken has never tried to emulate. Neither have George or Ralph, for that matter. Three boys who would barely know the difference between a fuse box and a generator.

'I'll go and find out.' Ken gets up, crunching his knuckles. He stretches his arms extravagantly, aware his muscles are visible even under his knitwear. Or at least they would be if there was enough light. Still, he thinks he spots Sherie's head turning towards him before he heads in the direction of the door.

'I'll come too,' says Ralph, brightly, as though a trip to the dusty basement is all he's wanted for Christmas.

'I don't think—'

'I want to come,' says Ralph.

Ken sighs.

'Two minds are better than one,' says Sherie.

'OK,' Ken says. 'Come on, Ralphy Boy.'

'Don't call me that,' Ralph snaps, but still follows behind Ken, treading a little too close for comfort. Like an eager puppy, Ken thinks with irritation.

'So what are we going to do with the fuse box?' Ralph says as they step through the door to the basement steps and start to tread their way down. Both of them are just in their socks and Ken feels the cold stone through the material as though he's just shoved his feet into the freezer.

'I have no fucking idea,' Ken says.

'You sounded like you did,' Ralph says, sounding disappointed.

'Yeah, well,' Ken says, without finishing his sentence. He

would have thought it was obvious. If Ralph realises, he doesn't say. Perhaps he's here for the same reason. Three brothers competing for a girl's attention. It's like a romcom. Or a classic Hollywood musical. Or something worse.

Their trip to the basement is unsuccessful. There are switches, wires, boxes on walls that look 'dangerous as fuck' according to Ralph. Ken flicks a few things, squinting in the harsh white light of a torch. Presses a button. Nothing happens.

'I feel like we've come to a part of the Death Star,' Ralph says, 'but we don't know how to bring it down.'

'Christ, you're not fucking twelve, Ralph.'

'You don't have to be such a prick to me, just because you don't know what you're doing.'

'I do,' Ken lies. 'In fact, let's go to the generator.'

'To the generator?' Ralph gasps, looking shocked, as though Ken has suggested they fly to a warzone.

'Yeah. You don't have to come.'

'You're going out in the *storm?*'

Ken walks past him and begins to climb the stairs. 'I repeat, you don't have to come. Might get ya jammies wet, wee laddy,' he says.

'Oh fuck off, I'm not even wearing pyjamas. These are just... comfy clothes.'

'Go back to the lounge.'

'I'm not going in there,' Ralph hisses, lowering his voice as they get to the top of the cellar steps.

'Why? Worried she's blowing him already?' Ken chuckles.

'Well, *yes*,' Ralph says. 'I'm coming with you.'

But his resolve is tested when they reach the kitchen back door. Ken pulls on some old Wellington boots he thinks used to belong to his grandfather. Ralph pulls on some of his trainers.

'It's awful,' he shouts after Ken as they walk towards the outbuildings. Ken has to agree, but he doesn't verbalise it. The force of the wind is extreme. Even for someone raised in the

Highlands, Ken's shocked by its force, and the searing cold burn rushing across his skin. He walks as fast as he can through the deep snow lying across the courtyard to the flaking, rough wooden door of the building in front of him. Once he's inside, he collides with something solid. No, not solid. It seemed to be changing shape and form in the fraction of a second it takes for him to fall, whatever it is coming down with him.

'Woah, you all right?' Ralph asks.

Ken feels a pain on his top shoulder where he's landed on something sharp. 'What is all this?' he says through gritted teeth, trying to get up off the dusty floor, pushing aside the strange mass that fell on him. Ralph has had the presence of mind to bring the torch and shines it on what appears to be an enormous plastic bag.

'I think it's sheeting. Big plastic sheeting,' he says as Ken brushes his jeans. He pushes aside the large cylindrical roll that he's fallen over onto and the many metres of plastic that have unravelled from it.

'Christ, they do have some toot in here,' Ken says, squinting in the darkness.

'I think the gardeners use it for the plants. You know, in the cold weather.'

'Well, we're certainly in the midst of that.'

Ralph shivers. 'God, Ken, I'm not sure how long I can be in here.'

Ken chuckles. 'You scared?' He navigates his way around various other obstacles towards the unit near the wall he's fairly sure is the generator.

'No, it's just... the clutter. It bothers me. Don't you ever find that untidy places are like loud noise?'

'You do come out with some odd shit,' Ken says, reaching a hand out. Before he can touch the generator, however, Ralph's frame in the doorway is bathed in a warm glow. The lights in the kitchen, along with the outside wall lights, have come on.

'Ah, it looks like it's back anyway,' says Ralph. 'Not sure it was worth risking our lives after all. Or my sanity.' He laughs, even though Ken doesn't think anything's very funny. His shoulder is still hurting and the cold is starting to become unbearable.

'Let's get back,' he mutters.

As they're walking through the kitchen, Ralph starts musing about what they'll eat for Christmas lunch the next day. 'Thank God the turkey was delivered before the storm, though I don't know how to stuff it – unless that's been done already?'

'Shut up,' Ken says, coming to a stop.

'What?' Ralph says, loudly.

'Shush!' Ken hisses. 'I'm trying to listen.'

'What—' Ralph starts to say again, but then he stops. The answer is obvious. Shouting is coming from the main part of the castle. Or at least, a very heated discussion.

'So you're one of *them*, are you?' comes an angry female voice. Sherie's enthusiasm for George must have thawed pretty quickly, Ken thinks as he treads as carefully and quietly as he can up the three steps that lead to the corridor.

'One of who?' says George, surprise in his voice. 'I don't understand why you're so—'

'So what? What am I? Angry? Too loud?'

'You haven't told me what you meant. I'm one of *them*. What the hell is that supposed to mean?'

'One of those guys. The ones who charm a woman into bed and then want nothing more to do with her.'

'That isn't fair,' says George, now sounding exasperated. 'We just had a nice evening. You seemed cool with it. I didn't expect any more from you.'

'It's not just that. It's that you never really asked me anything. Not in Florida, not in the pub, and definitely not since.'

'Asked you *what*?'

'Exactly! You don't even know. You took the bare-bones info I'd volunteered and left it at that. You didn't ask about my parents. I told you I didn't have siblings, you didn't ask me that. I told you about my plans for Christmas, you didn't ask any questions about that either. You talked about yourself. How you want to go into politics but may explore banking or hedge fund management or some posh money shit first. Which might all be fascinating to you, and I don't mind listening, but it would be polite to ask me something in return. Give me a chance to talk about myself.'

'Well, if I'm so awful,' he says, 'why did you come here in a snowstorm? Why did you risk your life to come and find me? Don't think I fell for that nonsense you spouted about getting lost. The station is pretty easy to find from the pub. So why bother turning up and then spend Christmas Eve brazenly trying to flirt with me in front of my brothers?'

'I wanted to give you a chance!'

'A chance? You wanted a shag, right? Or you liked the sound of Christmas in a castle and thought you rather fancied a life like that for yourself. Do you think you're the first gold digger I've encountered?'

'How fucking dare you? How can you say those things to me?'

'Easy. Because they're true.'

'I'm not staying here to listen to this.'

The noise of furniture being shifted. Perhaps she is pushing her way past the coffee table or the sofa. Seconds later, there's the sound of a door. The French windows. Then the gust of the storm.

'Sherie, for God's sake, don't be ridiculous!' George shouts.

'Fuck off!' she shouts back. Then there's a loud rattle as the door slams.

'Well, good fucking riddance,' George calls after her. But it's unlikely she'll be able to hear over the roar of the storm.

'She'll die out there,' Ralph says, turning to look at Ken, apparently aghast.

He nods. 'Come on.'

They retrace their steps, back through the kitchen, pausing to pull on their footwear. Then back out through the door into the courtyard.

'Sherie!' Ralph shouts.

'We need to go around the side,' Ken says to him, pointing around the wall of the castle. He leads the way through the snow. Ken's shocked at how deep it is – deeper than just a matter of minutes ago when they crossed the courtyard to come back inside.

He spots her immediately. A shape walking huddled through the snow, away from the castle. The wrong way. If she carries on, she'll end up heading down a slope in the direction of the loch.

'Hey, stop!' Ken calls out.

She does stop. He runs over to her, as fast as he can in his Wellington boots wading through many inches of snow.

'Jesus, I'm cold,' she says, teeth chattering, turning towards him.

'Come back inside,' he says. 'You'll freeze to death out here without a coat.'

She bites her lip, looks close to tears. 'I didn't want to go back for it and have to talk to that prick.'

Ken laughs. 'He can be a prick, but that's no reason to die in a snowdrift.'

'Come back with us,' says Ralph from behind him.

She pauses for only a couple of seconds more, then nods.

They re-enter the castle through the kitchens. He tells Sherie to sit by the Aga and Ralph says he'll make her another hot drink.

'Perhaps put something a bit special in it this time,' Ken says. 'Something from the drinks cabinet?'

Ralph nods. 'Sure.'

'That would be grand,' Sherie says, nodding, shuffling her chair closer to the heat, holding her hands out to warm them.

When Ralph returns, clutching a bottle like a trophy, he says that George has gone.

'Gone as in gone outside?' Ken frowns. 'Are his coat and shoes still there?'

Ralph shakes his head. 'I think I heard noises upstairs. Probably just sulking.' His eyes move over to Sherie, who is looking at the floor. Ken takes the bottle of brandy from Ralph and takes over the making of the drinks.

Half an hour later, they've returned to the living room. Ken has built up the fire, Ralph is laughing and joking with Sherie about something funny that happened at his school. He's flirting with her, Ken can tell. He can't criticise. He's flirting too.

He's aware of sounds upstairs. He thinks George might be running a bath. Part of him thinks he should go and check on his younger brother, check he's OK, but he doesn't want to leave this cosy, light-hearted little oasis. George would just make everything tense and negative again with whatever strained relationship he now has with Sherie. So typical of him – barely known her five minutes and already he's getting it wrong. Ken has tried to nudge him in the right direction in the past, tried to teach him the right way to get a girl to like him, but he's always brushed off Ken's advice, telling him to mind his own business. So he only has himself to blame.

Ralph's halfway through a rather risqué anecdote about a game of truth or dare he played in the dorms at school, with Sherie laughing in exaggerated embarrassment, when Ken's phone starts buzzing in his pocket. He takes it out.

'Who is it?' asks Ralph.

'It's an international number – probably Mum.' He answers and says, 'Hello?'

'Ken? That you?' his mother's voice says at the end of a crackling line.

'Yeah, it's me,' Ken says, getting up off the sofa, planning to take the call out of the room. But then there's a beep and the line disconnects.

'I'm going to try to call her back upstairs,' he says to Ralph and Sherie. 'Better signal up there.'

He turns to go, but something touches his hand. It's Sherie. She's holding onto him, her fingers on his, her thumb slightly rubbing against his skin. 'Come back soon, though,' she says. He looks into her eyes. Sees the faint smile on her lips.

'Absolutely,' he says. He winks at her. Then walks out of the room.

NINETEEN
GEORGE

CHRISTMAS EVE 2025

I'm not sure which one is my father. And that's what I'm here to find out.

George thinks he must have misheard. This young man can't have just said that. It isn't possible. Can't be.

'I think you need to explain more fully,' his grandmother says into the stunned silence.

The man nods. 'I'm nineteen years old. I was born in September. So my mother... um... conceived me in December the previous year. This is a little awkward. Her name was Sherie Maclean.'

As soon as he says her name, George takes a step backwards. He feels as though the stranger has produced a knife he's been concealing and has suddenly announced his real intention is to slay every single one of them. He feels his back hit the mantlepiece, knocking over a metal Christmas ornament, causing a clatter, but nobody reacts. Everyone's face is on Tommy. Waiting for him to continue.

'I'm aware this might be embarrassing, but I've just got to say it,' he goes on.

'Please do,' Eileen says, firmly.

He takes a deep breath. 'Twenty years ago, the Christmas before I was born, my mother was at this house. She'd got lost in the snow and sought shelter here. At Lemire Castle.'

He's interrupted by a sound. It takes a second or two for George to realise it's Ralph. He's uttered one word. 'No.' George understands. It's the word he'd like to utter, if he were capable of speech. 'No, this can't be happening,' Ralph adds, his voice rising.

'Hold on, Ralph,' his mother says, then turns back to Tommy. 'I'm sorry, but I think you've made a mistake. We don't know a Sherie Maclean. Nobody of that name has ever been a guest here, to my knowledge. Could you have got the wrong house, perhaps?'

Tommy shakes his head. 'I haven't made a mistake. I understand this is awkward, but I'm certain of both the name of the house and the date. Twenty years ago this Christmas.'

She continues to look disbelieving, then something changes in her expression. 'Oh...' she says, then looks up at Eileen in front of her. 'We weren't here. Mother, we were in America. We'd gone to the funeral of your friend Violet. We couldn't get back to England because of the storm. All flights to the UK were cancelled.'

'I remember it well.' George hears his grandmother speak and he turns to look at her. She's frowning and peering at Tommy with narrowed eyes. Then she says, 'I'm going to have to sit down.' She takes a seat on one of the sofas, then looks back at the visitor. 'So, your mother believes she became pregnant by one of my grandsons.'

'This is all lies,' George says, the words rushing out of him, tasting unpleasant in his mouth, like vomit. He suddenly feels very cold. Much colder than when the door was open to the storm outside.

'It's not, I promise you,' Tommy says. He looks up at him, his expression almost apologetic, then turns back to George's mother. 'And it's not that she wasn't sure which of your sons she had sex with. It's that... well... she had sex with all three of them.'

Silence descends once more. George thinks he really might vomit this time. Then someone says, 'Fuck,' in a slow, drawn-out way. It's Kite, from over on the other side of the room. George sees Ken's head snap round to face him. 'Kite, please go up to your room.'

The boy shakes his head. 'No chance. I want to hear this.' He takes a step towards the centre of the room and looks at Tommy as though he's examining a fascinating animal he's never seen before. 'You mean... you could be my brother?'

Tommy nods. 'I think so. If it was your father's sperm that—'

'That's enough,' Ken says, marching forward and grabbing his son's shoulders.

'Yes, this is sick,' George says, also stepping forward. 'I don't know what perverse game you're playing, but I won't have you sitting there saying things like this in front of my mother and grandmother.'

'I've heard the word "sperm" before, George,' Eileen says, her eyebrows raised. 'I know all the facts of procreation, I can assure you.'

'This isn't happening, this isn't fucking happening,' Ralph says, leaping up from his seat, his voice breaking into a sob, his hands going to his face. George can hear him starting to enact one of his calming rituals, reciting bones or joints or something medical. The behaviour would alarm him or ignite his fraternal protective instincts if his mind wasn't already spinning.

'I'm not having this,' George says. 'It's completely impossible.'

'Kite, *out*,' says Ken, roughly dragging his son towards the door.

'Fuck off, Dad,' the boy says. 'Just because you've been having weird foursomes with your brothers.'

'It wasn't a foursome!' Ken shouts at him.

His words are like a gunshot. Everyone in the room stares at Ken. George feels a plunging sensation in his stomach. Ken's just made a massive mistake. And from the look on his face, he knows it.

'*It*,' says his grandmother, pointedly.

Ken has gone bright red. 'I meant to say, nothing happened.'

'But that isn't what you said, is it, Kenneth?' she says. 'Your phrasing makes it sound like you know full well what this young man is talking about.'

Ken looks appalled with himself. 'I... I didn't... didn't mean...'

'I think Ken meant to say just that,' George says, hurrying to prevent any more linguistic fiascos. 'It wasn't anything because nothing happened.'

'Just shut up, *shut up*,' Ralph says. He seems to be going through some kind of internal unravelling. 'I can't... I can't cope with this.' He gets up and walks very quickly out of the room.

After a few moments, Claire says, 'I think I'd better go after him. He's always been... rather emotional.'

'No, leave him for now,' Eileen says. 'I have to say, Ralph's reaction rather confirms that our unexpected visitor here may be telling the truth. Or at least, the truth as he sees it.' She turns her sharp eyes to Tommy. 'My name is Eileen. If what you are saying is correct, that would make me your great-grandmother.'

Claire stands up. 'Oh, this is ridiculous.'

'I agree,' says George. 'I'd like you to leave. You're clearly a con artist or someone who has come here to make trouble. Maybe this is part of an elaborate stunt or something. Why did you come here on Christmas Eve of all days? Where is this Ms

Maclean? Why are you telling us all this out of the blue? You could have written a letter if you thought you had a claim to the family silver.'

His grandmother lets out a hollow laugh. 'George, really. The family silver isn't up for grabs, so to speak. I thought I made that clear.'

'It's a fair question,' Tommy says. 'I'm sorry I came tonight. The truth is, it's been a difficult time. I thought I could wait until the new year, but... well, in answer to your other question. About where my mother is. You see... she's dead.'

George dimly becomes aware that Ken has come over to stand next to him. Perhaps he hopes for some telepathic sign that there's a plan. That this is going to be OK. Then George notices movement from Tommy. A shuffling of the shoulders, as though he's about to remove his coat.

'I wouldn't bother taking that off,' George says. 'You won't be here much longer.'

'George, we're not sending him out into the storm, and that's final,' his grandmother says. 'Tommy – is it Thomas? I'm not a fan of abbreviations.' Before the young man can say anything, she carries on. 'Thomas, I'm very sorry to hear about your mother. And I think it is very clear that there is something going on here and I would like to get to the bottom of it.'

Tommy nods and looks as though he's trying to smile. 'Thanks. She died in a car accident. It... it was awful.'

George hears a gasp escape him. He closes his mouth quickly, cross with himself for not keeping control of his emotions.

'And this was recently?' Claire asks, looking confused. 'Then why didn't she come and find us before then? Say she did come here twenty years ago, when my sons were here and they... gave her shelter.' George sees her eyes flick over to him and Ken by the fire, before returning to Tommy. 'Why not come and have it out with my sons before her death?'

Tommy leans forward. 'Because she was in a long-term relationship with another man at the time. And he's spent his whole life thinking he was my father. But he wasn't. I was able to talk to my mother before she went in for surgery after the crash. Surgery she didn't survive. She knew there was a chance she wouldn't. And she wanted to tell me the truth. The fact that she had been on the pill when she was with my father, but missed doses when she...' He glances in the direction of George and Ken. 'When she met your sons. She kept the secret for years. Now, I feel like it's time I learned the next part of the story. I want to find out who my father is. My real father.'

George sees his grandmother nod, then get shakily to her feet. 'Well, I've got a lot to think about.'

'You're going?' George says. 'What... we haven't... Granny, I don't know who this young man is or how he's managed to convince you, but none of it—'

'Stop insulting my intelligence, George. You're not helping your case. I'm sorry, but I really need to lie down. I'll talk to you all in the morning.' She turns back to Tommy. 'I would like to speak to you privately, but I don't have the strength now. Please come to my rooms at 8 a.m. Someone will point you in the right direction. Our housekeeper Alexandra will find you a guest room to sleep in tonight. Or one of my grandsons will. It seems they're no strangers to being hospitable to unexpected guests needing shelter from a storm.' She walks towards the door, then says, as a parting shot, 'And there was I thinking like I had the monopoly on family bombshells this evening. Goodnight to you all!'

Then she is gone.

TWENTY
GEORGE

CHRISTMAS EVE 2025

George stands in front of the fireplace, feeling the backs of his legs growing rather warm. But he doesn't care. He could burn to death right here on the hearth rug and it still wouldn't be enough to shock him out of the dizzying spiral he is in. He looks at Tommy, sitting there blinking. In spite of his ruffled hair, he looks strangely perfect. A handsome young man. Angelic, almost. Like the innocent college heartthrob in a trashy romance movie. Looking at him, George wonders if he can see the ghost of Ken within his good looks. Both have similar sandy-blonde hair and strong jawline. Or is he just imagining it? He looks over at his older brother. Ken's eyes aren't on him or Tommy. They're on the floor. He says, 'I can't get my head around this.'

Claire stands up. 'I don't think it takes a rocket scientist to work out.' She steps forward and puts her hand on Ken's shoulder. 'Take Kite up to his bedroom.' He does as she instructs. Kite follows his father without complaint.

Then she looks over at George and says, 'Do as your grandmother says. Find Alexandra and ask her to sort out a guest room for our visitor. Or perhaps you could show him to a room.'

George stares at her for a few seconds. Her tone is more resigned than calm, as though she too has grown weary and just wants the evening to be over.

'Fine.' He goes over to Tommy and says, 'Come on, up you get.'

Tommy, looking a little bewildered, gets to his feet.

'Politely, George,' his mother cautions. He doesn't respond. Just starts walking out of the lounge. He can see Tommy in his peripheral vision, following him.

This is so insane, he thinks to himself. *Mad. Impossible. Terrifying.*

Out in the saloon hall, Alexandra is up a stepladder, fiddling with the garlands along the outer bannisters.

'Alexandra,' George begins. She turns around as they come into the hall. At that moment a loud crack of thunder can be heard, followed by a flash visible from the stained-glass window on the far wall. Then there is a shriek. Alexandra has fallen off the ladder and thudded onto the floor.

George instinctively rushes forward to her, but Tommy gets there first. 'Woah, you OK?'

She seems shaken more than hurt and manages to get herself to her feet, though she doesn't speak.

'Alexandra, are you hurt?' George asks. She looks shocked and dazed and still she doesn't respond. She raises a hand to her temple, staring at them both. 'Alexandra, you're worrying me. Did you hit your head?'

If she's hit her head on the stone floor, that could be disastrous, George thinks. It's unlikely any emergency services would be able to get within half a mile of Lemire Castle for some time, with the storm worsening by the second. Just as he thinks this, the lights on the hall Christmas tree to their right start to flicker and then go out. Then the chandelier cuts off too, plunging them all into darkness.

'Shit,' George says. He reaches for his phone, but it isn't in his pocket. He must have left it in the living room.

'Have you got a phone?' he says to Tommy.

'No,' he says. 'I dropped it on the way. Couldn't find it in the snow.'

He's about to ask Alexandra to turn on her phone torch when he hears his mother calling out.

'George, I think the power's out.'

'Yeah, you don't say!' he shouts back, walking in the direction of her voice, vaguely making out the glow of the fire from the open doorway. His thigh collides with a side table, causing him to gasp in pain.

'George, are you there?' his mother says, getting close. 'Maybe you should check the—'

Before he can finish the sentence, the lights bloom back into illumination. The tree lights default to a twinkling setting and the effect makes George's vision swim.

'What happened? Other than the brief power cut?' Claire asks, looking around.

'Alexandra fell and hurt herself,' George says, rubbing his bruised thigh.

'I'm fine, honestly,' Alexandra says, moving away from Tommy and the ladder.

'Did you hit your head? You could have a concussion.' Claire steps forward and looks at her. 'Come through into the living room. George, can you take over?'

He stares back at his mother, not getting her meaning. Then he sees her nod in the direction of Tommy, who's now standing awkwardly to his left.

'Oh, right, yeah,' he says.

'Some dry clothes and perhaps some toast or soup might be nice, too,' Claire says.

'Oh, there's no need,' Tommy starts to say, just as Alexandra says, 'I can do that, I'm honestly fine.'

'Nonsense,' says Claire, putting an arm around her. 'Now come and sit down by the fire and we'll see if we need a first aid kit.' Alexandra limps a little as she's led out of sight into the living room.

George feels suddenly very uncomfortable, left alone with Tommy, who he's aware is staring at him. 'Well... follow me.'

He begins to climb the stairs. He hears the creak of the young man close behind him. Taking a left down a corridor on the first floor, he shows him into one of the smaller guest bedrooms. It feels cold as he goes in, and he walks over to the radiator and turns it on. He surprises himself with this kind gesture. Although perhaps it isn't kind, he thinks. Perhaps it's just something to do, keep himself busy, so he doesn't have to look at this bizarre, impossible stranger.

When he does look at him, Tommy is putting his coat on the hook on the back of the door. He can't think of what to say to him and has a sudden compulsion to run from the room, run from the castle, out into the snow. Bury himself in a snowdrift and pretend none of this is happening. But instead, he just says, 'I'll get you some dry clothes.' He leaves the room, heads back out to the landing and then goes along to his bedroom. As he does so, he passes Ralph's room and can hear the unmistakable sound of him sobbing inside. He pauses for a moment, wondering if he should go in and comfort his brother. But he realises he doesn't have any words of comfort. He doesn't know what to say, because there isn't anything that will explain this.

He returns to the room with some of his pyjama bottoms and a T-shirt in his hand. 'You can wear these,' he tells Tommy.

The young man is watching the snow, but comes away from the window when George speaks. He takes the pyjamas. 'Thanks,' he says. George sees him shivering as he pulls off his navy jumper and starts to unbutton his shirt. He imagines the melted snow has probably soaked him through. He suddenly feels bad he's just brought two items of clothing with him – he should have brought a warmer top, maybe a dressing gown, underpants and socks. He's feeling sorry for him again. And as he notices this, he wonders if there's something else to his feelings. Something, perhaps, paternal.

No, he thinks to himself. *It isn't true. It isn't possible.*

'We'll find out, you know,' George says. 'We'll find out what you are. Who you are. Because you can't be who you say you are. You just... can't be.'

Tommy frowns at him, taking off his shirt. He doesn't look cross. Just confused and interested. 'Why not?' he says. 'I mean, I understand it might be embarrassing that you had a fling with my mother, but why does that make it any less likely to be true? Is there some other reason?'

The final question sends an ice-cold jolt through George's spine. Keeping eye contact with Tommy, he at last says, 'I'll let you get changed. I'll have some food sent up to you.'

Then he leaves.

Out on the landing, he almost walks into Ken.

'Is he in there?' Ken asks, nodding at the room George has just come out of. He nods and signals to Ken to follow him. He goes down the next corridor and along to Ralph's bedroom and opens the door without knocking.

'Hey, get out!' says Ralph. He's huddled on the floor. The room is in disarray – the duvet dragged off the bed and wrapped around him, the pillows scattered.

'I know this is awful, Ralph,' George says, coming to a stop in front of him, 'but going to pieces isn't going to solve it.'

'I've already gone to pieces,' Ralph croaks, his voice hoarse from crying. 'It's all over. It's happened. I'm finished. I don't know... I don't know if I can take much more of this.'

George glances at Ken, hoping for some help in what to say

or do next, but he's just watching Ralph as though he's some unusual animal he'd rather not touch.

'OK. Here's the plan of action. We need to figure out who he is, how he found out and why he's lying,' George says.

Ralph stares at him with red, bloodshot eyes. 'You think that's a plan?'

'We could try to make him talk,' Ken says, cracking his knuckles.

'We're not in one of your movies,' snaps George. 'He's not some member of a terrorist cell you can beat the truth out of. He's an impostor and a liar, but we need to tread carefully. Otherwise the whole question about Granny's inheritance is going to be the least of our worries. We could be looking at prison.'

Ralph winces and pulls the duvet closer around him. 'Don't say that word.'

'What do you think Granny will say to him?' Ken asks. 'It's a bit odd, isn't it? Her inviting him to her rooms, on Christmas morning.'

George shrugs. 'I'd say that's pretty typical. A deliberate provocation to make us worry she's about to divert all that koala sanctuary funding over to him instead. She's winding us up.'

'Porcupines,' Ralph whispers, as though to himself.

George carries on. 'We need to find out how he knows... what he thinks he knows. Why he's lying.'

Ralph sniffs loudly and sits up. 'What makes you think he's lying?'

'Because,' George says, lowering his voice, 'dead women at the bottom of deep lochs don't tend to go on to give birth to children.'

TWENTY-ONE
CLAIRE

CHRISTMAS EVE 2025

Once everyone's upstairs, Claire finds herself drifting. She walks from the living room to the library, then out into the hallway. She takes in all the Christmas lights on the impressive trees in each room. The uneaten mince pies. The crackle of the fire. She feels like she's in mourning. Not for a person, but for the Christmas that's been ruined. Ruined by fallout and anger and shock and, now, confusion. Scandal, even.

I'm your grandson. One of your sons is my father.

Her feet carry her upstairs. Without even thinking about it, she goes to the first of the guest bedrooms. Sees a light under the door. She reaches for the handle and goes in without knocking. The young man is awake, sitting on the edge of the bed, in a pair of pyjama bottoms that look too big for his slender, small frame. He really is quite beautiful, Claire thinks. The thought doesn't stem from attraction, but rather more the way one would admire a painting or a sculpture. She's suddenly taken back to a time when she stayed with an old man named Hector, a now deceased friend of her father's, who collected works by the painter Henry Scott Tuke, an artist who had produced many pictures of young men. She found them so exquisitely beautiful, she wasn't able to turn away, like a spell had been cast over her. And a similar spell holds her very still now, as she looks at the male figure sitting on the edge of the bed. Eyes on her.

'Err... Hello?' Tommy says. He sounds unsure, as though trepidatious about what's to come, the word going up at the end like a question. A question she doesn't really have an answer for.

She stands still, staring at his face. Wondering, for a fleeting second, if she can see Ralph in its smooth, boyish features. Then, as he turns his head slightly, she's convinced she notices the jut of Ken's strong jaw. George's piercing eyes.

'What do you want?' he says, laying his hands flat on the bed now as though about to push himself off the mattress.

'Just wanted to look at you,' Claire says quietly.

Then, just as suddenly as she walked in, she turns and leaves, closing the door behind her.

Her mind races during the short walk to her bedroom. She's telling herself off for missing her chance to question the visitor on her own, away from the emotive struggles of her offspring. But when she looked at that young man – that strange, almost otherworldly boy – she felt like she was looking into a deep abyss. And it scared her.

Once in her room, she goes to the cupboard in the corner and reaches for an old, leather-covered box at the back, up against some folded clothes she hardly ever wears. She takes the box out, opens it, then picks up the first photo inside. Then another. They're of her, her old life, when she studied in London in her twenties. A picture of her graduating from the Royal College of Music. She smiles sadly to herself, then looks at the next picture. An old family photo of her and her husband

and parents with the boys when they were young. There's a framed version of it somewhere in the castle, though she's become pretty good at filtering out things that upset her. It was taken not long before the two men's tragic deaths in the loch. Before that terrible day.

The bodies being dragged out of the water.

The emergency services, the flashing lights, the kind voices telling her there was no hope. They were gone.

She barely notices George coming into the room at first. Only dimly registers his attempt to get her attention.

'What?' she says, hurrying to put the pictures back in the box.

'What were you looking at?' he asks.

'That doesn't matter,' she says. 'What do you want?'

He looks confused by the question. 'Well... to talk. About, you know, Tommy. The things he said. Because it isn't true, Mum. It really isn't. I—'

She holds up a hand. 'I really don't want to talk about it right now, George. Really. It can wait until the morning.'

She puts the lid back on the box, lifts it up and carries it to the wardrobe. Once she's put it back in place and closed it, she looks over to him, hoping he's left her in peace. But her son's still standing there.

'I'm not sure if you've come to offer me comfort and reassurance, or if you want me to give those things to you, but right now I can't, I... I just can't. I'm tired.' She kicks off her shoes and sits down on the side of the bed. Then, almost to herself, she says, 'Do you know, sometimes I wonder how a mother can reach my age and really not know her own children at all.'

In her peripheral vision, she sees George still standing in the doorway. When the silence goes on too long, she turns her head. He opens his mouth, as though he's going to say something. The expression on his face, the intensity in his eyes, suggests it's something he's finding difficult to say. Something momentous. A confession, perhaps. Then he stops. Gives her a little nod and walks out of the room. Leaving her alone with her thoughts.

TWENTY-TWO
GEORGE

CHRISTMAS EVE 2005

George is lying in the bath, hating himself and the whole world. He doesn't know how he managed to mess up everything with Sherie; it just seemed to happen by itself. He hadn't really meant all those things he shouted at her. Or at least, he doesn't think he did. He can't be sure now, a little while on, whether he believed them to be true or if he just wanted to lash out. To break whatever there was between them before it could properly begin. And the whole blame can't rest on him, surely? He isn't the one who made up some flimsy story about being lost in the snow just to track down a fling. She's the weird one. If he'd done that to a girl, manipulated his way into her house, it would be seen as stalkerish behaviour. But she seems to think that kind of stunt is cute and sexy. She's clearly seen too many romcoms, he thinks with a sigh as he lets himself fall back into the water, allowing it to close over his head.

Underneath its surface, he thinks about drowning.

Thinks about his father and grandfather, who slipped under the surface of the loch, never to return. Their bodies were recovered, of course, but not them. The people inside them had gone. A foolish accident. A 'tragedy', people called it. He wonders what it was like for them to drown, to not be able to breathe, to struggle and panic and then lose all energy to fight. The thought doesn't horrify him. Memories of the incident don't feel traumatic, exactly. Just sad, in a dull, aching sort of way. A sore area in his mind. Pain, loss, grief. And guilt. All there, just below the surface, not quite raw but not quite gone. Like pressing a bruise that hasn't fully healed. And probably never will.

When he comes up for air, he doesn't notice what's different about the room at first. Then he sees him, standing there above him, causing him to start.

'Fucking hell, Ken,' he says, the movement causing water to slosh onto the floor.

'You gave me a fright,' Ken says, frowning at him. 'You didn't answer when I knocked.'

'I gave *you* a fright?' he says, gasping, wiping water from his eyes. 'God, you could have given me a heart attack.' He feels the accelerated beat against his chest, the fizz of adrenaline coursing through him. He looks up at his older brother and as he does so he realises why his sudden presence alarmed him. It wasn't just the surprise. It's an uncanny likeness Ken had at that angle. When George first focused on him, as he blinked the water from his eyes, Ken wasn't Ken at all. He looked like his grandfather. Like pictures of him when he was young. And even his face when he was older. That face that could switch from kindness to cruelty so quickly.

'George, what's going on with you and that girl?'

George rubs at his face again, not because he has water in his eyes, but to buy himself some seconds of thought. Then he says, 'I don't think I'm made for a relationship, Ken.'

His brother scoffs. He sits down on the storage chest by the edge of the bath, then says, 'Aren't you a bit young to come to a conclusion like that? She can't be much older than you are. I don't think she's proposing marriage.'

George shrugs. 'I don't know what else to say. We had fun, but that's all. It wasn't anything serious for me, certainly not the foundation for a lifelong connection. But she apparently felt differently.'

Ken looks amused. 'That's not what I heard,' he says. 'It sounds like she was pissed off you didn't ask her anything about her. That you treated her more as a disposable item than a human being.'

'God, you've got a nerve,' George says, his eyes wide.

'Don't get all outraged,' Ken says, raising a hand. 'I realise I'm not exactly an advert for relationship stability.'

'To put it mildly.'

'I'm just saying,' Ken says, 'She thinks you treated her poorly. The trick is, even if you want something without strings, is to make them think it was their idea.'

George rolls his eyes, 'Now who sounds sexist?'

Ken gets up. 'Mum tried to phone a moment ago. I managed to get her back for a bit, in time for her to say they've cancelled all the flights for tomorrow too. It looks like we're alone for the time being. Us and Sherie.'

George doesn't say anything to this. He just rubs the end of the bathtub with one of his toes, thinking.

'Well, I'll leave you to your ponderings,' Ken says. 'I better get down to the living room before Ralph has his wicked way with our guest. Or she with him.' He winks at George and goes to leave.

Before he goes through the door, George says, 'Do you ever think about Grandad?'

He can tell, from his peripheral vision, that Ken is staring at him in a very different way than he was before.

'Think what about Grandad?' he says, quietly.

'About... what he used to do.'

He sees Ken straighten up. 'No, I don't. I made a choice to be strong, George. Resilient. You should too.'

He turns to leave, but again, George interrupts him. 'Don't you think it's a good thing. That he died. A good thing he died before he could start on Ralph?'

He looks at Ken now. He wonders if Ken knows what he's trying to say. Wonders if he already knows. Has always known. Then he lowers his eyes. 'I just wish Dad hadn't died too. That he hadn't been in the boat when...'

He trails off. A few seconds of silence pass between them. Then Ken says, 'I don't think you should be dwelling on all that right now. Not ever. But if you're feeling sad... well, don't feel you have to come back down to the living room. Ralph and I will find Sherie a bed for the night. Then we'll try to have a nice Christmas Day tomorrow. As nice as possible.'

George says nothing. Eventually, Ken goes through the open door and closes it behind him, leaving him to his thoughts. Thoughts that drift across his mind like the small islands of soap bubbles on the surface of the now uncomfortably cool bath water.

TWENTY-THREE

KEN

CHRISTMAS EVE 2025

Ken is looking for George when he spots him coming out of their mother's room.

'What were you doing in there?' he asks him. 'What were you telling Mum?'

George shoots a glance at one of the doors to their right. Ken doesn't get the hint and carries on. 'I don't think we should be having private conversations with Mum or Granny or anyone until—'

'Just bloody shut up!' George hisses, then nods again in the direction of the guest bedrooms. Ken understands then. His mouth forms a silent 'Oh', then he nods.

'We should find Ralph,' George says very quietly.

'He's in his room,' Ken says. 'I've tried. I can hear him crying. I think he might be talking to himself too, in between the sobs. It sounds like he's having some kind of breakdown.'

'Yeah, well, I think we'll both be joining him in that soon if we don't get to the bottom of this,' George says as he leads the way towards Ralph's bedroom. He pauses outside and Ken watches as he presses his ear to the door.

'Is he still doing it?' Ken asks. 'The talking? Like, muttering to himself?'

George nods.

Ken shakes his head. 'God, he might as well write what we did in big fucking capital letters on his forehead. He's making it so obvious.'

He sees George's eyes flash, probably a reaction to the words *what we did*. Ken bites his lip. He knows he's a liability, knows he messed up downstairs when his outburst threw suspicion on him and his brothers. But the tense atmosphere was fast becoming unbearable. And the worst thing is, he's not sure how they're going to get out of it.

George moves away from the door and gives it a soft tap with his hand. 'Ralph? Ralph, it's me, George. Can I come in?'

He tries the door. It opens and George goes to step inside, but suddenly there's a bang as the door slams back shut. 'Leave me alone!' Ralph calls out, followed by the sound of something being dragged along the ground. Ken grows impatient and leans forward, trying to reopen the door, but whatever Ralph has wedged beneath the handle is blocking it from turning.

'Now what?' Ken says.

George beckons him down the corridor to his own bedroom. Inside, he closes the door and says, 'What are we going to do?'

Ken blinks at him. 'What? That's my question. I was going to ask you that.'

'Why do I have to come up with all the answers?' George asks, looking exasperated. 'Why not you?'

'Because you're the politician,' Ken says, then wishes he hadn't. 'Sorry, I didn't mean to be snarky.'

George's facial expression is unreadable. 'It's OK. But we need to stay on the same side... we need to have each other's backs through this. Through whatever *this* is. And I'm sorry I was a dick towards you downstairs.'

Ken looks at George and George looks back. 'This is how it used to be, isn't it?' Ken says. 'Us two, talking things out. Confessing to each other. Helping each other work things out, usually away from Ralph. The two big brothers, protecting him. When did we stop talking?'

His brother just continues to stare at him and then shrugs. Ken isn't sure if the action is annoying or endearing. Or a mixture of the two. He has a sudden urge to hug him, to bring him close, tell him they'll always be on the same team. Always fight each other's fights. But then George says something, very quietly, interrupting his thoughts. 'Do you ever think about the moment... the moment it happened? When she...?'

These aren't the words Ken wants to hear. Not the response he was hoping for. He closes his eyes in an effort to mentally push away the images that swim before him. But it just makes it worse. In the darkness, the body of a young woman comes forward, clear and detailed, as though he were in front of her now. As though she died just seconds ago...

'I never think of it,' Ken says. 'But at the same time, it's like I always do. It's never gone. I'm never free of it. Never free of *her*.'

When he opens his eyes again, he sees George staring at him. 'I know exactly what you mean,' he says.

Ken nods. Then he turns to go. Before he's through the door, however, he turns back and says, 'If you did know something about all this, about Tommy, about what happened back then, you'd tell me, right?'

George frowns, tension in his face creasing his brow. 'Of course,' he says.

Ken looks at him. 'All right,' he says. 'But it wouldn't be the first time you've kept a secret, would it?'

Then he exits the room.

TWENTY-FOUR

KEN

CHRISTMAS EVE 2005

In spite of the warming, Christmassy atmosphere, filled with movies and mince pies and, rather incongruously, some spicy battered chicken fillets Ralph found in the freezer, Ken can't keep disquieting thoughts out of his head. Can't stop thinking about what George said about his grandfather. It hadn't quite been Christmas, when he and his father died, but almost. Mid-November. So the festive season that year was very much impacted by it. And Ken's grief at losing his father was coupled with another feeling. A feeling of relief. Because he knows what George meant. It was a good thing his grandfather had died. Before things could get worse.

'Ken? You still with us?' Ralph prompts. Ken looks over and sees him waving from the two-seater sofa. He's sitting very close to Sherie. Almost nestled amongst the folds of the big comfortable dressing gown he fetched to keep her warm.

'I'm... feeling a bit sleepy,' he says. His eyes are facing forward, resting on the TV. A trailer is playing for the Christmas Special of *Doctor Who*, set to air the following day.

Apparently, it's entitled 'The Christmas Invasion'. The words make him shiver. He feels as if his laid-back Christmas has been invaded. Invaded by this unknown girl, their unexpected guest, who has very much made herself at home. And invaded by something else, too. Doubt. Suspicion. The feeling that upstairs, George is hiding something. Something that's just out of reach...

'It's only half past ten,' Ralph says. 'And besides, I'll doubt you'll get any sleep from the racket of the storm.'

'Yeah, stay for a bit,' Sherie says, smiling at him.

Ken sees Ralph's expression change with almost comical speed. 'Although if you're tired, best get to bed,' he says, clearly realising he might have just talked his way out of the chance of some alone time with their attractive guest.

'You can sleep here,' Sherie says. 'Budge up, Ralph.' She nudges him playfully in the ribs. 'Make room for your older brother.' She looks at Ken, then pats the space next to her. Sensing he might live to regret the decision, he parks himself down next to her and feels the warmth of her body as she snuggles into him.

'Gosh, your abs are like rocks,' she says, giving the right side of his chest a tap with her fist, as though knocking on a door.

'Mine aren't bad, either,' Ralph mutters.

Ken laughs. He knows it's unkind, but the childish ridiculousness of his little brother's insecurities both frustrates and amuses him.

'It's not funny,' Ralph says. He stands up and tugs off his snowflake-patterned jumper and T-shirt all in one go.

'God, your chest is so pale it's blinding,' Ken says, trying his best to settle back into his normal, playful self. 'It's literally offensive to my eyes.'

'Fuck off,' Ralph says, sticking a middle finger up at him, then clenching his arms. 'Look, muscle, see.'

Sherie laughs, then hits Ken's chest again, this time more of a slap than a knock. 'Don't be so harsh.' She turns back to Ralph. 'You look very fit, I promise you.'

'Yeah, like a Labrador puppy in that gangly stage before it knows how to use its limbs,' Ken says with a smirk.

Ralph collapses back on the sofa with a springy thud. 'Prick,' he mutters.

'Ah, come on,' Sherie, says, leaning over. Ken sees her hands on Ralph's chest. They then travel down a bit further to his stomach. 'There's a certain allure to him, I must admit.' She starts taking off the dressing gown. 'It's getting a bit hot in here.' She transfers her attention back to Ken. Hands on his knees. Snaking upwards. He feels a part of his anatomy getting excited in spite of himself.

'I think we should all lose some of our clothing,' she says. The forwardness of this makes him raise his eyebrows. He's about to say something, but she turns her head back to Ralph. And by the look on his face, he knows what she's suggesting.

'What about... what about George?' he stammers, sounding nervous but unable to keep the excitement from his voice.

Sherie chuckles. 'If I said George could go fuck himself, would that surprise you?'

'Knowing George, he's probably doing just that.' Ken laughs. 'But why have you gone off him? What's going on between you?'

Sherie tuts. 'Let's just say, he's yet to learn how to treat women. He has *a lot* of learning to do.'

She turns back to Ralph. His eyes are on her as though she's made of solid gold. He's entranced. Bewitched. Dazzled. In other circumstances, Ken would be too, but wild though he is, his mind is elsewhere tonight.

He pulls himself up off the sofa.

'Where are you going?' Sherie says, looking disappointed.

'This isn't for me,' Ken says. He surprises himself with these words. He had a reputation at drama school as the guy who slept with anything with a pulse, the bloke who wouldn't miss a party, the one who'd wake up in a bed with three other people and consider it to be a quiet night. But at this moment in time, he can't seem to separate himself from the images in his head. The images of two bodies being recovered from the loch. Just metres from this very room. And this memory mingles with a feeling of pain. In his chest. His legs. He has his right hand on his abdomen now. On a mark he knows is there, under his T-shirt. He looks back over at Ralph's torso. Free from any marks or scars.

Words start to echo in his mind, almost as clearly as when he heard them spoken, less than an hour ago upstairs.

Don't you think it's a good thing? That he died... before he could start on Ralph?

'Have fun, you two,' he says. He's aware his voice sounds strange. He feels as though he's speaking in a room with little oxygen, his words disappearing as soon as he's said them. But Ralph and Sherie don't seem to notice or care.

Once out of the living room, he heads upstairs. He can see the glow of George's room down the corridor, the door open. When he reaches it, though, he finds it empty. The guy can't still be in the bath, Ken thinks – he'll be as shrivelled as an old crisp packet. He's about to continue to his room when he sees something on George's bed. A folder, or photo album. Though the contents don't look like photos. They look like newspaper cuttings. He walks into the room and over to the bed. Yes, they are newspaper cuttings, slipped underneath clear plastic sleeves. Preserved.

Even before he reads the headlines, he knows what they'll be.

DOUBLE TRAGEDY ON LOCH LEMIRE

He closes his eyes, but can still see the words.

DROWNED JUST METRES FROM THEIR HOME

'Hey, what are you doing?'

George's angry voice makes his eyes snap open. Ken ignores his question.

'What are these here for?' He gestures to the album on the bed. George steps forward and closes it. Holds it close to his chest for a few seconds. Then lifts the mattress and shoves it underneath.

'You shouldn't be poking around my stuff.'

'You *saved* newspaper reports? Can't you just look them up on the net?'

'I read them at the time and I just couldn't throw them away,' George mutters.

'You've been keeping them under your bed for three years?'

George says nothing. He sits down on the bed, looking up at Ken. And Ken looks down at him, thinking about what to say next. After a few seconds, George gets into bed properly, pulling the duvet up to his chin. 'I'm going to sleep. I take it you showed Sherie to a guest room?'

Ken shakes his head. 'She's in the lounge with Ralph.'

George frowns. 'With Ralph?'

Ken nods. 'Yeah, it's why I left. Didn't fancy seeing him getting it on with her.' He's not really thinking about his words, doesn't appreciate that George might have an emotional reaction to this. His eyes aren't on his brother. They're on the space at the lower part of the mattress where the newspaper album was tucked out of sight.

TWO BODIES.
PRONOUNCED DEAD AT THE SCENE.
CLEMENT WEYMAN, 82, AND HIS SON-IN-LAW ALFRED, 61.

'They're doing *what?*' George says. 'What's fucking wrong with her? Is she doing this to punish me?' He leaps out of bed, pulls on some pyjama bottoms, then heads for the door.

Ken opens his mouth. Then closes it. Stays still until George is out of the room. Once alone, he reaches under the mattress and takes out the album. There are other newspaper articles inside. Clippings that show photographs of the two men when they were alive and smiling. And pictures showing the wreckage of his grandfather's boat. Pieces that were dragged to the edge. Or floated there.

His mind is whirring. He can almost hear it. A whirring and a clicking, like things slotting into place.

Then George is back.

'They're kissing,' he says. 'Come down and help me sort it out. Please.'

Ken continues to look down at the album. 'What's there to sort out? You go and stop them if you want.'

'No way! Or I will if you come with me. And put that back!'

When Ken doesn't move, George snatches the album from his hands.

'Fuck's sake,' George says. 'Why are you looking at me like that?'

Ken's now staring at him. Looking at his face. Eyes on his.

'It was you, wasn't it?' he says, quietly.

'I... what?' George says. His face is flushing now.

Ken knows. And it's clear George can see it.

'It was you. The hole in the boat,' Ken says. 'It was you, wasn't it? You killed them. Grandfather and Dad. They're both dead because of you.'

TWENTY-FIVE
GEORGE

CHRISTMAS EVE 2005

For a few seconds, George forces himself to believe he can hold it together. It's a lie. He keeps on saying it in his head, *hold it together, deny, hold it together, deny*, but he can't help himself. A strange noise, like a cough and a sob, escapes him, and he raises a hand to his mouth, then to his eyes, frustrated the tears have started to fall.

'Something happened... something in here,' George says, tapping his head with a trembling hand. 'It was as if something just flipped in my head. He'd been... he'd been hurting me that morning and said he wasn't finished. Said he didn't think I was taking his lessons on board. But I didn't understand the lessons, I didn't understand what he wanted from me. When I cried, he hurt me even more, saying the tears were a sign of weakness. So when I knew he was going to do it again later, I went outside... to the boat. It all seemed so easy when I did it. Like it wasn't me doing it, like my body was somebody else's. But it wasn't easy afterwards. It was... it was terrible. Really, really, terrible.'

'It's OK,' Ken says, getting up. 'It's OK. I understand.'

'Really?' George says, not trying to cover his tears now, allowing himself to fall into his big brother's strong arms.

'Yes, I do.'

They stand there for a bit, Ken just holding him, until eventually George lifts his head away from his chest. 'Will you tell Mum?'

Ken shakes his head. 'Of course not.'

George feels his lips trembling. He finds a crumpled tissue in the pocket of his pyjama bottoms and uses it to dab at his nose. 'You promise?'

'I promise,' says Ken. 'I mean... what good would it do?'

'That's what I thought. That's what I've always thought. I mean, it wouldn't be fair on her. Wouldn't be fair on anyone. It's my secret. That I killed my grandfather. And while I was at it, I killed my own dad without meaning to. It's awful. Like some twisted Shakespearean shit, but real.'

'Yeah. All of it taking place in the shadow of a Scottish castle. We just need three witches and a moving forest.'

Although he doesn't laugh, George feels a sudden rush of love for his older brother. That he is able to find humour in a moment like this, and deploy it like ointment to a wound.

'I think you're mixing up *Hamlet* and *Macbeth*.' George sniffs. 'And maybe one of the historical ones.'

'I'm not mixing up anything, I'm repurposing,' Ken says, with a slight smile. 'I know Shakespeare inside out. I love it all. The muscular character, the rhythm of it. Much more satisfying and easier to deal with than life, if you ask me. Life is... harder to take hold of.'

The wind howls around them, getting louder by the second. George wonders if his confession has damned him – a ludicrous thought, since he doesn't believe in hell or sins or even evil. But there's something so raw and elemental about the noise of the storm battering the castle's walls that makes him almost believe in it. That his sins will be the ruin of them all.

'I think I want to sleep now,' George says. 'If I can.'

Ken nods. 'I'm sorry you've been carrying the weight of all this. I really am.'

A few more tears slip down George's face as he climbs into the bed once more and pulls up the covers.

'And I'll sort out the Ralph and Sherie thing going on downstairs. Try and be the responsible older brother. Make sure they don't bother you.'

George is grateful for this too, but now just desperately wants Ken to go. He suddenly feels exhausted. The same tiredness he had just over three years ago when he went down to the boathouse late at night when nobody would see. And the exhaustion he felt the next day, when all the chaos unfolded. When the drowned bodies were taken away. He just slept and slept after that. He wonders if he'll do the same now.

'You will be all right, won't you?' Ken asks, before he goes through the door.

'Yeah,' George says. 'I'll be fine.'

'We will talk about this. When... when I've had time to digest it all, too. We'll talk. But it will be OK, I promise.'

George nods into his pillow. Tries to say 'thank you' but it comes out as barely a whisper and he isn't sure if Ken hears. Then he's gone and George is alone once more.

The storm. His mother's and grandmother's absence. Sherie's arrival and subsequent weirdness. And then his confession about the most terrible secret he thinks he'll ever hold. All of it makes him feel like he's slipped into some warped parallel world. The strangest Christmas Eve he's ever had, he thinks as he turns off the bedside lamp and closes his eyes. If he has one Christmas wish, it's that tomorrow will be much calmer. That's what he needs. Just a calm, uneventful Christmas Day to lessen all the anxiety and disorientation he's felt this evening. That isn't too much to ask, is it?

TWENTY-SIX
KEN

CHRISTMAS EVE 2005

Ken isn't sure if he's surprised by what he's just been told, or if it's just confirmed what he's always known. He can't be sure now. It's hard to see through the fog of his mind, impossible to get some certainty. He had suspicions, but perhaps they just feel exaggerated in retrospect. George has always changed the subject when the topic of his father and grandfather's accident on the loch comes up. Either steered the conversation away onto safer ground, or if that hasn't been possible, he's left the room or withdrawn into himself. Ken has always just put that down to grief. And the buried trauma. Memories of what his grandfather did to him. To them both. And because of all that, Ken understood why George didn't want to dwell. Didn't want to revel in the pain. Didn't want to remember.

But it's more than that. It always has been. He sees that now. In the midst of all that anguish, anxiety and horror, George had a burning guilt that outstripped anything his brothers felt. Anything his mother or grandmother could feel. He alone had a part in their deaths that went beyond any other member in the family. Ken is so desperately sorry for him, he feels he might break with the pain.

Not wanting to talk to anyone, and forgetting he promised George to check in on Ralph and Sherie downstairs, he goes straight to his bedroom. He doesn't bother turning the light on, just collapses onto the covers fully clothed, closes his eyes.

Misdeeds must be punished, Kenneth.

His hand goes to a space on his hip. Then another on his thigh.

It's important for a man's character to endure pain.

He presses his hand hard into his skin. Even though the wound healed long ago, he knows there's a very small mark there. A tiny scar that has never faded. He takes hold of that area now and pinches.

Those who endure find freedom quickly. Close your eyes. This will all be over soon.

A noise makes him jolt upright. There's someone coming through the door. At first, he thinks it's George. Wonders if he needs to continue their discussion. Exorcise whatever ghosts of the past are lingering between them. But it's a female figure that steps forward into the darkness.

'I came to see if you were OK.'

Ken reaches out to his left to turn on the bedside lamp. Blinks at Sherie. 'If I'm OK?' he says, frowning.

She nods. 'I was passing on the landing, you sounded upset. Were you talking to yourself?'

He raises a hand to his head. 'Was I?' He hadn't realised, but can easily believe it. It's as though time has become a book and he is slipping between its pages, dipping in and out of chapters. It's George's fault for taking him back there. Now he feels mentally stuck. And he has a beautiful girl in his room looking at him as though she's his mother and he's a poorly child.

She reaches out. Touches his cheek. He backs away, then stands up and goes over to the window. Without looking at her, he says, 'What have you done with my little brother? Hope you haven't broken his heart.'

She laughs. A light, breathy sound. For some reason, it reminds Ken of summer. Sunshine and birds, perhaps. 'Ralph got a little over-excited. He's taking a break.'

He looks at her now. 'A break? What is this, a tennis match?'

She smiles. A flirtatious smile now, unmistakably so. 'Maybe. Do you like tennis?'

He shakes his head. 'No. I was good at sports, when I was a teenager, but I never liked them.' He gestures to the theatre posters on the walls around him. 'They wasted time when I could be doing drama. I set a goal for myself, when I was fourteen, to act in every play Shakespeare wrote before I turned thirty. I've still got some way to go, but I might manage it. Providing Hollywood doesn't steal me away. I've got auditions for some action movies in the new year.'

'Well, I'm sure you'd cut a fine figure as an action star – you have a great physique.' She comes a step closer. Then another.

'Are you going to start tapping my chest again?' he asks.

'Would you like me to?'

She comes to a stop, just a few centimetres from him.

'Why are you sorry?'

He frowns. 'What?'

'You were muttering, "I'm sorry, I'm sorry," just before I came in.'

He shakes his head. 'I don't... I don't think I was.'

She reaches forward and puts her hands on his arms. 'You were.'

He holds her gaze for a few seconds. Then he takes off his jumper and T-shirt. He points to a space on the side of his stomach. 'Here,' he says. 'This is where he first burned me. He used a tuning fork, the type you use for a musical instrument. He held it into the flame of a candle and then burnt my skin with it.'

He sees the shock in her eyes. It's as though he's just shouted at her or hit her or something. 'Who did?' she whispers.

'My grandfather,' he says. 'But of course, he couldn't do too much to my torso, in case the injuries – small as they were – were noticed when I was coming out of the shower or swimming in the loch. So...' He pushes down his tracksuit bottoms, then lowers the waistband of his boxers. The skin is still red from where he pinched it earlier. The flushed colour on his otherwise tanned skin highlights the small mark. A light, raised line. 'He had to start finding places that were less likely to be seen. Had to focus on areas that were usually covered.'

Her eyes are wide. Shining in the lamplight. 'Oh God, I'm... so sorry.' She reaches out and touches his hip. Her touch is gentle, fingers lightly brushing the scar.

'It wasn't sexual. Or at least, I don't think it was. I was never... you know, he never... it wasn't... it wasn't *that*. It was about pain and power. And masculinity.'

Sherie looks confused. 'Masculinity? In what way?'

'He was always very critical of what he called "weak men". Psychologically weak, physically weak. Not that he was built like a ton of bricks, you understand, it was more... it's hard to explain. It was about what was going on up here.' He taps his forehead. 'Being able to withstand painful or upsetting experiences. Being mentally robust. If you ask me, I think it was all tied up with his own experiences as a soldier. He endured things. He never told us completely, but there'd be hints. Suggestions of what went on.'

Sherie shakes her head, slowly, sadly, her hands still on him. 'That doesn't excuse it.'

'I know it doesn't,' Ken says, quickly. 'But I think it might explain it. At least, partly. It wasn't just physical damage he did to me. There'd be threats, too. Usually to do with withholding money. Threatening to disinherit my parents. I don't know if he ever would have done, but I was scared... and ashamed... and confused and worried and... well... that's probably enough on all that.' He pulls his pants back up, letting the elastic slap against his waist. 'Probably not what you were hoping for when you came in.'

'Don't cover it,' she says. She lowers to her knees, leans forward, pulls his boxers down – fully down, this time – although she doesn't seem to have eyes for anything other than the area of skin he focused on. She leans forward and kisses it, very gently.

'There,' she whispers.

Ken just stares at her. So she leans forward and kisses it again, moving further up this time, until she reaches the side of his stomach. Moving closer to the centre, she continues her journey upwards until she gets to his neck. Then his jaw. Then pauses, briefly, before putting her lips to his. She kisses him, lightly, not passionately. Then pulls back, just a little, and asks, 'Is this OK?'

'I... don't know,' Ken says. It's true. He doesn't. But he knows he's willing to find out. He closes the millimetres between them, leaning into her, kissing her back. Arms wrapping around her shoulders.

They're on the bed seconds later. Their gentle merging like a dance they're figuring out the moves to. Then they relax into each other and Ken feels the familiar tug of desire. And he gives in, completely.

He doesn't know how much time has passed when he rolls onto his back on the bed. The room is suddenly very hot. He can hear Sherie breathing.

'Are you OK?' she asks. 'God, you were... very passionate. Like an animal, possessed.'

'I am an animal,' Ken says, still trying to catch his breath.

'No, you're not,' she says. In the corner of his vision, he sees her roll over onto her side. She's looking at him, but he keeps his eyes on the ceiling. 'You wear an armour. Like George. And Ralph. Ralph's is the easiest to penetrate.'

'I'd prefer you not to use the word "penetrate" in the same sentence as my little brother's name,' Ken says, with a half-smile.

'I'm being honest. He hasn't learned to hide himself in the way you and George do yet. And I'm not talking about what we just did, not just that. I'm talking about how you are. It's like you're slipping into these roles you've carved out for yourselves. The fit, chisel-jawed womanising actor. The suave Oxford student hoping to go into politics. Ralph is still the skinny little puppy, but I'm sure he'll find his niche. He certainly spent a lot of time telling me about dermatological research science and the efficacy of medication and lifestyle changes on skin conditions. Didn't quite pick up that I wasn't interested.'

Ken props himself up onto his elbows. 'I don't want to talk about my brothers. Things are complicated. They always are in families. I think our family more than many others. We're... different.'

'Because you're posh and rich.'

Ken tuts. 'Don't start with that. My family were traders, originally, if you go back a few generations. Not aristocracy. No, our complications come from other places.'

There are a few beats of silence. Then Sherie says something that makes Ken think he's slipped into a dream.

'Is it because of the murder?'

He must have misheard her. Must have done.

'What?' The word is like fingernails on crumpled paper.

'I said is it because of the murder?'

Ken takes in a sharp, painful breath. 'Yes, I thought that was what you said.'

He stands up. Pulling himself off the bed, as though the sheets are made of glass, not Egyptian cotton. The floor, too, seems to be sharp and harsh under his feet. The temperature of the room, seconds ago throbbing with the heat of their exertions, is now filled with the chill of the storm raging outside. He looks at her with his mouth open, unsure what to say. It's like she's stabbed him.

Astonishingly, her expression is calm. 'I heard you and your brother talking. When I came upstairs. That the death of your dad and grandad wasn't an accident. I heard George say he killed them. But I understand.' She pulls herself to the end of the bed, but stays sitting. 'I mean, after what you told me and showed me, about the abuse, the violence, everything you suffered, nobody could blame you.'

He can't talk. His throat feels swollen, as though he's been forced to swallow boiling water.

Sherie seems to notice his concern. She gets up off the bed and comes over to him. Kisses him on the cheek. 'Don't worry,' she says. 'I'm not going to tell anyone.'

Then she leaves.

He stands in the middle of the room for a few seconds. He's trembling. Freezing, but unable to bring himself to go over to the bed and seek warmth. Then he finds his ability to speak has returned.

'Oh fuck,' he breathes, falling to his knees. Crouching down low, clutching his head, as though protecting himself from falling rocks. 'Jesus fucking Christ.'

TWENTY-SEVEN
CLAIRE

CHRISTMAS DAY 2025

Claire goes downstairs on Christmas morning, well aware there isn't going to be any happy unwrapping of presents. Even without the arrival of the unexpected guest last night, there has been too much bad feeling created by her mother for all that. But she doesn't expect to find commotion and panic.

'George, what's going on?' Claire says, when she sees him. He's in his dressing gown and slippers and trips as he hurries towards her.

'Have you been up to Granny's?'

She shakes her head. 'No. Why? What's wrong?'

He looks stressed. Worried. Like there's an immediate situation. Or an immediate danger.

'I think... I want to check first.'

'George, stop, tell me what's wrong?'

He was in the process of pushing past her, but pauses again and says, 'I think she's dead. I think she may have been killed. Murdered.'

'What?' Claire says, stunned. 'How... who...'

'Alexandra's locked herself in one of the bathrooms. She's crying. She was running down the corridor and Ralph heard her say "She's dead" and "killed".'

Claire's memory flits back to the night before. Her mother's words.

Unless anyone plans to murder me during the night, I shall see you all for breakfast tomorrow morning.

She knew. She knew one of them would. That's why she's done all of this. She's laid the bait. Set a trap.

Her mind begins racing. What if that whole thing with the visitor last night was part of it? Could he be the murderer? Maybe she'd paid him to come here to kill her. And one of her sons is about to be framed.

Unless one of them actually did do it. *I wouldn't put it past them*, she thinks. She's appalled she's had the thought, but she can't unthink it. As she stares back into George's eyes, she wonders if he's seen it. Seen the terrible truth bloom in her eyes.

'Mum, why are you staring at me? We need to get up to Granny's rooms... see if it's true.'

Ken comes into view now. 'Has anyone been up? Alexandra's still crying. Ralph can't get her to open the door.'

'I'm going up there now.' George goes past them and Claire follows.

'I'm coming,' she says. 'Ken, perhaps you should go and help Ralph get Alexandra out of the bathroom. We'll need to talk to her. And maybe check on Kite.'

'I'm here,' grunts Kite, wandering into view, hair sticking up, looking like he's just been dragged out of a deep sleep. 'What's all the fuss? It's early.'

'Nothing,' Ken snaps.

'What?' says Kite.

'Go to your room,' says Ken, gruffly.

'Well, merry fucking Christmas to you too, *Father*,' says

Kite, imitating his dad's English accent on the last word and storming off.

Ken doesn't comment and Claire has too much on her mind to admonish him. They carry on in the direction of the north tower, Claire wondering what they might find up there with each step. And what unfortunate truths will be part of that discovery.

At the top of the winding staircase, George pauses in front of her, as though collecting himself.

'Open the door, George, it won't be locked,' Claire says, getting impatient.

He puts out his hand. Before it touches the handle, the door opens. Eileen stands there. Fully dressed, hair made up, smiling. Alive.

'My, my, what a welcoming committee this snowy festive morning.' She smiles. 'Merry Christmas.'

They all blink at her.

'But...' George says.

'We thought...' says Claire.

'Is there something wrong?' Eileen says. 'I was hoping to have a little early breakfast before I talk to our unexpected visitor. I told him to come to me at 8 a.m.' She looks at her watch. 'Has anyone seen him?'

TWENTY-EIGHT
KEN

CHRISTMAS DAY 2025

Ken hears Eileen's question and knows what this means. Where they'll all be heading next. The guest bedroom, where the stranger resides. And, to his surprise, he has a sudden fear for his son. He can't explain it, the lack of logic or sense to his fear, and it unsettles him. There's no reason Kite should enter the guest's bedroom, but the concern grips him all the same.

He begins to run. Pushing past George and dashing ahead, down the stairs to the landing, then up the few at the other end that lead to the west side of the first floor.

'Slow down, Ken,' his mother calls after him, but he ignores her.

'Kite!' Ken shouts as he turns the corner into the corridor.

There's no answer. But he sees immediately that one of the doors is wide open. He comes to a halt, feeling out of breath and hot. He walks the last few steps to the room slowly. And then sees that the very thing he wanted to avoid has come true.

There is a body. The guest is indeed dead, sprawled out on the floor. And Kite is staring down at him.

He knows this isn't the first time Kite has seen a corpse. They saw one together, years ago, on the street in Los Angeles. It was shortly after the schools had re-opened when Covid restrictions had eased, and Ken was alerted that the boy hadn't turned up at school, skiving off with his friends to buy contraband items – candy, back in those days, before he graduated to alcohol and cocaine. He saw him and his mates crowded around behind police tape as they watched law enforcement officers processing a crime scene: a body on the sidewalk. A young man lying on the ground in a pool of blood. Ken parked his car illegally and raced over to his son, ushering him and his friends away. Not that Kite seemed upset or disturbed. In fact, Ken was quietly appalled at how little effect the scene had on his son and wondered after if it had warped him in some unseen way. Perhaps his son had been damaged in some way, and Ken had failed to protect him.

Now it is happening again. And he's failed him again.

Looking down at the young man in front of him, he thinks about how similar this scene looks to the one four years ago. This handsome guest room in a Scottish castle is, in many ways, light years away from an LA street. The patterned rug, the ornate wallpaper, the antique metal and glass Christmas ornaments on the mantlepiece, the four-poster bed, the thick falling snow through the window. All of it is so different. But the body is the same. The same position. Sprawled, the angle unnatural. Something about the arms and legs – jutting out at the sides. The pool of blood. And Kite's calm, untroubled expression. It's eerily familiar.

'Kite, come away. Now.'

Kite stays still. Perhaps his lack of emotion is a coping mechanism, Ken thinks. Maybe the buried trauma from that earlier moment is coming to the surface, latching onto a new crime scene. Finding a home within a new moment of horror. Then it will be reborn again, as trauma once more, and do more untold damage to his young brain.

'Kite, I said come away!' Ken says, injecting more urgency into his tone.

He's about to put his hands around him, drag his son away if he has to, when he hears the others coming in. 'Oh my God,' says a voice. 'So it wasn't Grandma.' He turns to see Ralph standing behind him.

At last, Kite speaks. 'Grandma?' he repeats, looking first at Ken, then at Ralph.

'Alexandra... she was crying,' Ralph says. 'I heard her say something about a murder.' He comes to a stop in front of the body.

Ken's protective instincts switch to his younger brother. 'Ralph, I don't think you should go any closer.'

He watches as Ralph takes in the scene. The splayed legs, the arms, the blood, the blank eyes. The object buried in his chest. A pointed-star Christmas ornament, a deep-red bloodstain around the wound, soaked into the white T-shirt he is wearing. 'I thought Alexandra said "She's dead",' Ralph murmurs. 'But she must have said "he". I thought she meant... I didn't think it was...'

He trails off. Then Kite raises a hand and points to the corpse's crotch. 'Look, he's pissed his pants. That happens, apparently. I heard it on a podcast. The bladder releases when you die.'

'That's enough,' Ken says, sickened by his son's words and the casual way he's said them. He closes his hands around the boy's shoulders and pulls him away from the body and out of the room.

'You're always dragging me,' Kite mutters.

Ken ignores him. He looks back into the room and says to his brother, 'Ralph, you should come out too.'

Ken sees Ralph give him a look. One with a meaning he

understands but wishes he didn't. There's more to all of this, he thinks. More than just a dead man on the floor. More than just a murder or a family inheritance disagreement. This whole situation goes much deeper than the here and now.

'Has anyone phoned the police or an ambulance?' Eileen says. She's at the doorway with Claire and George, the two of them with near-identical shocked expressions on their faces. His grandmother, on the other hand, looks relatively untroubled. The sense of calm normality extends to her outfit, too. Ken, his brothers and his son are all in their boxers or pyjamas, Claire is in her dressing gown, all of them are dishevelled and disoriented. His grandmother, however, is in a white trouser suit and black blouse, with earrings and a necklace, as though she's ready to go to a dinner party. They all stare at her. Nobody speaks at first, then George says, 'I haven't got a signal.'

'My phone's in my room,' Ken says.

'Same,' Ralph says.

'We could try the landline,' says Claire.

'Are you sure you guys want to do that?' Kite says quietly. Ken still has his hands on his shoulders. After a few seconds' pause, he turns him around. Everyone's eyes are on him.

'What do you mean?' says Ken.

Kite shrugs. 'I mean... isn't it obvious? Somebody killed him, right? Someone here. One of us.'

TWENTY-NINE
GEORGE

CHRISTMAS DAY 2025

George tries to hide his horror at Kite's proclamation. He glances at his grandmother and sees her raise an eyebrow.

The boy looks embarrassed and moves his eyes to the floor. 'Sorry,' he mumbles. 'It's just... I mean, I've seen crime shows. That's the deal, right? Surely it's better you lot think about this shit before you throw yourselves into police cells.' He shrugs. 'Just a thought.'

Eileen nods. She seems impressed.

'It's nonsense,' George says, feeling like he needs to speak up before Kite's statements begin to be taken as fact. 'None of us would do this. None of us would... would kill anyone.' He hates himself for the hesitation, for stumbling over a sentence that should have been said with the confidence of the innocent, not the insecurities of the guilty.

'Oh yeah?' Kite says, now looking at him. 'Then why has Uncle Ralph just bolted?'

George suddenly becomes aware of a thudding sound. He looks around just in time to see the legs of Ralph's red pyjama trousers disappearing around the end of the corridor. He steps past his grandmother and mother and hurries after him. 'Ralph!' he shouts. He can hear his brother's steps getting faster, the sound of him running down the stairs. 'Ralph! Stop, where are you going?'

Ralph doesn't answer. And when George reaches the bottom of the stairs, he's vanished.

'Where is he?' he hears Ken shout from up on the landing.

'I don't know,' George breathes, looking in every direction. Then a wave of cold air hits his bare legs, and a roaring, rushing sound reaches his ears. George heads to the library and sees that the French windows are open. He rushes over to them and can just about see a figure in the snow, heading downhill. Towards the loch.

'Ralph!' George shouts, running after him. 'Ah fuck!' he yells as the freezing snow makes his feet sting. He runs fast, gaining on his brother, just before he reaches the end of the slope that leads down to the jetty and the water beyond.

'Ralph, what the hell are you playing at? Come inside!'

Ralph has knelt down, on his knees in the snow. He's swaying, muttering, just as he was the night before, only this time his inner crisis seems to have escalated.

'What's he doing?' comes a shout from behind him. Ken's standing nearby, looking at Ralph with concern in his eyes.

'Panicking, that's what,' George shouts over the rush of the wind, large flakes of snow entering his mouth every time he opens it. 'Help me get him up.'

Ken helps George get him standing, Ralph neither protesting nor making the task very easy, still rocking his head, tears running down his face. 'Always waiting to be found...' George hears him mutter as he steers him in the direction of the castle.

'Back inside, Ralph,' he says.

'Want to stay...' Ralph says quietly.

'You've got bare feet, so if you want to keep your toes, that's not an option,' George barks, forcing him to march forward.

When they reach the library, George and Ken lead Ralph into the room, and he collapses on one of the chairs. Their mother, grandmother and Kite have all been watching from the windows and they step back, looking at him as he lies there, bunched up like an animal whose only wish in the world is to withdraw into his shell and never come out.

Blankets are found and laid on top of him. George manages to encourage him to sit upright and says, 'Ralph, you need to snap out of this, it really isn't helping.'

'Darling, why did you run?' his mother says, sitting down next to him and putting an arm around him.

George doesn't want to leave Ralph, but he's now so cold, standing there in his T-shirt and boxers, that he feels like he might collapse. 'I need to warm up,' he says, going to leave.

'I think we should all stay together,' his mother calls out.

'Once I have more clothes on,' he says. 'Otherwise you'll have another dead body on your hands.'

'I'll come too,' Ken says.

As soon as they're out the room, George is about to speak to Ken, but then he sees Kite following.

'What do you—' Ken starts to say, but George frowns and nods to the boy behind him. Ken glances at his son and says, 'Oh, right.'

Kite frowns. 'What, I'm not wanted? I'm fucking freezing too, you know, I need to get dressed.'

'Yeah, that's fine,' Ken says. 'But I don't want you going anywhere near the room where... I'll come with you.'

The boy sighs, but doesn't protest. At first, George is annoyed the lad's presence has stopped them from having a private conclave, away from the others, but as he heads to his room and pulls on tracksuit bottoms and wraps himself in a thick dressing gown, he's grateful for the moment of peace.

When he heads back downstairs, he feels like he's going into battle.

'Has he said anything?' he says, looking at Ralph as he walks in.

Ken and Kite enter behind him before anyone can answer.

'No,' his mother says. 'He's said nothing. I asked him why he ran out, but...' She trails off. George knows why. Because even though she wants to know the answer, he can tell she's afraid of what it might be. And what it might mean.

'Perhaps,' his grandmother says, in a much stronger voice, looking at Ralph, 'actions speak louder than words.'

THIRTY
EILEEN

CHRISTMAS DAY 2025

Eileen stares at her grandson, sitting bunched on the sofa like a frightened child. She narrows her eyes, thinking. Wondering.

'Maybe one of us should have a look around the crime scene,' says Kenneth.

She turns her gaze on Kenneth. 'Why do you want to go back in there?'

She sees his face starting to colour. 'Well, I... I just wondered... there might be a... you know, a clue.'

'Feeling nostalgic for your time in *The Mousetrap*, are we, Kenneth?' she says. 'I'm not sure any of you should go up to the guest bedrooms.'

'Why not?' Kenneth frowns.

George tuts. 'Isn't it obvious? In case we hide something or interfere with something.'

Eileen hears her daughter draw in a breath. She raises her eyebrows at her. 'Do you think differently, Claire?'

Claire opens her mouth, pauses, then says, 'I don't think any of us should go back upstairs. We've got too much to sort out as a family, so I think we should all... well, all stay put. Including you, Mother.'

Eileen is amused by this last comment. 'Is that suspicion?'

Her daughter looks very awkward and says, quickly, 'No, no, I mean... I don't like to think of you going near the corpse. It's not... it's not nice.'

'I can deal with death,' she says. 'It's the living we should be afraid of.'

Something on the mantlepiece catches her eye. She walks slowly over and picks it up. It's an ornament – a star, one of three dotted among the photo frames and the clock in the centre. 'I don't think I'll be able to look at those Christmas ornaments in the same way again,' Claire says, with a shudder. Eileen looks at the object in her hand. Thinks about the point of it cutting through flesh, muscle and bone. 'They were new for this year. I put some in every room, I thought they looked nice.'

Eileen moves her eyes to her daughter. 'Well, you might be one short next year. Although, since this is my last Christmas, it's not really something I'll have to worry about.' She sees a look of dismay in her daughter's face. 'Oh, don't look so sad. You'll be able to get some more. eBay, possibly.'

'Granny, I can't believe you're joking at a time like this,' George says, weakly.

She shakes her head. 'I'm not joking, George, I was being flippant. There's a difference.' She thinks for a few moments, then says, 'We will have to phone the police. But I don't see the harm in a little... family discussion before we do.'

Everyone is watching her intensely, waiting for her next words. Waiting, she thinks, for their orders. Good. This is how she likes them. They've been unruly for too long. Now she needs to bring them into line.

'Where is Alexandra?' she asks.

'She found the body and was upset,' Ralph says, in a small voice, taking Eileen by surprise.

'She was crying in the loo,' Kenneth adds. 'I think I heard her vomiting.'

'Right,' Eileen says, making a decision. 'I think we need to sort this out. We need to do a post-mortem.' Upon hearing her daughter's gasp, she rolls her eyes and clarifies: 'I'm talking figuratively, Claire, not literally. We need to go over what happened, how it happened and what we can do about it. Fear not, no scalpels are involved.'

'I don't want Kite to be here,' Kenneth says.

'Tough shit,' Kite says. 'You can't send me away, not now.' He's leaning up against the bookshelves, looking more belligerent than before.

'Yes, I can, actually, because I'm your father,' Kenneth snaps.

'But that's so unfair,' the boy says. 'I'm already balls deep in this, I want to know what happened.'

Eileen walks forward towards him, taking her time with each step. 'Kite, darling, I know you feel your father doesn't deserve much respect, and perhaps he has a case to answer there, but please don't make this difficult situation more trying than it needs to be.'

She sees her great-grandson open his mouth, about to interrupt, so she carries on. 'I appreciate you feel you are, um, "balls deep" in this little mystery, but please remember the situation you find yourself in involves real people, real death and real consequences. This isn't a game or a TV show, it's real life.' She watches as the boy takes in these words. He closes his mouth but still looks sullen. 'Also, I'm sure you can remember quite clearly that yesterday, when I went through the plans for my will, you are the only person I plan to leave money to. If everything goes my way, you are the only member of this family who will receive anything at all.'

Kite holds her gaze. Then he nods.

'I'm glad you remember,' Eileen says. 'Please don't make me reconsider my arrangements.'

The boy stares back, his eyes widening slightly. Then he nods again and walks away.

'Straight to your room, mind,' Kenneth calls out, but Kite doesn't answer.

'Well, that's one thing sorted,' Eileen says. 'Now for the rest of you. I don't imagine this next step will be very pleasant, but it has to be done. George, close the door.'

As it closes, Claire says, 'I'm worried about leaving Alexandra. She'll come out to find us all gone.'

Eileen nods. 'Yes, I know, but we haven't moved house – we're just a few rooms down. And while she gathers herself, it will be good to try to get things clear. I like the poor girl, but I think she's better off absent for this bit.' She reaches out and takes hold of one of the chairs to steady herself. Then she looks around her, her eyes settling on Ralph. 'Did you say something?'

Ralph jerks, as though he's been caught out. 'What? No.'

'It sounded like you were muttering something under your breath.'

'I... wasn't saying anything,' Ralph says.

'Right,' Eileen says. 'Although I'm not discouraging talking, you understand. After all, that's what we're here for.' She stares around at the rest of them and then claps her hands together. 'Who's going first.'

They stare back at her, looking terrified.

'Don't all rush at once,' she says. 'Come on, we don't have all the time in the world. First, I want to know everything about what happened on the night Tommy was allegedly conceived.'

'Don't we—' George starts to say, then stops.

'Yes, George?' Eileen says, as everyone turns to look at him.

'Well, I was going to say, isn't the more important topic for discussion... the big question... who killed him?'

Nobody is looking at him now. Every eye in the room is on

the floor. Everyone except Eileen, who is staring at her middle grandson with a mixture of admiration and impatience. 'Yes, my dear boy, but I was rather hoping that might come out naturally during the telling of the tale. Unless, of course, you're volunteering a confession?'

Claire reaches out and puts a hand on his arm. 'George hasn't killed anyone,' she says. 'None of my sons have.' She looks around at them. Eileen thinks she sees something imploring in her eyes. 'Have you?' she prompts, her voice quivering.

'Since you seem keen to speak, George,' Eileen says, 'perhaps you could start us off.' He meets her eyes now. She sees the resolve in there. His acceptance that the time has come. The time to tell them the truth.

'OK,' he says at last.

This word causes Ralph to let out a little sob. Kenneth shuffles his feet. Neither of his brothers' movements causes George to stop. 'OK, I'll tell you what happened. It's time. Time for all of us. I'm going to tell you everything.'

He looks as though he's about to say something else, but then a small voice from the sofa says, 'Don't. Please, don't.' It's Ralph. He's staring at his brother with wide, pleading eyes.

'We have to, Ralph,' George says. 'It's time. Time for all of us to face this. And we'll do it together.'

THIRTY-ONE
RALPH

CHRISTMAS DAY 2005

Ralph feels himself drifting into a satisfied sleep. He isn't used to this. He normally puts girls off – ends up too over-enthusiastic and they back away, thinking him adorable rather than sexy. He worried he'd made the same mistake with Sherie. He got a bit overexcited during the kissing on the sofa and thought, when she went off for a bit, that he'd ruined his chances. Presumed she'd settle in one of the guest rooms and he wouldn't see her again. So he was both surprised and relieved when she did return a little while later. She looked flushed and very awake, whereas he was sleepy. The Christmas tree lights, the fire, the shadowy corners of the room, the storm outside – all of it made him feel a bit weird, a bit trippy. He's never taken illegal drugs, but when he saw Sherie walking towards him, he felt he had some idea what that must feel like.

After they'd made love on the sofa, Sherie seemed keen to talk, but he could barely keep his eyes open. She said something about how she thinks she seeks out the company of guys because of her own history of abandonment. The words 'history of abandonment' pricked at his mind, interrupting his post-coital satisfaction. They felt performative, as though she was seeking attention or sympathy. Maybe he had been ungallant, not asking her more about it, but he didn't want to get into anything deep or soul-searching. He just wanted to sleep.

So he slept.

It's Ken who wakes him. He's standing in the room. There's a broken vase on the floor. He must have knocked it over. He looks outraged, or panicked, or both.

'What's wrong?' Ralph mumbles, raising his head. He's intermingled with Sherie. The sofa is big enough for them both, but only just.

'What the fuck are you doing?' Ken says.

'Err... sleeping. Why?'

Ken points at the figure next to Ralph. 'She came back down here to you?'

Ralph nods. He can't understand what his brother's making such a fuss about. Is he jealous or something?

'What has she said?'

Ralph's getting irritated now. 'Said about *what*?' Sherie stirs, his raised volume disturbing her. But she doesn't wake. He pulls himself off the sofa, taking care to take his arm gently from underneath Sherie's.

'I... she... Nothing,' Ken mumbles.

'Can't you just go back to bed?' Ralph says. He picks up his discarded loungewear bottoms from the floor, pulls them on, then heads to the door.

'Where are you going?' Ken hisses.

'For a piss! Is that allowed? What the hell is wrong with you?'

'Nothing,' Ken mumbles again.

Ralph yawns and brushes his fringe from his forehead as he wanders out of the living room and towards the main staircase. Halfway up it, he almost collides with George.

'What the fuck? Why's everyone walking around?' Ralph says, stepping back.

'I could ask you the same question,' George says, peering down at the light coming from the living room doorway. 'Did I hear Ken? Where's Sherie?'

'In the lounge,' Ralph sighs, pushing past his brother, heading towards one of the landing bathrooms.

Once he's relieved himself, he cups his hands under the flowing tap and splashes some cold water onto his face. His contented sleep has left him feeling woozy. He's cold and wishes he'd put his T-shirt on before he left the living room. He isn't sure what time it is, it could be 1 a.m. or 6 a.m. for all he knows, but he has a sudden need to be awake and alert.

He hears the shouting before he opens the door. The words are muffled, but he recognises Ken's deep voice, then George shouting too. He goes out onto the landing and immediately hears Sherie. 'God you're all the same, aren't you?!'

He wonders if this is about him, if they're rowing about him sleeping with her, or her fling with George, or her grievances with his sexist behaviour. He thinks back to what she said during the row the previous day. Something about him not bothering to ask her anything about her life or family.

'I can't believe you fucking told her,' George is shouting now.

'I didn't!'

'Stop shouting at each other,' Sherie says. 'Please!'

Ralph frowns. This seems like something else entirely.

There's a sound – like a clatter. Something falling over. 'I trusted you!' George yells. 'I thought you understood.'

'I did! I *do*!'

'Look, there's nothing to fight about, I'm not going to tell anyone,' Sherie says. 'Though I might reconsider if you keep acting like this.'

'Tell anyone what?' Ralph says, marching in. 'What are you fighting about?'

'Nothing!' George and Ken shout together, almost in unison.

'God, you're all mad,' Sherie says, 'Just leave me alone.'

'I don't understand, what's wrong?' Ralph says, taking a step forward.

'Get out!' Ken says, pushing Ralph away.

'Stop pushing me!' Ralph shouts at him.

Then Ken does something he's never done before. He slaps Ralph across the face. The shock of it stuns him, makes him reel backwards, unable to talk.

Sherie steps in then. 'Stop it, leave him alone!'

'Ken, this isn't—' George starts to say, reaching for him.

'Get off!'

'Hey, just—' Sherie says. Then she shouts. Or is it more of a scream? Ralph can't tell. Nothing in front of his eyes is making sense, the sounds hitting his ears are jumbled, as if he's slipped into a foreign language film halfway through the story.

The crash seems to echo around the room, then through his head, making it ache and pound, as though he's been hit again.

He hasn't. But he knows something has happened. Because the room has gone very still and quiet.

At first, he can't figure out what he's seeing.

The flickering fire. The glowing Christmas lights, like pin-prick stars in the blackness.

Then the body.

Sherie's body, lying on the on the hearth rug, next to the overturned coffee table.

And his two brothers standing above her.

THIRTY-TWO
KEN

CHRISTMAS DAY 2005

After Sherie left his room, Ken fell asleep on the floor. The fact this was possible is astonishing to him when he wakes up, cold and aching. He figures he just passed out from the sheer intensity of everything he had been feeling. Like a protective instinct. His brain must have just shut itself off for a moment. Shivering and grunting as he stretches out his limbs, he gets to his feet and pulls on his tracksuit and hoodie. He isn't sure what time it is; he isn't wearing his watch and hasn't a clue where his phone is. He just knows he needs to leave his room for a bit. It feels like a hive of discomfort and anxiety and the more distance he can put between it and himself right now must be a good thing.

He's wrong.

Somehow he knows he's going to find something disconcerting when he descends the stairs and sees the light of the fire coming from the living room.

Sherie is there. He sees her first. She appears to be topless, using the dressing gown she was loaned as a blanket. And entwined with her is Ralph.

She came back down here to be with him, even after she and Ken had sex. And not just that. After they spoke about his grandfather.

I heard that the death of your dad and grandad wasn't an accident.

Perhaps all that was a dream, he thinks now as he stares at the two bodies on the sofa. Perhaps, because it was so present in his mind, he imagined that whole part of their conversation. Maybe they hadn't had a conversation at all. He could have fallen asleep after and she left him there, bored and annoyed by him. If true, this would explain why she returned to Ralph. Perhaps to pay him back? Make some sort of statement?

She knows. It's no use. He can't get away from the fact. She knows something that could bring down the family. The damage this could do to all of them. To George. To his mother and grandmother. To Ralph, who loved his father and grandfather more than any of them. Mostly because he had no knowledge of the monster who used to lurk in this castle. The old man who, before too long, would have started to inflict his sick games upon him too.

While he's thinking, his eyes drift to the floor and settle on a cushion. Dark brown with a burgundy trim, the colours just about possible to make out in the low light.

He looks at the cushion. Then back at Sherie. Then back at the cushion again.

There's a crash. He isn't sure what it is at first, then there's a pain in the back of his right leg, and he realises he's knocked against a small table behind him. The vase that was on it is now lying in pieces on the floor.

Ralph is awake. He's looking up and blinking at Ken. 'What's wrong?' he mumbles. Ken isn't sure what's wrong. If there is anything wrong, or how much of it he's imagined. The cushion on the floor feels like it's burning his peripheral vision.

He looks away from it, focusing on his brother's face. 'What the fuck are you doing?' he says.

'Err... sleeping. Why?'

Ken points at the sleeping figure next to him. 'She came back down here to you?'

Ralph nods.

'What has she said?'

Ralph's looking increasingly annoyed. 'Said about *what*?'

Sherie stirs, briefly, but doesn't wake. Ralph carefully pulls himself off the sofa.

'I... she... Nothing,' Ken mumbles.

'Can't you just go back to bed?' Ralph says.

Ken thinks of how he woke just a few minutes earlier. Cold and aching on the old fraying carpet in his room. Like a man in crisis. Not tucked up comfortably in bed like a good little boy on Christmas Eve.

But he's never really been a good boy. He knows that.

Then he glances at the cushion again.

When he looks back up, he sees Ralph is almost out the room.

'Where are you going?' Ken hisses.

'For a piss! Is that allowed? What the hell is wrong with you?'

'Nothing,' Ken mumbles again.

He wants to be left alone. And at the same time, he's terrified of Ralph leaving. Of what it might mean if he does, if it's just him and Sherie here, left in a room of a thousand dark possibilities.

Ralph is gone.

They are alone.

He feels his pulse rising.

Then voices make him turn his head towards the doorway. Seconds later, George is storming into the room.

'What's going on?' he says, loudly, looking thunderous.

Ken feels embarrassed. Even though he's just standing there, watching a woman sleep, it's as though he's been caught doing something. Something dreadful.

Except now she isn't asleep. Sherie's sitting up. Pulling on her clothes. And asking the same question George is.

Ken looks at her. Then at George. 'She knows,' he says. 'She heard us talking earlier. She knows what you did. She knows everything.'

Time becomes unreliable for Ken that night. If someone told him that he and his brothers had stood looking at Sherie's body for a thousand years, he could easily have believed it. It's Ralph's movement that drags him back to the present. He thinks he sees something similar in George too – he looks as though his mind has taken him somewhere dark, only to jolt him back to confront the terrible truth of the situation in front of him.

'Oh my God,' Ralph says. He dives towards Sherie. Hands on her. 'I can't find a pulse.'

Ken feels like he should be doing this. He's the eldest. He should be taking charge. Sorting this out. But it's his teenage brother who's putting her in the recovery position, feeling her neck, tapping her face, trying to work out if she's breathing.

'Why are you two just standing there? Fucking help me! Do something!' he shouts at them.

George looks over at Ken. 'An ambulance...?' He says the words pathetically, as though he's embarrassed by how ineffectual and pointless they are.

'It might be... too late...' Ken says, his voice not much more than a scratchy whisper. He's looking at Ralph, watching him trying to get something from her, some glimmer of life. He takes his hand away from Sherie and holds it up. There's blood on it.

'Her head's bleeding,' Ralph says. He looks at Ken, then over at George.

'Did someone hit her?' he asks.

'What?' George says, frowning. 'Nobody hit her. What are you talking about? We didn't—'

'Someone fucking hit her! Or pushed her,' Ralph shouts. He turns to Ken. 'Like you hit and pushed me!'

'None of us touched her,' Ken says, though his voice is shaky, his words sounding false in his mouth. 'Surely you saw that.'

'It's dark, and you'd just hurt me and it… it fucking upset me, OK,' Ralph says, a tremble in his voice verging on a sob. He seems moments away from completely losing it. His face is so pale and contorted, it looks like a skull.

'Nobody hit her,' Ken says again, forcing a commanding note into his voice. 'Get away from her, Ralph. We need to talk about what to do.'

George is shaking his head. 'She just… just fell. One minute she was here, the next…'

Ken meets his gaze. They look at each other for a few seconds. Then Ken says, 'She fell over. That's it.'

Ralph rubs at his eyes. 'I still don't understand. What was happening when I came in?'

'We got into a fight,' George says.

'Briefly,' says Ken.

'I didn't mean… not physical… we just…' George trails off.

Ralph gets up. 'I'd better call them,' he says.

'Who?' George says.

'An ambulance, like you just said!'

Ken steps forward. 'Ralph, how on earth are they going to get an ambulance up here? Have you seen what it's like outside?'

Ralph glances at the window briefly, but waves his hand. 'It's just the snow. It snows every year, I'm sure the emergency services have learnt to deal with it.'

'Not like this,' Ken says. 'It's one of the biggest blizzards this century has seen.'

'Well, considering this century is only five years old, I don't think that's a very impressive record!' Ralph shouts. 'Phone for a fucking ambulance, now, or I will.'

George sits down on one of the armchairs with a thump. 'It wouldn't just be an ambulance, though, would it? It would be the police. Forensics.'

Ken sees Ralph's eyes widen in concern. 'But... there might still be something—'

'She's dead,' George says. 'And it's our fault. Accident or not, it's going to be awful. Really, really awful.'

'Err... *yeah*, because someone's dead. Things usually are.'

'You don't remember, do you?' George says, putting his face in his hands. 'All the fuss when Dad and Grandfather died.'

Ken feels a prickle of unease at the back of his neck.

'Of course I do,' Ralph says. 'I was a child, but not a baby.'

'No, you really don't,' George says, his voice wavering, as though he's about to cry. 'Things were really... feeling that any moment they might... I don't want the police here. I just don't.'

Ken steps forward, coming up close to Ralph, taking care to avoid the legs on the floor right near him. He puts his hands on his brother's shoulders. His skin feels cold to the touch. He pulls off his own hoodie and gives it to him. 'Put this on, you must be freezing,' Ken says.

'I'm not freezing, I'm fucking furious,' he says, his jaw jutting out as it always does when he's struggling with his emotions. But after a few seconds, he takes the hoodie and pulls it on.

'Ralph, you might feel like you've got your whole life ahead of you, I felt that way at sixteen, but you need to realise how quickly it can all change. All those years stretching ahead can be altered in an instant. One moment, that's all it takes. And this is the moment.' He looks down at Sherie's body. His heart is pounding so fast, but he forces himself to stay calm, purposefully slowing his breath. 'A dead girl in the house. A girl all three brothers have shagged. A working class girl lost in the Highlands, fucked by three posh millionaire guys in their castle. Can't you see how that looks? How sordid that sounds?'

'Why...' George starts to say, then stops.

'Why what?' asks Ken.

George hesitates, then says, 'Well, why would it have to be that way around, like, us looking like the... you know... dominant ones. If anything, she came after us. Fuck knows why she had sex with all three of us, but I think we're all agreed she was definitely the instigator.'

Ken rolls his eyes. 'You're so naïve, George. Society is inherently sexist.'

'Oh come on, I don't need a sermon on sexism from you, the king fucking womaniser,' George snaps.

'No, no, hear me out – you've actually proved my point. It's presumed guys will go around sleeping with whoever will take them. If a guy got stranded at a castle filled with beautiful women and spent his Christmas having sex with them, people wouldn't be that shocked because they *presume* it of a young man. But if a girl does it in a castle with a bunch of men, people suddenly get all prudish and weird. If she truly initiated it all, people would presume she was warped or damaged or had a hidden agenda. Or they'd presume the evil men all took advantage of her. The version of the story people just can't buy: maybe she found herself surrounded by attractive guys and wanted to shag them. And that's why we'd be fucked if this ever got out.'

George looks like he's thinking, his brow furrowed, eyes staring into the distance beyond Ken. Slowly he nods.

'Can you imagine how that will be twisted by every newspaper in the country?' Ken continues. 'Possibly across the world. They'll make TV documentaries about us. Journalists will never leave us alone. We'll be put on trial. It will follow us for decades, infecting every single corner of our lives. It will fucking *define* us, Ralph. I'll never act again. George can say goodbye to any chance of going into politics after university. I wouldn't bet on you getting very far with studying medicine, either. All because of one split-second mistake. How would any of that be good? Or fair?'

Ken can see his brother trying to get his head around all this information.

George raises his head. Focuses back on Ken.

'So what do we do?' Ralph asks, his voice becoming small. Like a child's.

Ken stares back, not at Ralph, but at George. There's an agreement between them. They both know it.

'We cover this up,' Ken says. 'This never happened. We heard her story. Nobody knew she was here. And they never will.'

THIRTY-THREE
GEORGE

CHRISTMAS DAY 2005

'I need you to come back into the lounge,' Ken says.

George is clattering around the cupboards. Taking out cereal boxes, packets of teabags, things the housekeeper usually deals with. 'It's like there's been an apocalypse,' George mutters, taking out a box of Nesquik powder that should have been used a year ago. 'Maybe I fancy jam or crumpets. Or toast. Or Cheerios, we don't have any fucking Cheerios.'

'George, there hasn't been an apocalypse, but there could be if you don't come back and start helping me.' Ken is close to him now. He's still topless, after giving Ralph his hoodie. George can see goosebumps on his arms. The sight is strange to him. He feels like he's seeing something oddly intimate. A bodily reaction out of Ken's control, whether due to the cold or the intensity of the emotion.

'Why are you looking at my arm?'

George is frozen, the Nesquik still in his hand.

'George, look at me, look at me. I think you're having a

panic attack or something. And I can't do panic attacks right now, we need to keep our heads above water.'

The last three words slam into George with force. He drops the Nesquik. The tub opens and brown powder shoots across the floor.

'Heads above water? Did you say that on purpose?'

He sees confusion in Ken's eyes, then realisation. 'No! Fuck, no, it's just a phrase. I promise you.'

'No, it was a threat, Ken! A big fucking threat. I should never, ever have trusted you.'

'You can trust me! I'm your brother. Now stop fucking around in the kitchen, come back into the lounge, and help me sort this out. Ralph is alone in that room with a dead fucking body. He is seventeen years old. We're the older brothers. We owe him this. We need to protect him.'

George puts his face closer to Ken's. He can see every pore on his perfectly even skin. Its perfection feels obscene. As though the charismatic, handsome actor persona and everything that goes into creating it is what he's really keen on protecting. Not Ralph, or him, or any other member of the family. Ken's looking after Ken. George is certain of it. 'I can't go back in that room,' he says, his teeth clenched.

Ken slaps him across the face. It's so surprising to George, he wonders if it's actually happened or if his brain is playing tricks on him. But then it happens again, from the other side this time. 'Yes you fucking can,' Ken says. Then he slaps him again.

'Why the fuck are you hitting everyone today?' George shouts. He lashes out, but Ken's too strong. He blocks his hand. George isn't sure if he meant to punch him or slap him, but it makes little difference. He's unable to make contact, Ken stopping each attempt. So he pushes himself towards him, trying to knock him to the ground. It's like they're back where they were less than twenty minutes ago, fighting in the living room. A fight that would end in disaster.

They end up on the floor, Ken trying to hold him still while George flails and shouts and eventually weakens. His muscles stop resisting. His words turn into sobs. Tears fall down his face, his shoulders shake and Ken allows their struggle to turn into a hug.

'I'm trying to protect you and Ralph, too,' Ken says quietly into his ear. 'I promise you. And I know you're strong enough for this. The same way you were strong enough to make that hole in Grandad's boat. The same way you acted to keep your little brother safe. Find that strength within you now and use it.' He gives George a little shake on the last two words.

George stays still for a few seconds. Then, eventually, he nods. 'OK,' he says. 'I'm sorry I ran out. Let's go back.'

Before they can get up, however, a shadow falls upon them. Ralph comes into view, standing above them, frowning.

'Why are you both covered in chocolate?'

Both brothers stand and dust themselves down. George suddenly feels embarrassed and irritated with himself for crying. For allowing the panic to take hold of him. He fled the living room minutes earlier as though his life depended on it. The thought of seeing that poor dead girl on the floor for a moment longer felt intolerably painful to him. Now he feels foolish. Of course they need to go back. Of course they need to keep their cool and fix this.

'This might sound stupid,' Ralph says, 'and I feel awful for saying it, but... I think I might have an idea. An idea about what to do with... with the body.'

George and Ken stare at him. 'Go on then,' Ken prompts after a pause.

Ralph takes a deep breath. 'Well, you remember when we were out looking for the generator, in the storage buildings.'

'Yeah,' Ken says, nodding slowly.

'Well, that plastic sheeting. The roll the gardeners use to cover plants for the winter. I think we should wrap her in it.'

George and Ken look at each other. 'Right...' George says.
'And then what?' Ken asks.
Ralph takes a deep breath, and says, quite calmly, 'Then we put her in the loch.'

THIRTY-FOUR
RALPH

CHRISTMAS DAY 2025

The noise of the storm outside has been stressful for Ralph, but as he sits huddled on the sofa listening to George explain, he starts to find the roaring wind and tap of snowflakes on the window calming. Something to focus on. An ambient sound that helps him perform his more obvious coping rituals. But when George gets to the point about the plan – his plan – involving the loch, any sense of calm and being able to cope vanishes. He feels himself starting to rock forward involuntarily. His mother gets up and stands in front of him. At first, he thinks it's his movement that's disturbed her, but it's George's words that have made her separate herself from him. And he knows why. She must be appalled by him. He's appalled with himself.

'It was your idea, Ralph?' Claire says. 'Your idea to wrap up that poor girl's body and put her in the loch?'

He doesn't answer. But when silence falls, the feeling of everyone's gaze on him – judging him, perhaps even repulsed by him – means he eventually manages a short nod.

'My God,' his mother says. 'Is that why you ran down to the

loch this morning?' She looks out the window, even though the view is almost entirely obscured by the swirling blizzard.

'Mum... I'm... I'm so sorry,' Ralph says in the faintest of voices.

He sees her look over at George, then back at him. 'But how on earth could you think that was a solution?'

Ralph lowers his eyes, trying not to look at his mother. Instead, he focuses on his knees. The blanket has flopped down, and the two damp patches on the legs of his pyjamas are visible where he knelt down in the snow earlier. By the edge of the loch. The edge of that big, breathing mass – like a beast, lying there, covered in ice, dormant but alive. Harsh, elemental, perhaps even evil.

'Ralph?' his mother prompts, frustration now audible in her tone.

He looks at her, and says, still in his quiet, choked voice, 'There's so much you don't know yet.'

From behind his mother, he sees his grandmother nod. 'Indeed,' she says. 'Like how that poor, dead girl managed to give birth to that poor, dead young man.'

There's a pause, and it feels like everyone is digesting her words. Then George speaks.

'Well, we've got more to tell you, Granny, but I can promise you, that's a mystery to us all.'

Ralph looks at his brother, but his eyes aren't met. George is staring at his grandmother, eyes wide and pleading, as though willing her to understand. To convince her he's telling her the truth. She nods and tells him to continue, and George carries on explaining what happened that terrible night in 2005.

Ralph withdraws into his thoughts. Thoughts, memories, haunting images that will never go away. No matter what happens here today. No matter what retribution or absolution awaits him.

Then everybody jumps. A loud noise at the French

windows has caused every head in the room to turn towards them.

'Jesus Christ,' says his mother.

He understands her astonishment. The disorienting sense of history – both recent and buried – repeating itself.

Because there's someone outside. Knocking to come in.

THIRTY-FIVE
RALPH

CHRISTMAS DAY 2005

Ralph can't quite believe it's happened. He sits in the living room, looking at the body on the floor. He can hear Ken and George arguing in the kitchen, but doesn't pay attention to the snatched words that are just about audible. He can't quite believe how easily the solution comes to him. He imagines George and Ken are rowing about solutions – how best to cover up what's happened. Whatever that is. A fight gone wrong, apparently. An inadvertent shove, Sherie coming in between the brothers as they fought. Plausible, he supposes. But part of him wonders if it's the full story.

But that doesn't matter now. What matters is what they do next. Ken's little speech about this scandal following them through their lives hit him hard. It was well worded and well timed, and the effect on Ralph hasn't been one of despair or distress, but rather motivation and mental clarity. He knows what they need to do. Now he just needs to tell them.

He walks through the darkened passageway towards the

light of the kitchen. At first, he can't see Ken and George. Then he spots the tangle of legs and arms on the floor.

'Why are you covered in chocolate?' he asks. He spots the yellow Nesquik tub next to them. If the situation wasn't so serious, he'd have probably found it funny. He watches as they stand and brush themselves off, then tells them his plan, reminding Ken of the plastic sheeting they saw in the outhouses and how they could wrap the body and put it in the loch.

George looks like he's having trouble with the idea of doing such a thing, but Ken nods enthusiastically. 'Yeah. Yeah, I think that could work. We'd need to weigh her down, somehow.'

'There must be something in there we can use,' Ralph says, nodding to the back door of the kitchen, beyond which lie the courtyard and the storage sheds. 'There's so much shit in there, nobody would notice if we took some stuff.'

'We could wrap her in the hearth rug,' Ken says. 'Perhaps that would be safer. In case there's blood on it.'

George shakes his head slowly. 'That's the kind of thing Mum would obsess over. We should check it, but if it's clean, we should keep it.'

'Forensic people would be able to tell,' Ralph mutters.

'But there'll never be any forensic people here,' Ken says. 'We're going to make sure of that.' He steps forward and taps Ralph on the arm. 'We're going to do what you suggest. You've impressed me, Ralph. I didn't think you had it in you.'

He strides off down the passageway towards the main part of the castle.

'Err... where are you going?' George calls after him. 'I thought you said the plastic sheets were in the storage sheds?'

'I don't know if you've seen the weather, but it's fucking crazy out there. Even worse than when Ralph and I went outside earlier. I'm off to put on many hundreds of layers. I suggest you both do the same.'

THIRTY-SIX
GEORGE

CHRISTMAS DAY 2005

George does as Ken suggests. He goes up to his room and doubles up – even triples up – on clothing. He gets into some thick tracksuit bottoms and over those pulls on some jeans. He adds a workout vest under his T-shirt, then pulls on a long-sleeve top, followed by a thin jumper and then a thicker one. He finds an oversized old Ralph Lauren hoodie at the bottom of his wardrobe, so he puts that on too. When he glances at himself in the mirror, he wonders if he'll see a round ball of cotton wool rather than a person, but he still looks relatively ordinary. Too ordinary for a night like this. The worst night of his life so far. Or perhaps his second-worst.

He looks over at his bed. Wonders about looking at the photo album again, not as a source of guilt and horror, but of strength. A reminder he got through all that, and he'll get through this too. But he doesn't have time. Ken strolls in, looking similarly layered up, disturbing the flow of his thoughts.

'I'm ready,' he says. 'We need to go. From what I remember, the plastic is in a roll. It's quite large and heavy – I knocked it over when I went in – but I should be able to manage it. But I need you and Ralph to get something to weigh the body down. We should wrap everything together.'

He says all this in an emotionless, businesslike tone. As though he's discussing wrapping up a Christmas present to be shipped off abroad. Not someone who was, until recently, a living, breathing human being.

'Won't that make her difficult to lift?' George says. 'I mean... shouldn't we take her outside first, close to where we want to put her into the loch?'

Ken frowns. He appears to be thinking. 'I suppose. I was just worried about someone seeing.'

'Who's going to be walking around in weather like this? As far as I know, we're the only ones here. Any staff are on Christmas holidays, in their homes in the village, or even further afield. The only people nearby are Hamish and his father, and they'll be asleep and wouldn't be able to see anything from their cottage, even if they're not. Nobody's going to be taking a walk around the loch at 3 a.m. on Christmas morning.'

Ken nods. 'You're right. So... what do you suggest?'

George sighs. Nods to himself. 'We take her to the storage sheds. Wrap and bind her in there and include some bricks or other heavy objects. That will save us having to cart everything into the living room and then trying to carry it all out again. Then we can carry or drag the... package... through the snow down to the loch.'

After reaching this agreement, they head down the corridor to the room at the end. Ralph's bedroom. He's sitting on the floor, pulling on some thick winter socks over his regular sports socks. He looks as though he's concentrating hard. It reminds George of how he looked as a child when working away at building impressively complicated Lego sets. As he watches him, George realises he's saying something. Mumbling to himself.

'*Hinge. Saddle. Condyloid.*'

The words reach him, but he isn't sure what they mean.

'*Ball and socket. Plane. Hinge. Saddle.*'

George looks at Ken. They share a look, then George turns back and says, 'How are you doing, Ralph?'

He stops his mumbling but doesn't look up. 'I'm not very good,' he says.

'Well, that's bloody obvious,' says Ken.

Ralph continues to sit very still on the floor. He isn't crying or shaking. But George still feels like he can see something falling apart in the boy's face. Like his soul is disintegrating from within.

'What were you saying? Just now, those words you were repeating?'

Ralph pauses, then says, very quietly. 'Synovial joints. In the human body. The ones I was reading about before... reading about earlier. Reciting them over and over makes me feel calmer.'

Again, George glances at Ken, who shrugs. 'Right.'

There's another pause. Then Ralph says something in a clearer voice. And the clarity seems to make his words all the more terrible.

'I can't believe what we're about to do was my idea.'

He's right. George knows that. This idea should have been cooked up by either him or Ken. After all, they're the ones responsible for this mess. But instead, their way out has come courtesy of their lovable puppy of a little brother. A quiet mastermind in lamb's clothing.

'It's a good idea,' Ken says firmly. 'And we're going to pull it off.'

Ralph stands up. He keeps his eyes on the floor. 'It makes me think I'm... bad.'

'You're not bad,' George says.

'No, you're not,' Ken says. 'But how you act now is important. We've all got to be brave. You've got to be brave, Ralph.' He stops talking for a second, then says, in a deeper voice, 'Cowards die many times before their deaths; the valiant never taste of death but once.'

George tuts. 'God, you're crass. I really don't think this is the time for you to show off your experience with Shakespeare. I know you want us to be eternally impressed you played Hamlet in fucking Eastbourne.'

'It wasn't from *Hamlet*, and I didn't mean it to be crass,' Ken says.

'Well, it was,' snaps George.

'And it isn't fair to call me a coward,' Ralph chips in, looking angry now.

'I'm not,' Ken says. 'That wasn't what I was trying to say. You're not a coward.'

Silence falls among them. Then, in a very small voice, Ralph asks, 'What am I, then?'

'You're the best of the three of us,' George says.

'You're a survivor,' says Ken.

THIRTY-SEVEN

RALPH

CHRISTMAS DAY 2005

Ken and George lift Sherie – or 'the body' as she has become – and carry her through the darkened hallways and passageways, down through the kitchen and out the back door.

In the storage sheds, they lay her on the plastic sheeting. Ralph wonders if he's grieving as he looks at her peaceful face. He thinks it's peaceful. It's dark and shadowy, even with the dim side lights on, so he can't tell properly. But he hopes it is.

'This is the end of everything, isn't it?'

He isn't sure why he says it, just as the body starts to disappear, with Ken unwrapping more of the plastic and laying it over her face.

'We can't be having that sort of talk,' Ken says.

He sees him glance at George. It isn't the first time they've shared a look like this. They're worried about him. How quickly the dial can change, he thinks. Half an hour ago, it was George having the meltdown. Ken's doing his best to be the macho, commanding leader, but even he is out of his depth here. But despite their struggles, his older brothers are doing their best to be exactly that – older brothers. And they're worried about him.

They should be, he thinks.

This night has broken him. Seventeen years old, and he's already irreparably wrecked. He didn't kill her. But it's still destroyed him. Every little domino of decisions that caused each piece to tip them towards this moment. The moment which sees him about to help illegally dispose of a body.

Hinge. Saddle. Condyloid. Ball and socket. Plane.

'Ralph, why don't you go back inside the house?' George says, as though he can read Ralph's mind.

'What?' he says, looking up. George has his eyes on him, his breath visible in the freezing air.

'I didn't like what you just said,' George says. 'About this being the end of everything.'

'We might need him to help carry her,' Ken says, as he places a brick alongside the first coating of the body, then adds another layer of plastic on top. 'We need to weigh the package down as much as we can.'

'You're a fucking weightlifter,' George says. 'I'm sure you can manage it.'

'And I don't need to go back indoors,' Ralph says. 'I'm fine.'

Neither George nor Ken raise any further objections. Ralph isn't sure why he's rejected a chance to limit his involvement. It would just feel wrong to withdraw now. Like a mathematical equation that hasn't been properly formulated. Like a form that hasn't been filled out correctly.

So he stays. Stands there. They wrap the ends with binbags. Tie the package with rope, then with tape, then with more plastic sheeting. Until eventually Ken stands back and says, 'OK, I think that's enough.'

'You sure?' George asks.

'I don't fucking know, George, this is my first dead body.'

Ken doesn't raise his voice, but the words have a harsh sting in them. Ralph sees George flinch.

'I'm sorry,' Ken says. 'I don't mean to... I'm just tired. And stressed.'

'I think that's probably an understatement,' George says. 'It's OK, let's... let's just carry on.'

Carrying on means lifting the body and carrying it out into the cold.

And it really is cold. Their short excursion to the generator room and storage sheds was nothing compared to the blistering ferocity of the harsh wind and stinging snowflakes as they carry the wrapped package through the snow.

At least it's downhill, Ralph thinks, as they make their slow journey down to the loch. He thinks they're just about keeping to the pathway, but they could be far off. The snow has transformed the whole surrounding area into a different world, beyond anything Ralph has seen before. It makes any wintry dustings of the past feel like mere heavy frosts.

'We haven't discussed how far,' Ken shouts back behind them.

'How far what?' George says. But Ralph knows what Ken means. They haven't discussed how far into the loch they need to take her. Nobody's tested the ice. They don't know whether it will be a case of tipping her in from the edge of the little snow-covered jetty, or if it will be thick enough to drag her far out across the surface. But that would involve smashing through further on, which feels like a thoroughly foolish thing to do.

They save the debate for when they reach the jetty. Ken's in favour of stepping out onto the ice carefully and trying to drag the body some way out. George tells him the plan is insane. Ralph isn't sure. He can't quite remember what he envisaged. What he imagined when he suggested this plan. In his head, the ice hadn't been there. They would just tip the body – the package – into the loch, and it would sink without a trace, and they'd go on with their lives. If they could.

If he isn't too broken.

Discussion about the topic can't continue, however. Because they're not alone.

'Hello!'

At first, Ralph thinks the man's shout is a trick of the wind. The howling, the roaring, a noise that can easily play tricks on troubled minds. But if anything, the blustering and battering is starting to calm. Ralph's sure the storm isn't raging quite so aggressively as it was when they first went out to the storage sheds. The easing off helped them get to where they are now, at the edge of the loch. But it's also led to another sort of exposure. Another risk they didn't think was worth considering.

The risk of being discovered.

THIRTY-EIGHT
GEORGE

CHRISTMAS DAY 2025

George stares at the male figure knocking on the library windows. For a moment, he thinks it's Tommy, resurrected from the dead, here to bring carnage and retribution upon them. Perhaps he'll wander in, still wearing that blood-stained T-shirt, the Christmas ornament still wedged in his broken chest, the wound dripping as he ambles into the room and sets about killing them all.

This doesn't happen, of course. And as George blinks, staring at the figure, he realises he knows who this is. 'It's Hamish,' he says, stepping forward. He opens one of the French windows as everyone watches.

'Sorry to disturb you all,' Hamish says, leaning forward, looking around. 'I heard shouting and saw people running about near the loch. I thought I should check on you.'

Everyone continues to stare. George tries to find some words, something he can say to dilute the oddness of this situation. 'Ah... yes... err, thank you.'

'I did try to phone,' Hamish says. 'Couldn't get through.'

His eyes scan the room again. Pause on Ralph, huddled on the sofa, the blanket bundled around his feet.

George is about to confirm again that they're all fine when his grandmother speaks.

'That was very kind of you, Hamish, but as you can see, there's no problem here.'

Hamish's expression suggests he isn't convinced. 'Haven't had a storm this bad since 2005, I'd say,' he says. It's the wrong thing to mention, and maybe he senses it, because his next comment feels like an awkward sidestep. 'Unwrapped all your presents, then?' He's clearly trying to sound jolly, but seems to realise he's being too familiar. No matter how many times George has told him to relax in his and the family's presence, he is still staff. He isn't family.

Claire steps forward, and in a tone that indicates she too feels Hamish has overstepped, tells him everything is fine and wishes him a happy Christmas.

Hamish gives her a nod, then closes the door. George latches it shut and watches as the figure departs, disappearing completely into the blustery whiteness of the storm.

'I suppose it was nice of him to bother, in such conditions,' Claire says. 'I hope I didn't sound too rude, but I was afraid he just wouldn't leave.'

'It was a bit awkward,' George says.

'Yeah, and ironic,' says Ken.

George shoots him a look – one that's clearly clocked by both his mother and grandmother. 'What did you mean by that, Kenneth?' the latter says, her eyes fixed on him.

Ken appears to flail a bit, his mouth twitching, then he looks at George. Claire also looks at him, then back at Ken, as though she were at a silent tennis match. 'You're not...' she says, frowning. 'You're not telling me Hamish has something to do with all this, are you?'

'I think, perhaps,' Eileen cuts in, 'we should avoid jumping to conclusions before your sons have had a chance to explain.'

THIRTY-NINE

KEN

CHRISTMAS DAY 2005

'Hello!' comes the call again.

'Stand in front of the body,' Ken says sharply to both of his brothers.

'What?' George says.

'Just fucking do it,' snaps Ken. He can see the shape moving a little way along the edge of the loch, near the western stretch of the forest. 'I think it's either Robbie or Hamish.'

'What do we do?' breathed Ralph.

Ken's surprised at how well he can hear his little brother. He isn't speaking loudly, and yet his words are audible. The storm's reduction is a blessing in some ways, but also a major risk. And that risk seems to have become a reality.

'Shit,' he says to himself. 'Stay here.'

He sets off walking through the snow as fast as the dense, powdery drifts will allow. It takes him a good few minutes to reach the trees, perhaps more, and it's only when he gets close to where the man is standing that he can see it's Hamish, fully dressed in his outdoor gear, as though going for a walk in the snow at 4 a.m. is a normal thing for him to do. At the same moment, he realises George has followed him. He wants to shout at him for not doing what he's told, to tell him that he can handle this himself, but he can't now, with Hamish very much within hearing distance.

'Are you boys OK?' Hamish asks. 'I came to check on you.' Even though he's only ten years older than Ken, he has a fatherly nature – more so than his father, Robbie, who has always appeared sullen and unapproachable.

'You came out here for us? At this time?' Ken asks. 'That's... kind.' He glances back at the edge of the loch. To his relief, Ralph is only just about visible, hidden by the way the perimeter curves around. But he thinks he can still just about make out the thing on the ground next to him. The thing Hamish absolutely must not see.

'Can we go a bit further into the trees?' Ken says. 'Get out of the wind?'

Hamish nods and leads the way deeper into the forest. 'Your mother phoned last night and said she and your grandma were unable to get back home, so you boys would be alone for Christmas. I offered for you to come and spend Christmas Day with my dad and me, but she said you'd probably prefer just to stay in the castle, just wanted to make me aware. I couldn't sleep because of the storm and could see the courtyard lights on at the back of the castle, and a lot of the downstairs lights too. Thought I'd walk up to check you were all right.'

In other circumstances, Ken might have been rather touched and impressed by this act of caring and dedication, but right now it irritates him. 'We're fine, honestly,' he says.

'Yeah, all fine,' George adds, nodding.

Hamish looks confused. 'So... why are you all outdoors? You weren't going to go onto the loch, were you? The ice might seem thick, but I wouldn't trust it.'

George nods, a little too hurriedly in Ken's view. 'Sure, sure.'

There's a silence amongst them, Hamish looking expectant. Ken's not sure what for, then realises they haven't answered the main part of his question. 'Oh, we... Ralph had a fever.'

'He was sleepwalking,' George says, barely a second later.

Ken frowns at him.

'He was sleepwalking *and* had a fever?' Hamish asks. 'Is he OK?'

He takes a step forward, as though about to walk out of the cover of the trees to try to spot the unwell sleepwalking boy. Ken silently curses in his head. Why did he mention Ralph at all? He just wants to tell Hamish, well-meaning though he is, to fuck off and mind his own business. He is, after all, staff.

'We've got it in hand,' Ken says, raising a hand in reassurance. 'We said we'd come with him for some air. Just needed a stroll in the snow. We've been cooped up in there for too long, as you can imagine.'

Hamish nods. 'Yeah, you can say that again. It's more than a little suffocating in the cottage with my dad. He's had the flu. For a bit, I thought I'd have to take him to hospital, but he's turned a corner now and is up and about. Eating some more. Hopefully he'll enjoy his Christmas dinner. Perhaps that's what Ralph's got. The flu, that is.'

'Maybe.' Ken nods at the same time as George says, 'Nah, I don't think so.'

Hamish raises his eyebrows again. It must be obvious something else is going on here, but politeness and a sense of deference to his employers' family is apparently holding him back from questioning them with more vigour.

'I'm sorry to hear about Robbie,' Ken says. 'Does he... can we do anything? Do you need medication?'

Hamish shakes his head. 'There's not much to do, other than hot drinks and paracetamol. And we have both those things in abundance, thank goodness. As I said, he's much better now. But thank you, I appreciate the offer.' He gives them a smile.

Ken and George smile back.

Go, Ken thinks with all the mental energy he has left, as if the sheer force of the word will make Hamish retreat. *Just fucking leave.*

'Well, we should all get back to our beds,' Hamish says. 'I can't imagine there'll be much driving around here for a day or two, even in the Range Rovers, but do shout if you boys need anything. You can call any time.'

'We will, thank you,' says George.

'Definitely,' says Ken.

They turn to leave as Hamish begins to walk back through the wood away from them. Then he stops. 'Oh, I almost forgot,' he calls out.

Ken's heart is beating hard. *What now?*

Hamish smiles at them widely again. 'Merry Christmas!'

Ken laughs and gives him a thumbs up. 'Yeah, same to you, man.'

Hamish waves a gloved hand and continues on his way.

'*Man?*' George says. '"Same to you, *man*"? Bit weird.'

'I was trying to sound casual,' Ken says, wincing.

'I think you just sounded strange.'

Ken pushes him, 'Well, you shouldn't even be here – you should have stayed with Ralph. Just... come on.'

He marches past him through the last stretch of trees and out into the open. But he doesn't get very far before he freezes.

Ralph is no longer at the edge of the jetty. And neither is the package. The body. They're both gone.

FORTY

GEORGE

CHRISTMAS DAY 2005

Both brothers gasp. At first, George doesn't understand. Where could Ralph have disappeared to, with the trussed-up package that took two of them to move?

Then something catches his eye.

'Oh my God,' George says, pointing.

Through the thick falling snow, two shapes become visible. Ralph. And the package. Both of them on the ice.

'No!' Ken says. He starts to run as fast as he can through the snow. It isn't very fast at all and after only a few strides he falls over. 'Ralph!' he shouts, spitting ice out of his mouth.

'Ralph!' George calls out, too. The figure comes to a stop. George can just about make out what he's doing. 'Ralph, don't!'

He's dragging the body. He's come to a stop on the ice and it looks as though he's pushing the package into the ice.

'Ralph, come back now!' Ken roars.

'Hamish will hear!' George says.

'Shit,' Ken says, nodding. 'You're right... I'm... I'm going to have to get him.'

The wind may have died down, but the snow is getting thicker – so thick that it's becoming almost impossible to make him out in the darkness.

'I can't see him,' Ken says, striding ahead.

'I can't either... I can't even see where the fucking ice begins and the ground ends.'

'I know. I... I can't see him,' Ken says again, the panic now plain in his voice.

George knows what he's thinking. He knows what's going through his mind, the terrible fear gradually becoming a reality. He's gone through the ice. In his attempt to dispose of the body himself, Ralph has gone through the ice. And the two of them are going to have to explain to their mother why her youngest son has died, frightened and cold, in the depths of the loch. The same loch that took the lives of her husband and father.

'Ralph,' George says, but the word is just a whisper, lost in the night air.

'You shouldn't have left him,' Ken says.

'Don't blame me!' George says.

'I'm going out to find him.'

George takes hold of his arm. 'You're bigger and heavier than he is. If he's gone through the ice, you definitely will.'

'*How* can I stay here when he might be drowning out there? How can I fucking do that?'

The two brothers stare at each other. Then George sees something over his brother's shoulder. Something solid and moving. Coming towards them through the darkness.

It's Ralph. George doesn't think he's ever been so relieved to see someone.

Ken makes a noise halfway between a gasp and a shout. Both of them rush forward until they reach him. He's trying to get back up onto the jetty, the edge of it defined by a mountainous ridge of snow. He's struggling, his feet failing to get purchase on the seemingly never-ending cascade of white powder.

'I've got you,' Ken says. George watches as he pulls him up onto the jetty. The two collapse to the ground, Ken hugging the shaking boy as though he's never going to let him go again.

'You fucking idiot,' Ken says. 'You didn't have to do that. You didn't have to do it alone.'

'I just... wanted... to... get... it... done,' Ralph says through chattering teeth.

That's when George realises there's something very wrong about him.

He's not wearing his big outdoor coat. Or his hoodie or jumper. He's in his short-sleeved T-shirt. And he's a worrying colour – his skin seems to be an ill-looking grey-blue.

'Where the hell is your coat?' George asks.

Ken lets go of him and steps back, taking him in. 'Jesus, Ralph – where are your clothes?' He touches the boy's bare arms with his gloved hands, even though he can't feel them through the material. 'We need to get you inside.'

Ralph nods. Then he slumps back into Ken as though he's unable to keep standing. George takes off his own coat. 'Here, Ralph, wear this. I'll be fine while we get back up to the castle.'

Ralph gives a small nod and allows himself to be helped into the coat. Then they walk, with Ken supporting him and George leading the way back up to the courtyard, past the storage buildings and through the back door into the kitchen.

'Come over to the Aga,' Ken says. He pushes Ralph down into a chair. 'George, go and build up the fire.'

George nods and runs out of the room. His face feels like it's burning as he adjusts after being out in the cold. He has to resist delaying things by stopping to warm his own body by the embers of the previous fire and begins to add wood to it. Once it's crackling in a satisfying way, he takes off his gloves and is about to leave the room when his leg knocks up against something. It's the edge of the still upturned coffee table. And he can see a very small mark on one of the legs.

A small, dark red mark.

He thinks back to the events in this room. Barely two hours ago, Sherie was a living, breathing human. How quickly everything can change. Now this little drop of blood appears to be the only thing left of her.

She knows what you did.

He can still hear Ken's voice echoing through the room. The moment he realised what he meant. What he was referring to. What Sherie knew. And how, in that moment, he understood. Understood that they could never let her leave.

George reaches into his pocket and takes out an old tissue. He uses it to wipe off the single drop of blood. Sets the coffee table the right way up. Then he throws the tissue on the fire and watches it burn.

FORTY-ONE

KEN

CHRISTMAS DAY 2005

In the hours that follow, as dawn starts to break in the form of a dull, grey smudge against the landscape, Ken focuses his attention on getting Ralph warm and back to good health. He's concerned, though, that even once he's been warmed on the outside, he still seems chilled from within. In some ways, he knows what that feels like. He wonders if he will be able to cope with the weight of what they've done in the months and years to come. A lifelong heaviness, dampening every nice moment, every happy exchange or bright day or instance of joy.

No. He can't think like that. He shakes his head as he waits for Ralph to get into some warm, dry clothes. Ken has never been one for excessive rumination. He leaves that to his younger brothers. No, he's the doer, the one who takes the reins and grabs the initiative with all his strength. What occurred today was damage limitation. That's all.

He looks in through the doorway of Ralph's room. He's bundled up again, though this time in a dressing gown rather than outdoor gear.

'Ralph, just tell me what happened to your clothes,' Ken says, going in. 'Where did your coat go?'

A tear slips down Ralph's face. A single, solitary tear. But he doesn't burst into sobs. He sits on the edge of the bed and then says, 'I got it caught. On... on the body. One of the ropes got through the buttonholes in the cuff when I was dragging it out onto the loch. I could see a hole in the ice to push the body into, but when the rope got caught, I just had to get the coat off. I felt like it had touched the body... her body... and then I felt like I was burning. Felt like the cold air was actually, like, fire or something. So I took my jumper and hoodie off too. They... they went into the water. They were soaked when I was pushing the package into the hole. I couldn't reach and I didn't want to. So I just left them and walked back to you and George.'

Ken listens to this. Then tells Ralph he understands. 'But you shouldn't have ever gone out onto the ice on your own. That was... fuck, that was so dangerous.'

He shrugs. 'It had to be one of us, in the end. I'm the lightest. I could just about drag the... the package. And besides, I was worried that Hamish would come down to where we'd been standing. Worried you and George wouldn't be able to put him off, that he'd interfere. I figured it was just safer to get rid of her... of it... quickly. As quickly as possible. So I did.'

Ken surveys his little brother. He realises he's not just seeing a boy anymore, but the outline of the man he is becoming. A stronger, more independent man than he would have expected. Although he still isn't happy with the risk he took, Ralph has, after all, shown an initiative he wouldn't have thought him capable of.

'I'm proud of you,' Ken says. 'Even though we've had a terrible night, I'm proud of how you've got through this – how we've all got through this.'

There are a few moments of silence. Then Ralph says one word, very quietly. 'Proud.'

Ken isn't quite sure if it's intended as a question, but he responds as if it is. 'We're brothers. We stick together and look after each other. I think that's a good thing to be proud of.'

Ralph is silent again, then lies back down, pulling the dressing gown close around him. Then he rolls over onto his side, facing away from Ken. After a while, in a low voice, he says, 'We just tried our best to cover up a death. We wrapped up the body of a woman – a real human being – and were all ready to throw her in the loch to save our own necks. So I'm sorry, but I can't see anything in that to be proud about. Nothing at all.'

Ken decides to leave Ralph to catch up on his rest. He checks on George, who's asleep in the kitchen, his face resting on the table. Ken suddenly finds himself ravenously hungry, as though the stress of the night's events has drained him of all energy. He starts to pull out things from the fridge – eggs, a packet of bacon that's just about within date, along with hash browns from the freezer. He cooks everything up in one pan, adding in the frozen hash browns, not caring that they should be oven-cooked. They finished the bread earlier on Christmas Eve, save for a few crusts. He grabs these, loads the contents of the frying pan between them and eats it all like a sandwich, egg yolk and bacon grease running down his fingers onto the tabletop.

George wakes up while he is eating. He takes a look at the food slipping through Ken's hands and then rushes to the sink and vomits.

'You OK?' Ken says, looking over at him.

'Yeah,' he pants, then spits. He turns on the tap and drinks straight from it.

'I was hungry,' Ken says, because he doesn't know what else to say.

'I can see that,' mutters George.

Ken nods. 'Perhaps you should get some sleep. I mean, proper sleep, in a bed. You probably feel awful.'

George shuts off the water, but is still staring at the sink. 'I do feel awful. But I don't think it's because I've been sleeping at the kitchen table.'

Ken sighs. 'I guess not. Oh, I solved the mystery of Ralph's lack of a coat.' George turns towards him. Ken explains what Ralph told him.

'God, I can't help seeing him going through the ice,' George says, shaking his head. 'I know it didn't happen... but it could have so easily.'

'I know,' says Ken. 'But we were lucky. He didn't. He managed it. Our little brother, the saviour of us both. And to think, he's the only one who isn't responsible for her death.'

George frowns at him. 'What do you mean? I'm... wait, you think we're both responsible?'

Ken raises his eyebrows. 'Well, yeah. Sherie wouldn't have died if it wasn't for us.'

'She wouldn't have died if it wasn't for *you*,' George says, his voice taking on a sudden force it didn't sound capable of seconds before.

Ken feels his face flushing. 'You pushed her, George. *You* did that.'

George looks astounded. 'It was... it happened when... it was during our scuffle... I didn't... You can't blame me for—'

'I don't blame you,' Ken says, getting up and coming over. He washes his hands in the sink and dries them calmly. Then he looks at his brother. 'I can understand why you did what you did.'

George is shaking his head now. 'I didn't... that's not...'

Ken pats his shoulder. 'You protected us. The family. Our futures. I'm proud of you. I'm proud of all of us.'

George is looking at him with a complicated expression that Ken can't read. Then he says, 'You're working hard on this brave, strong performance, and I know why you're doing it. But you're going to crack, Ken. It may take days, it may take years, I don't know. Just now, when I was in the living room, I thought we'd done the right thing too... that her ever leaving this castle would have been too much of a risk. But any certainty I have... well, it feels wafer thin. Like it could go at any moment. And in the end, that isn't certainty, is it?'

Ken tightens his grip on him. 'Don't be so defeatist. I wasn't lying when I said we were survivors. So just... fucking survive. OK?'

George looks as if he's about to say something. Then he freezes. Both of them do. Because from the corner of the table comes a ringing and buzzing sound. Ken's mobile is ringing, the vibrations making it shift across the surface. It's been there since the day before. Ken's almost forgotten it exists, since signal is so infrequent, particularly when a storm is raging. He goes over to the table, picks it up and answers it.

'Hello?'

'Darling, it's me,' says his mother's voice at the end, surprisingly clearly.

'Oh... Mum, hello,' he says.

He hears a slight tut, probably because he's called her 'Mum' and not 'Mother'. Then she says, 'Well, I'm pleased I've managed to get through to you. I couldn't sleep, so I've come down to the hotel lobby. It's very nice here. The Ashtons did offer us their Upper East Side apartment, but Granny didn't want the hassle of moving. I realised just now that it must be morning for you and your brothers. I thought I'd phone to say merry Christmas.'

'What?' Ken says, rubbing his temples. He thinks he has a headache coming. The mixture of the cold air and lack of sleep. To say nothing of the stresses of the night.

'Christmas, dear. Merry Christmas.'

'Oh, yeah, sorry.'

'Don't tell me you've forgotten,' she says. 'Goodness, all it takes is for me to be absent and the festivities go out of the window. I suspect you wouldn't have even tried to phone me or your grandmother if I hadn't made the effort.'

Ken sighs heavily in answer to this. He returns to his seat at the table and begins to scratch his nails across the surface.

'Anyway, I hope you're having a good little holiday without us,' she says. 'What have you been up to? All safe inside from the storm, I hope?'

'Up to?' Ken says. He looks up and sees George staring at him. 'Nothing much. We haven't been up to anything, really.'

'No mischief, I hope,' she says. 'I do worry about the three of you alone. I tried phoning little Ralphy but I couldn't get through to him. His phone might be off.'

'He's asleep,' says Ken, yawning. 'It's still very early here, Mother. In fact, I think I'm going to go back to bed for a bit.'

'Oh, very well,' she says, sounding like she's yawning herself. 'Just make sure you have as lovely a day as possible, even without all the usual festivities. You'll probably be relieved when we get home and everything goes back to normal. And we'll make Christmas next year extra special to make up for this one.'

'Yes,' says Ken. 'Yeah, it's a strange Christmas. But we're dealing with it. I can't lie, I'm glad this is a one-off. I'd like everything to go back to normal.'

He says goodbye and cuts the call.

'Still in New York?' George asks.

Ken nods.

'You can, you know,' George says.

'What?'

'You said you can't lie. But you can lie. You lie very well.'

Ken lets out his breath, slowly, thinking. 'Yeah, well, it's just a phrase isn't it, *I can't lie*. And quite topic-specific. But then, I'm an actor. It's what actors do. We lie for a living.'

'You always lied the best out of all of us, when we were kids. I remember you lying to Mum and Dad about having done your holiday homework. Or any jobs you'd been asked to do. It always seemed to come so naturally to you.'

'Where's all this going, George?' Ken asks, feeling his patience waning.

George chews his bottom lip for a few seconds, then he says, 'I guess I'm just worried about how well I'm going to pull it all off. All the lying. Going forward.'

Ken gets up. His whole body feels like it is weighted with lead. Or bricks. Bricks wrapped up close to him with rope and tape, ready to sink him to the bottom of a loch.

'You want to be a politician, don't you? My advice: get fucking used to it.'

Ken goes to leave the kitchen, but George speaks again. 'So what happens now?'

Ken shrugs. 'Well, it's like I just said to Mum. This Christmas is a one-off. An anomaly. I think it's best for all of us if we just pretend it never happened.'

FORTY-TWO

EILEEN

CHRISTMAS DAY 2025

Eileen has listened to her grandsons' story. The telling of it took some piecing together. Occasionally, they'd contradict each other. Sometimes Kenneth would get frustrated by the way George was explaining things. Other times, George would accuse Kenneth of trying to diminish his culpability. Ralph was the most silent, and when he did add his own view or share his memories, they were often vague. He evaded more than the others. This makes Eileen suspicious. Suspicious that there's something more than what is being said. But that takes a backseat to the feeling of disappointment and shame she feels. Shame that her grandsons could have done something so awful. To dispose of a woman's body, cover everything up, not tell anyone for years. Treat that young girl like she was just a piece of flesh, like a scrap from a table flung aside, useless and discarded. It's horrible to think about.

'So she died after falling over during a tussle between you both?' she says, pointing a finger at George and then Kenneth.

They both nod.

'And you were arguing about who got to sleep with her?' she says, not bothering to hide the distaste in her voice.

'Well,' Kenneth says. 'We'd all slept with her, of course. That's what caused the row. When we found out Ralph had, too.'

'If I hadn't tried to break up the fight... if I'd just—'

'You need to stop blaming yourself for that, Ralph,' Kenneth says.

Eileen takes all this in. 'And there was nothing else? No other element to the argument?'

She sees George and Kenneth exchange a look. 'Why would there be?'

Eileen says nothing for a moment. She's not stupid. It's clear there's more. She glances at her daughter, who has her head in her hands. She wonders if it's even harder for Claire. Hard for a mother to hear about her sons doing such sordid things. 'I don't understand,' she says, looking up, her eyes red.

'It was an accident,' says George.

'No, I mean... about the young man.'

There's silence for a minute. Then Kenneth frowns and says, 'Sorry?'

'Tommy! The young man upstairs lying fucking dead on the fucking carpet of his room!'

The boys look stunned. Eileen wonders if it's their mother swearing – a rarity in itself – or the realisation that a major issue still remains, even after their confessions. Two major issues, in fact.

'They'd forgotten,' Eileen says. 'They'd forgotten about the corpse upstairs. You see, my dear, for your sons, inconvenient dead bodies at Christmas are two-a-penny.'

Kenneth kicks the leg of an armchair angrily. Everyone jumps except Eileen. She just narrows her eyes at him. 'Of course, your mother's right. This might get us closer to understanding what happened to our unexpected guest, but it doesn't give us a definitive answer.' She folds her arms and glares at each of the brothers in turn. 'Anyone care to own up?'

Nobody speaks.

'Or perhaps someone could solve the other big mystery on the cards,' she says. 'How does a dead woman give birth to a child?'

Again, silence greets this.

'Fine.' She stands up. 'If nobody has anything to say, I suppose we'll just have to wait for the police to get it out of you. It would have been much more helpful if we could have ironed out the facts before they trampled over our home, our family, our secrets. But it seems like you've all chosen the hard route.'

Her speech does what she intends. Before she reaches the door, somebody speaks.

'There's something else. Something we haven't told you,' Ralph says.

She turns to see he's stood up too and is facing her, his lip trembling.

'I'm not a fan of Americanisms,' Eileen says, 'but I think the correct phrase for this moment is *You don't say.*'

Ralph nods. 'I'm sorry. I shouldn't have kept it back, but I've never been able to tell anyone. It's driven me mad. For years. I've always felt like this whole thing was my fault. I told myself that if I hadn't interrupted the argument, Sherie wouldn't have fallen and hit her head. But that's not all. There's something nobody else knows. And it explains everything.'

Eileen notices Kenneth, George and Claire's faces all staring at Ralph. All of them look trepidatious. Worried. Unsure what he's about to reveal.

'Sherie's alive,' he says, with a sob. The tears fall down his face. 'Or at least, she was when I last saw her.'

FORTY-THREE
RALPH

CHRISTMAS DAY 2025

'Ralph, what are you talking about?' George asks, staring at his brother.

Ralph struggles to hold his tears back. He dabs at his eyes, trying to get a handle on his emotions. He can't believe he's about to share this. Something he's kept buried within him for years, like a splinter or piece of shrapnel that's remained under the skin, infecting him. Poisoning him. And one day, possibly killing him.

'She wasn't dead. When we tied her up and took her out into the snow.'

Ken's staring at him, mouth open. Then he says, 'Ralph, you're... you're wrong. I'm sorry, but you really are. That was a dead body we tied up. I could... I could feel it. She felt dead.'

'How would you know?' Ralph says. 'You felt for a pulse and when you didn't find one, you presumed. You were so busy thinking about how to cover it all up that you didn't realise she had just been knocked out. And she came round.'

George is shaking his head, muttering, 'No... no, this isn't... she can't...'

'She did,' Ralph continues. 'Just before we were interrupted, outside, when Hamish called out to us, I'd seen movement. Or rather, I thought I had. Something moving amidst the sheeting.'

'Why didn't you fucking tell us?' Ken says, his voice strained, hard as nails, his jaw jutting out.

'Because I was worried you'd kill her!' Ralph shouts at him. 'I thought you'd take one of the bricks you'd packed to weigh her down and use it to murder her properly. Remove all doubt. And I didn't want that. So when you and George disappeared to stop Hamish from coming over, I unwrapped her. And she was there, alive, coughing and gasping, trying to get free.'

'I can't believe this...' George says, still shaking his head. Then he looks up. 'Your coat. Shit, that's where your coat went.'

Ralph nods. 'She was upset and cold.'

'Of course she was upset and cold!' his mother cuts in. 'Jesus Christ, that poor, poor girl.'

'I told her to run,' Ralph says. He's aware his voice has taken on a low, almost monotonous quality, but it's the only way he can tell them everything without breaking down completely. It's like an automated machine has taken over his brain. 'I told her to get away from the loch, from the castle, before you got back. I said she wasn't safe.'

'I can't believe you think—' George starts to say, but his grandmother puts up a hand.

'Let him talk,' she says.

'She said she wanted to go to the police. I said she needed to see a doctor, because of the head wound. The storm was lessening. The wind wasn't as harsh, but it was extremely cold. I gave her my jumper and coat, told her to head for the village. I said I'd distract Ken and George while she escaped. I said I'd convince them she'd gone into the loch. Convince them she was still dead.'

The silence that follows is dizzying. Ralph almost feels the room swaying with the magnitude of what he's just said, as though the castle walls and the people surrounded by them are one and the same. One big mass. An unwieldy, fragile beast that could fall if someone pushed too hard.

'But she didn't go to the police?' his mother asks, eventually.

Ralph shrugs. 'She said she was going to. I told her I understood. But apparently not.'

'So, just to be clear,' Eileen says, 'she just disappeared off, into the snow?'

'Yes,' Ralph says, simply.

Ken's now the one shaking his head. 'You stupid fucking child,' he says.

Something snaps within Ralph. He steps towards Ken. 'She made out she'd discovered something about you both that made you want to kill her. I was terrified that she was right. Or, even if that wasn't true, I worried you'd still want to just keep everything hushed up. And that you might decide... decide it was better off if the plan to put her in the loch went ahead. Alive or not.'

George makes a sound that's a mixture of a laugh and a cry. 'You thought we'd be capable of that.'

Ralph sniffs. Dabs at his eyes. Then looks at his brother. 'Well... aren't you?'

George's eyes are very dark. Ralph can't look at them for long.

'You've kept this back for all this time,' says George, sounding weak with surprise. 'God... no wonder you're always on the verge of a breakdown. No wonder you've struggled. We were all scared of a secret that we thought was dead and buried. But for you, the secret has been well and truly alive all this time.'

Ralph nods. 'Yes. And every single day I've waited for her to come back into our lives. For a knock on the door, either from her, maybe demanding money, or the police to say she'd told them everything.'

'Instead, she went off and did something else,' Eileen says, smoothly. 'She had a baby.'

There's a pause while everyone absorbs this. Then Claire just says, 'Christ.' She gets up and goes over to the radiator. She holds her hands out for a bit. Ralph watches her, wanting to go over and say something to her. Apologise, perhaps. For being such a disappointment. For the whole awful mess. But a little bit of him knows it isn't entirely his fault. While he has never thought of himself as a hero in the story, he does know he saved Sherie's life that day. It's just that he feels like it isn't enough to eclipse everything else.

Before he can do anything or say anything further, his mother turns around and looks him in the eye. 'Did you kill that young man, Ralph? Did you kill Tommy?'

Ralph feels his jaw drop. He can't speak for a second, then says, 'I can't believe you'd ask me that.' He looks at his two older brothers. 'What about them? Why haven't you accused them?'

'Because,' she says, after taking a deep breath, 'they didn't know he could be telling the truth. In their eyes, he was an impossibility. But not to you. To you, his existence made perfect sense. And I think that might have done something to your brain last night, my dear boy. I think it may have driven you to murder. So I ask you again: did you kill him?'

FORTY-FOUR
EILEEN

CHRISTMAS DAY 2025

Eileen watches her youngest grandson wrestle with his mother's question. She's interested in the answer, of course, but isn't convinced her daughter is on the right track. Eileen often feels Claire misunderstands her children. Ralph isn't the type to go around stabbing people with Christmas ornaments. He's always been emotional, but in a kind, gentle way. Not the sort to fly into a murderous rage. Many aspects of her grandsons' confession this morning have surprised her, but she hasn't been surprised to learn that Ralph is the least guilty of all of them. He may have slept with the girl, but that was no crime.

She waits a few more seconds for Ralph's answer, and when it doesn't come, with the man just standing there staring at his mother, tears rolling down his face, Eileen decides to speak up. 'Claire, I think you're mistaken. It's true Ralph here was the only one who knew the deceased young woman wasn't, well, deceased. But I really don't think he would want to kill a young man who could be his own son.'

Ralph turns his shimmering eyes to look at her. 'Thank you,

Granny. I promise I didn't go near his bedroom. I didn't speak to him after he went upstairs. I didn't kill him.'

Eileen nods. Then she glances over at George and Kenneth. Kenneth has the tight, pinched look of a man who's trying not to explode. George is worryingly grey, as though he's dying inside. Neither says anything.

'Well, I think we're going to leave it there for now,' Eileen says, getting to her feet. 'I'm feeling a bit cold and tired. I'm going to retire to my rooms for a couple of hours and mull this over. Then we'll phone the police. During that time, if anyone wanted to come to my rooms and tell me anything – anything that might help our little predicament here – I would be very grateful.' She looks again at each of them in turn. When nobody replies, she walks out of the room.

She's on the upper levels, about to ascend the staircase to the tower, when she hears the sobs. Unmistakably female, coming from one of the landings. She changes direction and finds Alexandra sitting on the floor, her head in her hands.

'My dear, are you all right?' she says, coming to a stop in front of her. She reaches down and puts a hand on the young woman's shoulder.

Alexandra continues to cry and gives a shake of her head.

'I understand this whole situation is very upsetting,' Eileen says. 'It can't be pleasant to find a body like that.' She keeps her voice as kind and gentle as she can. But even so, she can't help feeling like the girl should pull herself together.

Then something occurs to her. All of a sudden, she has the feeling of puzzle pieces slotting into place in her head.

'Perhaps you should come up to my rooms,' she says, quietly. 'Then we can have a little chat.'

Alexandra raises her head, her red eyes meeting Eileen's. That's when she knows her suspicions are correct.

'Come on,' she says, tilting her head in the direction of the staircase up to her apartment. 'Let's get this straightened out.'

'I can't,' Alexandra whispers. 'It's awful. Really awful.'

'Perhaps,' Eileen says. 'But in my experience, there's always more than one way of looking at a situation. And I find even the darkest of days can be turned around with a change of perspective and a good, solid plan. So dry your eyes and come with me.'

An hour later, Eileen descends the stairs, heading down to the ground floor of the castle. On the halfway landing, she hears someone coming behind her from one of the first-floor rooms.

'What's happening?' the person asks.

She looks back to see that it's Ralph. His face is now dry, but she notices his lip still trembles as he meets her gaze. 'Come down to the living room,' she says. 'I've made a decision.'

She continues her journey and hears him hurrying to catch up with her. 'Granny, did someone come to talk to you? I thought I heard movement upstairs, but I wasn't sure... was it George? Or Ken?'

'Did someone say my name?' Kenneth says, stepping out of the library down the end of the hallway. 'What's happening? And has any decision been reached about food? Are we still having Christmas lunch? Where's Alexandra?'

'Let's go to the living room,' Eileen says again, resisting saying something sharp in response to his enquiry about lunch. 'Kenneth, please round up your mother and George.'

She goes into the room before any further discussion can be had. Inside, she asks Ralph to make up the fire and then sits herself down in the armchair by the Christmas tree. The chair that their uninvited guest sat in the night before.

The family assemble around her, with Kenneth and George standing by the nascent blaze of the fire and Ralph and his mother sitting on the sofa. Eileen notices Claire trying to lay a hand on her son's arm, but he pulls himself away. He apparently hasn't yet forgiven her for accusing him of murder. Claire looks hurt, then turns her eyes to Eileen.

'Enough of these theatrics, Mother,' she says. 'I know you get a kick out of ordering us around and keeping us on tenterhooks, but we need to come up with some sort of plan of action here. Every minute we leave that poor boy's body upstairs, we're making each one of us more and more guilty.'

'Be quiet,' Eileen says, frowning at her. 'There's something important I need to tell you.' She swallows, gathers her thoughts, deciding on the best way to word what she's about to say. 'A few minutes ago, I managed to get through to the police. They now know there's a dead body in the castle. They also know it was murder. They're currently unsure how long it will take them to get here. As you can see, the storm isn't quite as strong as it was, but the snowfall is still substantial. I think we're quite cut off for the moment. Once they arrive, they'll process the crime scene and make their arrest.'

The last word causes movement in all of them. Ralph leans forward. Claire raises a hand to her mouth. George jerks his head. Kenneth stays motionless.

'Arrest?' Claire says. 'Arrest who?'

'Me,' Eileen says, folding her arms. 'I've confessed to the murder.'

FORTY-FIVE
GEORGE

CHRISTMAS DAY 2025

'Lord, Mother, what are you talking about?' Claire says.

'She's covering for *him*,' George says, walking around the front of the sofa, pointing at Ralph. 'I think he crawled to the tower and confessed. I reckon Tommy tried to blackmail him or something. So he killed him.'

Ralph looks stricken. 'How can you say that, George? You're the murderer amongst us. We know that already.'

This causes George to feel a fresh new jolt of fury. 'If you're talking about Sherie, that was an accident. And it turns out she didn't die, according to you, so what's the fucking point of mentioning it?'

Ralph stands up, 'Why are you so keen for it to be me? Why not him?' He points at Ken. 'Or his son? Conspicuously absent, isn't he? Where's Kite got to, Ken? Sobbing in his room after confessing to Granny?'

'You little prick,' Ken says, lunging towards him.

'Boys, stop it!' Claire shouts, coming between them. 'All of you, sit down and let's listen to what your grandmother has to say.'

'But I have nothing further to say,' Eileen says. She stands up and strides towards the door. 'You're welcome to fight amongst yourselves if that's how you want to spend your Christmas Day. I'm going to go and get some things sorted. I imagine police custody might be a bit chilly.'

'Granny, please,' George says, feeling like this is his last chance to get to the truth of what's happening here. 'Tell us why you're doing this! Nobody here believes you actually did it.'

His grandmother looks at him. 'Is that so?' she says. 'Are you sure?'

George opens his mouth and closes it again. He doesn't know what to say to this, and by the time words return, she is already out of sight.

'She can't be serious,' he says, staring back at the rest of his family.

Nobody answers him. Ralph is still looking thunderous. After a few seconds, he pushes past him and leaves the living room. Ken follows suit, muttering about checking on Kite.

That leaves George and his mother. And he finds he cannot look at her. With his eyes on the old Persian rug beneath his feet, he says, quietly, 'Mum... I'm sorry...'

He can tell she's facing him, though still he cannot look up. She makes him wait a few seconds, then says, 'For which bit?'

He lets out a rush of breath. It catches in his throat and he coughs. His throat is tight. It's hard to swallow, as though he has a sudden bad cold. 'All of it.'

When he does, eventually, meet her eyes, he finds he knows what she's about to ask him before she says it.

'Was it really an accident, George? When you, Ken and Sherie argued in this room and she fell. Hit her head on this coffee table.' She nods to the piece of furniture separating them.

Keeps looking at it for a few more seconds, as though it might suddenly talk and give her an answer. Then she looks back up at George. 'Or was it deliberate?'

The snapping of the fire and the beat of his heart are the two loudest things he thinks he's ever heard. Then he says, 'Oh, Mum. I really wish I knew. But the truth is, over the years, things have become so muddled in my head, I'm not sure I know anymore. I'm not sure what is true... and what I hope to be true.'

She stays standing there for a bit longer. Then, as tears start to fall from her eyes, she walks towards him. Puts her arms around him. 'Oh my boy,' she says, and he stoops to rest his chin on her shoulder. 'My poor, poor boy.'

He's struggling to hold himself together now. His eyes settle on the falling snow outside. The frozen loch, just about visible in the dull morning light. It wasn't snowing when his father and grandfather went out on the loch, but the strange light reminds him of that day. And he finds he cannot bear it any longer. Through the tightness of his throat, he manages to say two words. 'There's more.'

Although the words are just a whisper, he knows his mother has heard them. He feels her grow tense. She pulls away from the embrace. 'Maybe another time, darling,' she says. 'I think we have more than enough to be going on with.'

Then she leaves the room, leaving George unsure if he's disappointed or relieved.

He ends up outside. Feeling so stifled and suffocated inside the rooms of the castle, he steps out into the deep, virginal snow, drinking in the freezing air. The flakes are still falling, but very slowly now, floating down as if they have all the time in the world. The opposite of the determined flow they've watched from the windows for the past couple of days. The sight that greets him reminds him of a quaint winter scene you'd find on a

Christmas card. Except the view in front of him isn't a country lane or a snowy churchyard. It's the slope down to a loch. Loch Lemire. An unavoidable part of his life.

The sound of his phone ringing pulls him away from his dark thoughts. He looks down to see Delia's name on the screen.

'Hello,' he says.

'Merry Christmas,' she says. 'I was wondering when you'd call.' He hears a touch of reproach in her voice. With everything that has happened, wishing his wife a happy Christmas has been far from his mind. Before he can answer, she goes on. 'We've had a lot of snow here. Is it apocalyptic where you are? It looked like it when I saw the weather report on the news.'

'Yes, it is,' he says, slowly. 'It's been apocalyptic.'

'Well, I hope you're keeping warm. It's been rather stressful here, too, to tell you the truth. Daddy had a terrible row with my brother last night. Cyril came home from university with two friends called Kev and Keith, who claim they are progressive anti-capitalist atheists, so they're shunning their traditional family Christmas and wanted to "crash" at our home. And by crash, they mean eat meals at the wrong time, drink all the mulled wine and leave the milk out of the fridge. They've barely moved from the sofa and yesterday requested we all watch some uncouth game show called *Taskmaster*, whatever that is, while lecturing my parents about the cost of living, various global conflicts and sodding climate change. Mummy eventually convinced Cyril to put them up in a hotel, but then the snow hit and it made leaving impossible. So we're stuck with them, two strangers on Christmas Day.'

'How awful for you,' George says, without enthusiasm.

'It really has been. One of them is from Basildon.'

'Delia, I'm sorry, I'm going to have to go,' George starts to say, but she's already talking again.

'And to top it all off, because of the row, Cyril's now refusing to eat Christmas lunch, even though the uninvited guests are still keen, but Daddy's saying he won't dine with two interlopers, so Mummy's currently preparing the food while sobbing. I've had to go back up to my room as she's got archive episodes of *Desert Island Discs* blaring out of the kitchen on full volume. Let's just say Gareth Southgate's music choices don't lend themselves to Christmas morning. The Stormzy remix of "Shape of You" was the final straw for me. Christ, this might be the worst Christmas I've ever had, and it's still only morning. I imagine yours has been a breeze in comparison. Talking of which, I hope you've got some positive updates when it comes to your meeting with your grandmother and the money situation. George? George? Are you even listening to me?'

George takes the phone away from his ear, lowers it, then cuts the call. He has a sudden urge to hurl it as far as he can – hopefully into the loch – but stops himself. He'll have to make some excuse later. Tell her he lost signal. But right now he just needs peace. Space to think. Or not think. Even though he felt he couldn't stand Delia's monologue for one more second, he's surprised to find that, in a strange way, it's calmed him. Somehow the absurd, stupid mundanity of her words and perceived troubles have had a soothing effect. It's as though the reminder that trivialities of the kind she's experiencing still exist is a relief. It's all still out there, he thinks to himself. The real world. A world where a 'final straw' is someone having the radio on too loud. And in a way, that's comforting.

The scent of cannabis pulls him from his thoughts. Then someone says 'Boo' behind him. He jumps back, shocked to see that he's not alone. Kite is there, leaning up against the side wall of the castle, puffing away on a spliff.

'Ha,' he says, exhaling with a laugh. 'Scared you, didn't I?'

George frowns. 'No,' he lies. 'I... wasn't scared.'

Kite raises his eyebrows. 'You sure? I'm good at sneaking up on people. Who were you talking to?'

'My wife.'

The boy smirks. 'Did you tell her about all the shit that's been going on?'

'No,' George says, then regrets it. 'I mean, I lost signal before I could.'

Kite nods but doesn't look convinced. George continues to frown, looking at his nephew. The flakes of snow landing in his short blonde hair. The calm way he takes another drag on the spliff. He reminds him of Ken. Shorter, skinnier, more belligerent and aloof. But still Ken.

'You shouldn't smoke that stuff,' George says. 'I was part of a Department of Health consultation on cannabis misuse. That spliff contains literally hundreds of chemicals. Some of which can seriously impact your mind, mood, cognitive function, perhaps permanently, with frequent use – especially in the young. Memory, coordination, paranoia. Even psychosis.'

Kite takes a step forward towards George and blows smoke in his face. 'Bring. It. On.' He laughs again, then says, 'I just wanted some less-than-fresh air. And the storm's stopped. Or are we in the eye of it? You know, like in disaster movies? When they have a short moment to get to safety before it all starts going crazy again? Maybe it'll bring the whole castle down and take us along with it.'

George holds his breath until the puff of smoke has floated away on the cold morning air. Then he says, 'Is that really a comment on the weather, Kite? Or are you employing metaphors?'

Kite smirks. '*Employing metaphors*? Is that what I'm doing?'

George pulls his coat closer to him. 'We should get inside. I thought you were supposed to be upstairs in your room, anyway.'

Kite shrugged. 'Got bored. It's kind of shocking how dull a murder can be when there are no cops or forensics guys or reporters or car chases.'

George nods. 'Yeah, well, this isn't a normal murder.'

He starts to tread through the snow away from his nephew. Then the boy says, 'I know something that isn't dull, though.'

George stops and turns around. 'What?'

Kite has the look of someone who's about to play his ace. 'I know who did it.'

George stays very still. 'How do you know that?'

Kite raises his eyebrows. 'Interesting that you ask *how* rather than *who*? You're less boring than you look, Uncle George.'

George doesn't like how the boy says the word 'Uncle', as if it's an insult. 'Just tell me,' he says.

Kite takes one more puff on the spliff and then tosses it into a snowdrift. 'How well do you know that servant woman?'

George stares at him. 'Alexandra?'

Kite nods. 'I listened at the door. I couldn't resist. I was getting bored, so I went along the landing. Saw her sobbing there, and your gran was asking her what was wrong. It sounded like it was a big deal, so I went up the stairs and listened. Alexandra spilt everything.'

'What? What do you mean?'

Kite exhales again. 'She killed Tommy. I mean, that's obvious, isn't it? Don't they always say, the butler did it?'

George feels himself shivering, but he doesn't think it has anything to do with the cold. 'I'm surprised you know about murder mystery tropes,' he says.

'People always think they know what I think and like and know and don't know. Or they don't notice me at all. Not sure which option fucks me off more.'

George waves an impatient hand. 'Just carry on.'

Kite pauses for a moment, frowning, then continues. 'That Tommy guy wasn't your son, or Dad's son or Uncle Ralph's son. He was a con artist. Your servant woman's boyfriend. Or ex-boyfriend. Sounds like a nasty fucker, from what she said. He was controlling her.'

George's mind is whirring, trying to compute every detail

crammed within Kite's succinct summary. 'Wait, so... so he wasn't Sherie's son. She never had a child?'

Kite shrugs. 'Don't know, but if she did, it wasn't him. From what it sounds like, I don't think she ever had a kid. The whole thing was a story.'

George is shaking his head, the weight of this new information making it ache. 'I can't believe she'd do this. Can't believe she'd put us through it.'

Kite makes a noise of disbelief. 'What, you know her well? *Really?*'

George ignores this comment. 'So she admitted to all this. She told Granny everything?'

'Yep.' Kite nods. 'It sounds as if she was on board with his plan but then she bailed out. They found out about Sherie, hatched a plan she wasn't sure about. But he went rogue and turned up without warning, hoping to blackmail each of you. Make you guys think he might be your son and you'd give him good money to just vanish again. All that might have worked, but Alexandra paid him a visit. Things got heated. She said it was self-defence.' He makes a hissing sound and shrugs again, as though he's not sure about this. 'I don't know. You'll have to ask her if you want any more details.'

George starts to walk away. He needs to do exactly this. Needs to hear it from Alexandra herself, get her to tell him everything.

'Oh, and she's going to leave her all the money,' Kite calls after him.

George stops so suddenly that he almost falls face first, down in the snow.

'Or a lot of it, at least. I don't know if the sloth sanctuary's still going ahead, or if the housekeeper pockets the lot. I'll leave you to thrash that out with your grandma. If you can try to find out if my 50k's safe, that would be great.'

George thinks the boy's finished, and he turns again to

leave, then he hears him speak once more. 'You think the storm's over, Uncle George, but you're so wrong. So, so wrong.'

George stares at him. '*What?* What more could there possibly be?'

To his surprise, Kite throws his head back and laughs. A laugh of bitter mirth. 'Oh my God, it might be the biggest bombshell of the week. It's going to blow your mind when you find out.'

'Find out *what?*' George says, marching back up to the smirking teenager, feeling like he might hit him.

Kite holds his gaze. Then says, smoothly, 'The truth about her.'

George reaches forward and grabs the lapels of Kite's coat. 'Who?'

Kite continues to smile. 'Alexandra, of course. Man, I can't wait for you to find out who she really is.'

FORTY-SIX
EILEEN

CHRISTMAS DAY 2025

Eileen listens as Alexandra tells her about Tommy. Tells her about her relationship with him, about his cruelty, his plan to extort money from the family.

'I'm so ashamed,' she says. 'Tommy was obsessed with money. It was like a mania. I understood it to some point, early on in our relationship I even admired his drive. But if I started to question it, he turned... difficult. So when we met Sherie and we heard about her story, he couldn't resist.' Tears fall down her face as she says this.

'My dear, you were in the grip of a manipulative, abusive man,' Eileen says. 'This is not something to be ashamed of. And it sounds like Sherie might have been planning blackmail herself, from what you tell me about your meeting with her?'

Alexandra nods. 'I think so. Well, maybe that's unfair. I don't actually know. She was sort of musing aloud. She was already in a bit of a state when we met her coming up the drive.'

'That's understandable. I imagine the memories of this

castle have haunted her for twenty years. In some ways, it was very brave of her to try to return, whatever her motives.'

Alexandra looks encouraged by this. 'I know... and I feel terrible she never got her chance to have it out with your grandsons. To talk to them. But there was nobody home that day, and I was with Tommy, so it made more sense to take her to the pub. She calmed down over a pint, told us everything. Completely poured her heart out. Said she'd once stayed here when stranded twenty years ago and ended up having sex with three psycho brothers who tried to kill her. Sorry, I shouldn't say "psycho", I realise they're your grandsons.' She sniffs and looks embarrassed, but Eileen doesn't interrupt. 'Anyway, Sherie said she escaped and meant to go to the police, but had trauma from the whole thing. The years went by and she never ended up reporting it. When I heard this, I wanted to tell you, wanted to find out if it was true, but Tommy was adamant we should keep it secret. We added her on Instagram, so when we saw, not long after, that she had been killed in a car crash, he acted like it was perfect. As though it was meant to be. He'd always looked young for his age, enjoyed using his good looks to charm people. He was fairly confident he could pass for someone aged nineteen, that he could play the part of a secret son who might have a claim to some inheritance. But the whole idea turned me a bit mad. I remember looking at that Insta post saying she'd died, and feeling like it was my fault somehow. And Tommy convinced me that by using her secrets as leverage, I was somehow honouring her memory. The whole thing was sick. Just self-interested lies he used to make me do what he wanted.' Her lip is trembling, and she raises her hands to her face, sobs consuming her. 'I was so pleased when I got this job! So pleased I was coming to work at Lemire Castle. And now not only have I ruined all that, I've killed someone under your roof. I've betrayed your kindness. I've betrayed the family.'

Eileen thinks for a bit, looking at the distressed young

woman in front of her. She didn't plan to do this now. The plan was always to allow the revelations to unfold after her death. Part of her liked the idea of dying safe in the knowledge that the drama would continue even after she exited the stage. But she decides now that it would be selfish. Alexandra's honesty, late as it might be, deserves honesty in return.

'You may have heard rumours, Alexandra, that my daughter and grandsons are not going to inherit my wealth and this castle after my death?'

Alexandra sniffs and looks up. Then she nods.

'Well, yesterday,' Eileen continues, 'I told my family I intended to leave the family fortune to an animal sanctuary. That wasn't entirely truthful. While it's true I have put aside a healthy six-figure sum to go to my friend's marvellous organisation Quills, Tails & Sleepy Sloths, that's not the full story.'

Alexandra blinks at her.

'It served as a good way of winding them all up a bit. I was getting tired of how entitled and presumptuous my grandsons were becoming. But the truth of the matter is, I intend for almost everything to go to you, Alexandra.'

She sees her eyes widen, her mouth open, but no sound comes out.

'I know this might sound a bit odd, but I assure you there is a reason.'

Alexandra blinks again, then manages to say quietly, 'Why me?'

'Oh, Alexandra, there is a lot you don't know. About me, about this castle, this family. My marriage. I, too, have had experience with... difficult men. My husband was no saint. Far from it. And although he was respected and made sure our family fortunes prospered, he had his own dark secrets. His own weaknesses.' She takes a deep breath and says, 'My husband had affairs throughout our marriage. I always knew it, and the done thing for a woman in my position, especially back then, was to turn a blind eye. So I did, or so it seemed on the surface. But in private, I used a family friend whom I trusted to keep tabs on my husband's conquests. And the day came when he told me that not only had my husband added a new woman to his repertoire, unlike the others, who were usually based in London or Edinburgh, this one was local to the Highlands. From Inverness. Her name was Ailsa Fraser.'

Alexandra gasps. 'But... I don't understand. That's my mother's name.' Eileen watches her frown of confusion turn into dawning realisation. 'No... no, it can't be. My mother always said it was a one-night stand... a businessman.'

Eileen nods. 'My husband was a businessman, so she was telling the truth in that respect.'

'Oh my God...' Alexandra says, her expression shifting to the floor. Her eyes continue to move, darting rapidly as though her brain is working in overdrive, shifting through past memories, past snatches of conversation, perhaps, trying to make sense of everything.

'I've known all your life. My husband paid your mother money to keep quiet. When he died, I made sure that it continued. And then, when your mother passed away, I continued to keep track of you. When I was informed you were looking for work, I decided it was time to bring you into the fold, so to speak. Our housekeeper, Mrs Sopel, had become too old for the job, poor dear, and we were keen to simplify our domestic staff. You had experience in both catering and cleaning. It all worked rather perfectly. It was no accident that an advert for a housekeeper's job turned up in your email inbox.'

Alexandra nods, slowly. 'Yes, I thought it was strange... but then, it seemed convincing. It said it was from a Highlands recruitment business. So... I'm... I'm family? I'm related to you all?'

Eileen shakes her head. 'No, not to me, of course. But to

Claire, yes. You're her half-sister. And to my grandsons, you are, technically speaking, their aunt.'

Alexandra shakes her head, slowly, as though struggling to process it all. Then she laughs. Not a sound of mirth, more disbelief and shock. 'Sorry, it's not funny, I just...'

'I understand,' Eileen says. 'As I said, all this would have come out upon my death when the will was read. There is some difficulty with Scottish law to do with disinheriting one's relatives. I think George is rather pinning his hopes on that. I can't go for totality, or at least not as total as I presented it to them in my little dramatic speech yesterday. But let's just say, the lion's share, including this castle, will be yours.' She swallows and chooses her next words carefully. 'You don't reach my time of life without having some regrets. It's human to have them and I try not to dwell. I think that sort of thing can so easily slip into self-indulgence. But one of my big regrets over the years was the presumption that, by turning a blind eye to my husband's affairs, I wasn't causing any harm. As I've already intimated, I think he did cause harm, I think he used women in an unpleasant way and it makes me rather ill to think about it now. While I wasn't his keeper, I've always wondered whether, if I'd made more of a fuss, I could have avoided the broken and disrupted lives that sometimes resulted from his affairs. So getting to know you, giving you a home here, with the promise of more to come, is, if it doesn't sound pretentious to say it, my atonement. A way of absolving myself from the things I've done. Or rather, didn't do. And I'm glad I've been able to do you the courtesy of telling you this face to face.'

She leans forward and takes the young woman's hands. Alexandra holds onto them, tight. 'It's so weird,' she says to Eileen, looking up into her eyes. 'Part of me has always felt like I belonged in this place. This castle has felt like home.'

Eileen nods. 'It is, my dear. That's only natural. And now, I must rest. I have a few things to sort out. I need you to calmly go downstairs and start preparing Christmas lunch. Do not phone the police, do not confess to any crimes, don't do anything that might incriminate yourself. I'm going to sort everything out, OK?'

Alexandra pauses. Then she nods. 'OK.' She gets up, dabbing at her eyes. 'And thank you. Thank you for everything.'

FORTY-SEVEN

GEORGE

CHRISTMAS DAY 2025

After his disorienting conversation with Kite outside, George enters the castle in a head-spinning daze. He barely registers where he's going — only realises his destination when he's outside his grandmother's rooms. He bursts into the apartment without knocking. At first, he doesn't see her. 'Granny?' he calls out.

She comes out of her bathroom with a glass of water in one hand and a pill bottle in the other. 'Goodness, George, why all this racket? Anyone would think somebody had been murdered.' She raises her eyebrows innocently at him and then withdraws back into the bathroom. When she returns, sans pill bottle and water, she looks at him and says, 'Sorry, forgive me for my little joke.'

George feels himself almost shaking with emotion. 'Little joke? Is everything a joke to you? This family? Our home? Our lives?'

She perches herself by the window in her chair and surveys him. 'George, have you been talking to Alexandra?'

He steps forward. 'No, Granny, fucking *Kite* has been talking to Alexandra. Or rather, eavesdropping on her. I just heard from my teenage nephew whom I barely know that not only am I losing my family home to a total stranger, it turns out she's not a total stranger. But Kite won't say any more, so I've come to ask you to explain!'

She keeps looking at him, not saying anything. Not moving. George finds it maddening.

'Well?' he demands. 'Have you not got anything to say? Nothing at all? I want to know the truth about the money and the truth about who she is. Who she *really* is!' He points in the direction of the door, as though Alexandra is standing there in person.

Eileen waits a few more seconds, lets out a long sigh, then holds up her hands. 'All right, George. Maybe I misled you a bit about the porcupine sanctuary.'

He isn't sure if it's the exaggerated sigh or the word 'porcupine' that makes him snap. Whatever it is, he reaches forward and grabs her wrists. He sees her smooth demeanour vanish, registers the look of alarm in her eyes. And with a rush of energy that feels almost shameful in its strength and speed, he realises he's glad. Glad he's managed to shock her. Glad he's taking control of the situation.

'Whatever the fucking truth is, whatever your goddam lawyers say, I'm going to fight this through the courts if I have to.'

Something seems to change in his grandmother's face. Her eyes narrow, and he sees something he hasn't seen there before. Hatred. 'Look at yourself, George,' she says in a tight, but still strong, voice. 'Look at what you're doing. Manhandling an old lady in her own home while you rant and rave about what? About money. About your own selfish greed. Your own sense of what the world owes you, what *I* owe you. Do you know what I did when I found out I didn't have long to live, before I disinherited you and your brothers? I had Michael Allerton and his consultancy firm produce in-depth investigative profiles of you. Of all of you. And what he uncovered confirmed my suspicions.'

This only serves to heighten George's anger. 'You did what? How dare you? How dare *he*? He's part of my legal team. I trusted him.'

Eileen laughs bitterly. 'Trust? You don't know the meaning of the word. Nor does Ralph or Kenneth, for that matter. Cheating on your wives and partners, drug misuse when it comes to Kenneth, not to mention his neglectful parenting. You're all just awful. Truly awful.'

For one terrible moment, George actually thinks about dragging her out onto the balcony and throwing her off.

And he knows she's seen it in his face. There's something close to fear in her eyes. A challenge, too. As though part of her is daring him to do it. Finish this whole terrible saga by killing his own grandmother.

He takes a deep breath. Then he lets go of her arms and leaves the room. Not knowing where he's going or what he's going to do. He just knows, if he were to stay, things wouldn't end well for either of them.

He's halfway down the stairs when someone says his name. 'George? Where are you going? Did you just go to see your grandmother?'

He sees his mother at the bottom of the stairs. She's holding three wrapped presents. She sees him looking at them and says, 'I know it's strange, but I thought... well, we might as well unwrap them. It is Christmas morning, after all. And we may not get time, once the police get here.'

He looks at the neatly wrapped box-shaped objects for a few moments, then raises his eyes to his mother's face. 'Where's Alexandra?'

She looks taken aback by the abrupt question. 'I think she's in the kitchen. She's making a start on lunch. Why?'

George doesn't reply. He just walks past her and heads in the direction of the small flight of stairs that leads down to the kitchen. He's going to get to the bottom of all this, once and for all. No matter what the cost.

FORTY-EIGHT
GEORGE

CHRISTMAS DAY 2025

George doesn't have a plan when he walks into the kitchen. Or at least, nothing more developed than demanding that Alexandra explain everything. The truth about who she is. In the back of his mind, he has a sneaking suspicion where this might be going, but he's afraid to admit it to himself. If the past twenty-four hours have taught him one thing, it's that anything is possible. The most unlikely things can become true. One's worst nightmares can be made real. And everything one thought one knew can be reframed in a second.

Alexandra is sitting at the kitchen table, peeling vegetables. George walks in from the corridor and steps inside. She looks up. Sets down the potato peeler.

'You're... making Christmas lunch as if nothing's happened?' George asks, looking at the vegetables in front of her.

'Yes, well, it is my job,' she says, with a sniff. 'Your grandmother thought Christmas lunch might be a nice thing to have, after everything. She asked if I could still make it the best I can, although I'm quite late in starting.'

George waits for a moment, staring back at the young woman in front of him. He can tell she's been crying, but her cheeks are now dry.

'I suppose making a belated Christmas lunch is a small price to pay for thirty-five million.'

He sees her jaw tighten when he says this. Then she picks up the potato peeler again and starts scraping away. 'I didn't think she was going to tell you,' she says, quietly. 'And I don't think I'm getting that much, exactly. I'm sure it will become clear. Anyway, I suppose it's best. Get it all out in the open.'

'You killed Tommy,' George breathes. It isn't a question. And Alexandra doesn't confirm or deny. She just carries on peeling the potatoes.

'You don't seriously think we're going to let our grandma hand you our family money? You? Some random kitchen girl?'

'It's not just the money,' Alexandra says. 'The castle too.'

George clenches his knuckles. He can feel that familiar surging sensation. Blood rushing to his face. Muscles tightening. 'We'll fight you in court. Every step of the way. I don't pretend to be an expert in inheritance law, but I'm pretty sure this can't be done in whatever dramatic, sweeping way my grandmother has implied. And I reckon she knows that, and this is just one of her vicious little wind-ups. The thought of you living in this castle is ridiculous.'

Alexandra gives him an odd look. 'But I do live in it. Already.'

'I think you know what I mean,' George says.

She narrows her eyes. 'Oh, you mean, you don't want me living here if I'm not a servant. Not in my rightful lowly place, is that what you mean? Well, don't worry, I'm not going to kick you out straight away. I'll give you time.'

'Time?' George says. '*Time?* You're fucking insane. This

place will never be yours. I don't know what sob story you've sold my grandmother, I don't know what tenuous connection to the family you've managed to trick her with, but it won't work. I'm not going to allow this. None of us are.'

Alexandra remains very still. 'I haven't tricked her or sold her anything. In fact, I was just as in the dark as you were about... about certain things.' She sniffs again and wipes a single tear away. Then she says, in a voice so quiet he almost doesn't hear it, 'I'm your aunt.'

George feels destabilised, as though the ground has started moving. 'My... my what?'

'I'm your aunt. Your mother is my sister. Or half-sister. Your grandfather and my mum... well, you get the idea.'

He stares at her sitting there, her eyes averted. He isn't sure if this is what he suspected and hoped wasn't true, or if it's a shocking surprise, something he never expected. 'You'll never be part of this family. You're not like us. And you're a murderer.'

Alexandra twists on the bench to face him. 'Oh really? That's important to you, is it? We all keep versions of ourselves secret, George. Tommy was a horrible part of my life. Being with him was horrible. Being without him was horrible, too, for different reasons. And killing him was both the worst and best thing I've ever done. But you're forgetting that I'm not the only one who has killed in this house.'

George leans forward. 'You're forgetting that the big twist of the day is that Sherie didn't die here. Ralph let her go and you met her in a bar. So that means I didn't kill her. Sorry if that's inconvenient for you.'

'I'm not talking about Sherie,' she says. 'I'm talking about your father. And your grandfather.'

George feels himself going cold.

'What? Did you just forget about that? Or did you deliberately leave that aspect of your story out when you did your big confession to your mum and grandma earlier?'

George is now slowly shaking his head, although no words are coming out of his mouth.

'Don't worry, I didn't mention it to Eileen. I didn't think her finding out her husband was a child abuser would do my cause any favours. And I'm truly sorry, George, that you went through that. It's horrible to think that the man who fathered me, the man who my mother slept with, was capable of such a thing. Sherie alluded to it, when I spoke to her. She knew that's why you boys were so fucked up. While it doesn't excuse the things you've done, I think it makes it easier for me to understand.' She takes a breath and bites her lip, her eyes going glazed for a few seconds. Then she refocuses and continues. 'I reckon you've gone through your adult life feeling like a bad person trying your best to be good. But really, I think you're a good person who just did a bad thing because of what was happening to you. Like so many of us. You're not the only one who's been hurt by people who are supposed to love you.' She stands up, causing the chair to scrape loudly across the floor. The sound digs into his brain, making his head hurt. He feels like a dead weight, as though he might collapse at any moment.

'You think... you think I'm a *good* person, do you?' He clenches his fists harder. His knuckles crack.

'Let's just be sensible about this, OK?' Alexandra carries on. 'I'll say nothing. You don't cause me any complications. And you'll do your best to try to dissuade the others from doing anything disruptive. I've worked so hard all my life in jobs I've hated. I've been pushed around by men. Neglected by my family members. I've scraped by, put up with shit, been damaged and bruised by life. So I think it's my fucking time. My time to take rather than be taken from. And if a Scottish castle and millions of pounds is what's on offer, I'm going to damn well snatch it with both hands.'

FORTY-NINE
GEORGE

CHRISTMAS DAY 2025

I should have told them. I should have told them. I should have told them.

George thinks this to himself over and over as the cold air of the courtyard bites at the exposed flesh of his face and hands. He hasn't put his coat back on. He couldn't risk waiting a single second.

I should have told them.

He knows why he left out the details about his father and grandfather's deaths. What he did to the boat. How it was all his fault they drowned. At the time, when he was recounting the story of Sherie's visit twenty years ago, he told himself he was sparing his mother and grandmother. Sheltering them from an uncomfortable truth. The most terrible of truths. But that wasn't true. He was doing it for himself. In the end, he always does things for himself.

And that's what he's doing now, as he carries Alexandra's body over the snow and through the door of one of the storage buildings.

Bodies. That's what his life has been. The body of Sherie, presumed dead, dragged to this same place. First here, into the dusty dark, and then destined for the depths of the loch. The bodies of his father and grandfather. Taken to the shore, ambulances and paramedics waiting. Attempts to revive them proving fruitless. Now he has another. Another that will define his life. Another to add to the collection, the faces which will fill his head and become more a part of his identity than anything else. More than his work, than the good he tries to do. More than his wife, who has no idea what her husband is capable of. More than the father he might one day become.

Yes, that's it, he thinks as he wraps Alexandra's body in plastic sheeting. He's doing this for the child he and Delia will have one day. His son or daughter will need a father to look up to. A respectable figure. A member of parliament. A responsible husband, a dutiful son and grandson, a kind parent. Not a killer.

The plastic covers her face.

Not a killer.

He weighs the wrapped package with bricks, tools, anything else he can find.

Not a killer.

He drags the body outside.

Through the snow.

Heading for the edge of the loch.

EPILOGUE
CLAIRE

TEN MONTHS LATER

This Christmas will be different. This has become Claire's mantra. It's been with her all year, like a distant beacon, but now they're into October, it's become ever-present. Something visible on the horizon. *This Christmas will be different.*

She has just placed the order for the Christmas trees for Lemire Castle for the approaching season. This is the first time she's been allowed to choose them, now that her mother is dead. Eileen liked Claire to take care of the admin, but never saw her as a decision-maker. Now Claire can make all the decisions herself. She isn't living in her mother's shadow. The threat of disinheritance no longer hanging over her, like a permanent sword of Damocles.

Claire thinks back to that awful Christmas last year. How by the time the police arrived, her mother had taken her own life – an overdose of her tablets. She left a detailed note beside her bed, confessing to killing Tommy. At least that kept things easier for the rest of the family.

The only strange thing they've had to contend with – or

rather, *another* strange thing, since everything about that whole business was strange – was how their housekeeper Alexandra had absconded and vanished into thin air. George explained that she had been involved with Tommy and was embarrassed that he'd ended up at Lemire because of her. Apparently, that was why she'd slipped away without saying goodbye. That was the official reason, anyway. There's more to it than that, as Claire well knows. There are, however, things that Claire still doesn't know and has no wish to know. She thinks back to how she stopped George from confessing something to her, that Christmas morning in the library, when it looked like all the revelations had come out and there was nothing left to tell. But there's always something more to tell. Claire knows this. And she's learnt that the key to tranquillity is to know when to dig and, crucially, when not to.

On that terrible Christmas Day, when she looked out of the window and saw George dragging something towards the loch, she knew in an instant what was happening. All the pieces fell into place. Him asking where Alexandra was. Her mother talking to her just before she took her own life. Then reading her mother's letter that laid out the truth. The full truth, at last. Claire never expected to be in such a position. A moment when she'd have to decide to cover up her sister's murder – a sister she never knew she had. But she'd do it to protect her son. To protect the family. And to keep her home.

She knew her mother had used their family friend Michael Allerton and his consultancy firm for various things over the years, and she decided that he, along with their family lawyer Jacob Wakefield, would be the best first port of call. She apologised for contacting them on Christmas Day but told them time was of the essence. 'I need a will to go missing,' she explained. 'A recent will that my mother made. I presume that won't be a problem?' The two men assured her they would see to it. As she'd put the phone down, she thought to herself that, no matter how much the world changed, sometimes it still did come down to who you know. 'Keep your friends close,' her father once told her, 'and the *useful* friends even closer.'

Overall, things have undeniably worked out well. She's inherited the castle. The boys have a healthy chunk of money each. George and Delia have a baby on the way. Ken and Kite have moved to the UK: a lovely old house in Hampstead, offering them a more homely, quiet existence compared to their lifestyle in LA, with Ken returning to his roots as a 'serious' actor on the London stage. Even Ralph and Mara have patched things up. Claire suspects the money might have had something to do with that, but she's not about to make waves. Best not to stir the pot. That was her mother's hobby. Now she's gone. And they can all have a nice, proper Christmas, free from all that drama.

Getting up from her writing desk and closing her laptop, Claire lets her reading glasses hang down and looks out at the loch. The water is a bit choppy. A rippling sheet of steel. The dark clouds suggest rain might be coming. And she thinks she can make out something else. Flashing lights. Red and blue.

Then comes the knock at the door.

Hamish stands there. His brow is creased, a worried expression on his face. 'They've found a body,' he says.

It takes a while for the sentence to make any sense to Claire. It feels like she's fallen into a strange vortex of time where horrible events are doomed to repeat themselves. Slightly altered and skewed each time, but still the déjà vu remains.

'A father and son were out in a boat and found her,' Hamish continues.

'Her?' Claire asks. It's all she can say.

Hamish nods. 'Yeah, a young woman, or so they think. Wrapped in plastic sheeting. The police are down there. Came up through the road on the north side. They'll probably be here soon.'

Claire feels faint. She thanks Hamish and walks away, leaving him standing outside. She hasn't got the time or energy to waste on niceties.

She returns to the living room. Resumes her spot looking out at the window, then takes out her phone. When George doesn't answer, she leaves a message on the landline. 'George, call me back when you get this. Something's happened.'

Her phone buzzes a few minutes later.

'Mum, Delia's just said you've left a cryptic message on the answerphone. Why can't you just ring my bloody mobile like a normal person? You've got her all worried. Again.'

She doesn't say anything at first. She can feel the pulse of her heartbeat through her fingers. The vibrations cause the phone to shift in her hand. She holds on tight. Finds the words.

'I know what you did,' she says.

She hears a breath on the other end. 'What did you say?' George asks.

'They've found the body,' Claire says, her voice taking on strength. Purpose. Her thoughts becoming more ordered. 'We don't have long. We need to come up with a plan. To protect you. To protect all of us. To protect the family.'

A LETTER FROM B P WALTER

Dear reader,

I want to say a huge thank you for choosing to read *The Winter Visitor*. I really hope its twists and wintry chills kept you turning the pages! If you did enjoy it, and want to keep up to date with all my latest releases, just sign up at the following link. Your email address will never be shared and you can unsubscribe at any time.

www.bookouture.com/b-p-walter

I hope you loved *The Winter Visitor* as much as I enjoyed writing it. If you felt it was a good read, I would be very grateful if you could write a review. I'd love to hear what you think, and it makes such a difference helping new readers to discover one of my books for the first time.

I love hearing from my readers – you can get in touch through social media.

Thanks,

B P Walter

KEEP IN TOUCH WITH B P WALTER

www.bpwalter.com

instagram.com/bpwalterauthor
facebook.com/BPWalterAuthor
x.com/BarnabyWalter

ACKNOWLEDGEMENTS

Thank you to my wonderful family: my partner, Leno, my parents, sisters, uncle, and to Rebecca and Tom and all my close friends. Special mention to my gran, who passed away while I was writing *The Winter Visitor*. Thanks to my agent, Joanna Swainson, rights director Hana Murrell and everyone at Hardman & Swainson, and to my editor Ruth Tross and the whole team at Bookouture (and thanks so much for such a delightful and warm welcome to the imprint!). Thanks to Lizzy Barber, John Boyne, Fiona Cummins, Jackie Kabler, Simon Masters, Lauren North, Marion Todd and Michael Wood for all the WhatsApp chats and lunches that help break up the book writing. I'd like to say a massive thank you to all the readers and booksellers who have picked up my books and taken the time to recommend them and leave reviews online. I'll always be extremely grateful.

PUBLISHING TEAM

Turning a manuscript into a book requires the efforts of many people. The publishing team at Bookouture would like to acknowledge everyone who contributed to this publication.

Audio
Alba Proko
Sinead O'Connor
Melissa Tran

Commercial
Lauren Morrissette
Hannah Richmond
Imogen Allport

Contracts
Peta Nightingale

Cover design
The Brewster Project

Data and analysis
Mark Alder
Mohamed Bussuri

Editorial
Ruth Tross
Sinead O'Connor

Copyeditor
Laura Gerrard

Proofreader
Becca Allen

Marketing
Alex Crow
Melanie Price
Occy Carr
Cíara Rosney
Martyna Młynarska

Operations and distribution
Marina Valles
Stephanie Straub
Joe Morris

Production
Hannah Snetsinger
Mandy Kullar
Nadia Michael
Charlotte Hegley

Publicity
Kim Nash
Noelle Holten
Jess Readett
Sarah Hardy

www.ingramcontent.com/pod-product-compliance
Lightning Source LLC
LaVergne TN
LVHW041623060526
838200LV00040B/1411